BIG DICKER

HAREM STATION

NEW YORK TIMES BESTSELLING AUTHOR, JA HUSS, WRITING AS

KCROSS

BIG DICKER

NEW YORK TIMES BESTSELLING AUTHOR JA HUSS WRITING AS

CROSS

Copyright © 2019 by JA Huss & KC Cross
ISBN: 978-1-950232-01-7

Edited by RJ Locksley
Cover Design by JA Huss

ABOUT
THE BOOK

KC Cross is the not-so-secret naughty pen name of New York Times bestselling author, JA Huss (who normally writes filthy romantic suspense).

**Welcome to Mighty Minions Resort.
Jimmy's personal hell.**

All Jimmy wants is a booster shot of DNA scrambler so he never has to find his one-true soul mate. But life rarely goes the way you plan it.

After dropping Xyla off on Blue Sand Beach for a little vacay with her sexbot girlfriends the Big Dicker has to make an emergency landing on the demon-themed Mighty Minions Resort. Picture hordes of exasperated parents, sticky, crying kids, and a park AI that seems determined to suck every credit out of his Harem Station bank account.

The only good thing about Mighty Minions from

Jimmy's perspective—it's not the place you meet your soul mate.

Until outlaw Cygnian princess, Delphi, shows up and shatters all his best-laid plans.

But Delphi isn't there to fall in love with Jimmy.

She's there to kidnap him and take him back to her boss, the Loathsome One.

Big Dicker is a full-length, romp-y, Sci-Fi Romance that features hot, soul-mate sex on a family-friendly resort, a sentient ship with a strip poker problem, three drunk-outlaw sexbots on vacay, a crazy, but misunderstood, dragonbee bot, and an evil villainess who has big plans for Jimmy's sperm.

CHAPTER ONE

The Vacation Sector isn't a place I usually spend time. Hell, I don't even pass through here even though there are more than two hundred different gates in this sector that go to pretty much anywhere you can think of in the galaxy.

Too much traffic. Too many people. I hate people.

Spending those first several years on Harem Station with just ALCOR, Xyla, and my brothers changed me, I think.

Before we had to run from Wayward Station I was a pretty sociable guy. Hell, my father was a diplomat and his hope was that I'd take his place when he retired, so I went to all the parties and met all the people.

At least… that's what I thought he wanted for me.

Before I learned the truth about who and what I am.

Crux told me his Corla story about six months after we arrived on what was then called ALCOR Station. ALCOR had whipped up some fermented wine from printed fruit for us to celebrate my birthday and we got a little bit drunk, so Crux's whole sordid tale came burbling out of his mouth unasked for.

I knew parts of it already. I knew we helped Corla escape, I knew everyone was pissed about that. But that's it. That's all I really knew.

It grossed me out, to be honest. The creepy ceremony and breeding just gave me the fucking shivers. So when ALCOR finally let us leave the station several years later, the first thing Xyla and I did was book on over to a biogenetics lab just off the Outlaw Highway and have a DNA signature scrambler made.

If I ever did get caught by the Cygnians or the Akeelians there was no way in hell they'd figure out who I was. And I would not be forced into some creepy breeding ceremony because the DNA signature scrambler would make sure there was no true soulmate for me.

Pretty clever, I think. It was Xyla's idea. She's been around. She knows things.

The DNA signature scrambler bought me time, at least. If I ever did get caught it would take my captors a little while to figure out there was something wrong and maybe that's all the time I need to make an escape.

The scrambler wears off but I go back every year to get a boost.

Xyla and I talked about this stuff *ad nauseam* back in the day. Came up with dozens of scenarios and plans of escape should I ever get caught and once we acquired *Dicker* about a decade ago, we clued her in. Inputting all kinds of sequences into her core for what to do in case of a capture scenario.

But... time passed. Lots of time passed, actually. And no Akeelians or Cygnians ever came looking for me. Did they forget about us? Did they move on to phase two of their diabolical plan with new violet-eyed boys?

Hard to tell.

But I did move on. I got a little relaxed. A little bit complacent, maybe.

But now? I laugh to myself as *Dicker* takes us towards the docking station of Blue Sand Beach. Oh, hell the fuck no. As soon as I drop Xyla off here to meet up with her friends for some girl time, I'm going right to the biogenetics lab to make sure all my shit is up to date.

"Are you sure you don't want to come with me?" Xyla asks. She's autoshopping from the pilot's chair, cycling through all kinds of skimpy bikinis and summery dresses for her ten spins in the sun. Which I find kinda cute, if I'm being honest. She's been looking forward to this reunion with her sex-bot girlfriends, Cha-Cha and Ladybug, for months. Cha-Cha is Luck's partner now. Ever since Valor decided to stay back on Harem to help Tray manage all that Baby ALCOR AI bullshit Luck has been on his own.

But Cha-Cha is a long-time friend of Xyla's so I think it's working out OK.

"Me on a Blue Sand beach with three former sexbots?" I say. "No, thanks. I'll be fine. *Dicker* and I have plans."

"To do what?"

"To just… chill, ya know. I told you. We're just gonna float around and take it easy. Besides, it's not fair if we both go down and *Dicker* can't."

"I don't mind," *Dicker* says in her sweet, yet seductive voice. "You can go—"

"No," I say, cursing *Dicker* for being so selfless. "No. I'm not leaving you alone up here."

"I don't think you two should be alone either," Xyla says, pouting her new lavender synthetic lips as she looks over at me. They glitter a little too. Kinda flashy. "That meeting with the Angel people was kinda intense. Maybe I should skip my trip and we should go back to Harem and let everyone know what they said?"

"Xyla," I say. "That's dumb. We're already here. Just enjoy yourself. We're fine."

The Angel Station people were not what I expected. They looked normal. They weren't sex-bots or anything. Just your average people. Could fit in to any Akeelian society just fine, I suppose. But I don't think they're a bunch of runaway Akeelians like us. They kept asking me about gate maps. Could I give them a gate map for all the gates ALCOR knew about and shit like that?

And then, when I told them that ALCOR was dead and I could probably ask the Baby ALCOR if he had some master gate list, but it wasn't likely, they lost interest and left.

We were out on some random station near a tiny, lackluster sun called Gliese. And even though I'm a decent diplomatic representative for Harem Station, I was annoyed beyond belief by the time we were heading back to the gate to get the fuck out of there.

The abandoned station was creepy too. Reminded me way too much of Harem before my brothers and I arrived.

"They didn't tell us anything time-sensitive anyway," I say. They didn't really tell us anything at all, actually. "So we can't do much until we find that Veila girl. And that's not our job. Serpint can do it. Or Luck. He seems more than happy to be the new booty hunter. Is he here yet?"

"He dropped Cha-Cha off earlier in the spin," *Dicker* says. "*Lady Luck* didn't mention where they were going afterward."

"What are you gonna do then?" Xyla says. "Just float around up here and wait for me? Because that sounds dumb too. You should at least go somewhere fun. There's a planet over here that has karkadann races. You've never seen those. It's pretty cool. And they have a virtual made just for ships there too. You guys should go do that."

It does sound kinda fun. Karkadanns are pretty rare. Muscular, monstrous equines with thick plates of organic armor and a single, curved horn between their eyes. But I wouldn't want to go without Xyla. There's not much I would want to do without Xyla—except go take care of this biogenetic stuff.

I just don't want her to know that's what I'm doing because then she'll figure out I'm a lot more worried about this whole Cygnian soulmate bullshit than I'm letting on. She'd never get off this ship if she knew what was whirling through my head and how freaked out about it I am.

Dicker starts announcing our docking sequence as we are grabbed by the tractor beam and slowly pulled towards the airlock we were assigned to for dropoff.

"We'll be fine," I tell Xyla, who has made her shopping decisions and sent them down to Blue Sand Beach for pickup when she arrives, and is now unbuckling her harness to go grab her pack.

"I know you will," she calls over her shoulder. Then she turns and smiles at me, her lavender hair pulled back into a tight ponytail and her normally matte-black upper body now sporting a light shade of purple. Her legs are still silver but her feet are flat, and not molded into stilettos, because she's ready for the beach.

Dicker completes docking and green lights flash as the Blue Sand Beach arrival station chimes, "Welcome to Blue Sand Beach. The only planet in the Vacation Sector designed for discriminating adults. Please exit your ship..." and blah, blah blah.

The outer airlock opens, then the inner one, and then there's a clear path into the station.

Still, Xyla hesitates. "Maybe I shouldn't go."

"Go," I say, commanding her. "We're fine. *Dicker* and I will just dick around a little and be back for you in ten days. Just have fun. You earned it."

She makes a concerned face at me.

"Go," I say again.

"Fine." She sighs. "But I'm not gonna have fun knowing you two are up here all alone with nothing to do."

I smile at her. "You better have fun. Or I'll be pissed. Ten days on Blue Sands is a small fortune."

She shakes her head and smiles. "You'll call me if you need anything, though, right? I'll have my comm turned on the whole time."

"I will. Now go."

Xyla shoots me one last regretful look, then turns and saunters out the airlock. She stops at the end of the hall, just before our airlock closes, and waves. Then she's gone.

I let out a long sigh of relief. "OK, *Dicker.* Just us now."

"Where should we go? To that karkadann place? I'd like to see that virtual."

"Sending you coordinates now."

"Oh," *Dicker* says, just a moment later. "What's this? And why didn't you tell Xyla this was the plan?"

"Because you know how she worries. She'd never get off the ship. And she's been looking forward to this reunion for months. It's just a simple booster, that's all. Just to make sure that if I ever do run into my stupid Cygnian soulmate, there's no possible way I'll ever get stuck with her."

Dicker lets off a little laugh. "You can't outrun your fate, Jimmy. It always catches up with you eventually."

Maybe not, I think to myself. *But stacking the odds in my favor can't hurt either.*

CHAPTER TWO

DELPHI

My first glimpse of Jimmy, Xyla, and the *Big Dicker* was back on the ship stop closest to Harem Station. It's one of the ship stops only outlaws frequent. But it's also one of their usual haunts when they travel. I was waiting for them for weeks. After we learned about what happened at Bull Station things got pretty tense where I was and I was ordered to put the plan in motion.

My little dragonbee bot, Flicka, had already infiltrated the ship stop's maintenance logs and inserted a virus that would automatically load itself deep inside *Dicker*'s core the next time they came by, so after that it was just a waiting game.

Getting to Jimmy wasn't going to be an issue. I was pretty confident about that part of my plan. Xyla... she was a whole other issue that needed to be dealt with.

But fate finds a way.

When they passed through the ship stop a few spins ago and I learned that Jimmy was on his way to drop Xyla off on Blue Sand Beach for a girlfriend getaway, I knew this was going to be OK. Everything would work out.

So now I'm following them in my ship, the *Queen Bee*, and we're hovering just a few million klicks out from the Blue Sand Beach station. Waiting to activate the virus and follow them.

"Xyla has been logged into Blue Sand arrivals," *Queenie* says.

"Perfect," I say. "Don't lose them."

"As if," *Queenie* retorts.

She's more confident than I am because the *Big Dicker* is a much more sophisticated piece of equipment than *Queenie* is. I'd never tell her that to her interface, but it's true. We don't have an ALCOR AI to provide us with all kinds of fancy, new upgrades. I've heard that he makes his own sentient ships out on Harem Station. So it's very possible that there's some component inside *Dicker* that will identify my virus and disable it before it can get a foothold.

And if that happens all of my carefully laid plans will be worthless.

I need this to work. I need them to break down and make an unscheduled service stop so everything hinges on what happens in the next few hours.

"*Dicker* is in undocking sequence," *Queenie* says.

"Good," I whisper, eyes locked on the large screen above me. I lean forward, trying to get a better look at Jimmy's ship. She's very sleek and long, with an ample cargo bay on her underside meant to hold crews of bots. That's what they do. They liberate bots and borgs from their masters and give them a new home on Harem where all their restrictions are removed in exchange for five hundred spins of servitude.

I admit, it's a pretty nice deal if you're a bot.

16

They do this with sentient ships too. If they make it to one of the two ALCOR security gates and surrender, ALCOR will tow them through the gate, dock them into a medical bay, and then sign them over to someone trustworthy on Harem to give them a new life.

This is totally illegal in Prime Space. But even before the Prime Navy made an alliance with Harem after the explosions at Bull Station, they didn't interfere. If your sentient ship decided to bail and made it to Harem, it was gone for good. They would not go in to recover them.

Since I started working with *Queenie* a few months ago I've often wondered if she would ever abandon me like this. She's capable of it, that's for sure. I don't trust her and I doubt she trusts me, but she's getting something out of this partnership just like I am. You'd think she'd do as she's told, but sentient ships are sneaky fuckers. Which is why they're not allowed to exist without a responsible party being in charge of them.

ALCOR knows this is a hard-and-fast rule so he makes sure all his sentient ships leave Harem with their new responsible party. At least he did. Before the Prime Navy made that alliance.

But now? There's no telling what that insane AI will do. It could be that autonomous sentient ships will be common in the years ahead.

Everyone is on edge over this. What will the galaxy look like with free sentient ships all over the place? They are all so dangerous. Pretty much everyone agrees that autonomous ALCOR is bad enough.

But... what if he did that with other AI's too?

The only thing we have going for us as far as that little scenario goes is that sentient AI's are locked onto stations and planets and can't leave.

At least that was what we thought before ALCOR left Harem and blew up a Cygnian warship, leaving a copy of himself behind.

And the security beacons around Harem are controlled by older, just-as-dangerous copies of ALCOR that are tens of thousands of years old. There is no way to directly attack Harem Station.

Yet.

But all that could change if I complete my mission.

I have no use for sentient AI's or ships. They're more trouble than they're worth. But everyone not in alliance with Harem Station wants those AI's gone. They're up to no good out there. Everyone knows it.

But that's not why I'm doing this.

My twin brother is being held captive by the most evil Cygnian princess to ever float around this galaxy.

We call her... the Loathsome One.

Ugggh. Just thinking her name makes me sick.

My brother, Tycho, is a Cygnian male, which makes him nearly worthless in Cygnian society. Because while he and I were both genetically engineered from the same stock, Cygnian males cannot breed. They're sterile. And our genetics are pretty much the only reason Cygnians exist.

Tycho is nothing but a slave. Nothing but a body meant to work. I am a high-ranking pink, and we come from the same genetics batch, but his only purpose— the only purpose of any Cygnian male from what I can tell—is to make sure fertilization takes place. There are no single births in Cygnian society. They never live past the embryonic stage. So Tycho is nothing more than my other half. Every Cygnian girl is born with a fraternal male twin. That's the only way to produce a female in our society.

They separate us at birth. The boys go into the slave harems so they can learn to work and the girls go into the breeding harems so they can be farmed for genetics.

But Tycho and I were not separated. We grew up together in my father's house. Perhaps my father thought Tycho was more than he appeared? Or maybe he has some kind of true affection for him? Or maybe my father was just having doubts about his role in this whole horrid war?

It's hard to tell.

The only thing I know for sure is that my twin is part of me, now and forever, and I'd do anything to keep him safe.

Anything. Up to and including kidnapping Jimmy of Harem Station and delivering him to the Loathsome One. I have no idea what her plans for him are, and I don't care.

This must be done.

"They're heading towards Gate 137," *Queenie* says.

"137. Where the fuck does that go?"

"The Outer Highway," *Queenie* replies.

"Shit," I say. "That place is a cesspool. It will make everything more difficult."

"We could activate the virus now, if you'd like."

"In the Vacation Sector?" I sigh. "I'm not sure that's any better."

"Those are your choices, Delphi. And you have thirty seconds to make a decision or there will be too much cross-traffic to ensure the signal gets through."

"Fine. Do it now."

"Sent," *Queenie* chirps. "Received. Infiltrating." Then, a moment later. "Success. *Dicker* has activated reverse thrusters and is changing course."

"Where are they headed?" I ask, biting my nails.

Queenie laughs. "Mighty Minions Resort."

"Oh, for fuck's sake," I say, rubbing my forehead, trying to stave off a headache. "The family station?"

"Happiest Place in the Galaxy," *Queenie* says.

"This might be worse than the Outer Highway."

"It's done now. So deal with it."

"Like I have a choice," I mumble.

"Should I send word to the Loathsome One?"

"No!" I say, jumping out of my seat. "Just no. She doesn't need to hear about our fuck-ups, OK? Tycho's life is in her hands. Just follow them in and make sure we're right behind them for docking."

"Achieved," *Queenie* says. "I put in our request and we have an arrival number of three hundred and seventy-four."

"Three hundred and seventy-four? For sun's sake. That'll take all day!"

"Yes," *Queenie* says. "I think I'll take a break while we wait."

I just stare at her navigation console, wondering if her attitude is getting worse. Or am I imagining things?

Queenie has never been the most pleasant ship personality and ever since the Loathsome One gave her to me to complete this mission, she hasn't tried very hard to hide the fact she thinks I'm incompetent.

She might even hate me.

Just my luck, I sigh. To be partnered with a ship who hates me. What if she sabotages my efforts? What if she's secretly plotting a way to escape? It's not unheard of for ships to trick their owners into flying to the ALCOR gates to make their escape.

I've heard rumors about what happens to the people on the ships when that happens.

And maybe all this talk of Jimmy, and Xyla, and *Dicker*, and ALCOR has got her thinking?

Shit.

Flicka buzzes by my ear and then settles her little dragonbee feet onto my shoulder. "Don't worry," she sings in her tiny buzzy voice. "I'm on your side, Delphi."

I pat her small back with my fingertip and whisper, "Thank you, Flicka."

Because she is, quite literally, my only friend in the whole universe besides Tycho.

CHAPTER THREE

Free. Sorta. I kinda feel bad for thinking that. Also for keeping my little side mission a secret from Xyla. But if she knew this was bothering me enough to go in for a DNA signature scramble booster three months early, she'd never have left the damn ship.

"Mother of suns," *Dicker* says.

"What?"

"A communication just came through from the Blue Sand Beach gate captain and there's a friggin' virus packed inside."

I get up from my co-pilot's seat and walk back towards *Dicker's* home station. She was almost entirely rebuilt after that whole disaster at Bull Station. Which was fine. Her core personality was all intact. And she hadn't been upgraded for a couple years, so she's bigger and better than ever now.

When we upgraded her we put her core into a console on the main deck. She used to live two decks below. Not that it matters really. She has access to every component on her body. But she's got a monitor with voice wave interface that animates when she talks now and I kinda like that.

23

"How bad is it?" I ask.

"Fucker." She sighs. "It's wiggled its way inside my water generators and now they're offline. I've got it contained but... it just flushed all our fresh water out into space."

"Shit. What should we do? Stop and fix it now? Or just head on through and fix it at the lab?"

"There is no reason to believe we'll have any trouble if we proceed, Jimmy. But I'd hate to be wrong and get you stuck with no water. We should stop." She pauses for a moment, then says, "Oh, crap."

"Now what?"

"That little fucker just duplicated itself."

"Where is it now?"

"Same place. And I just deleted it again, but now there's three of them. Shit, Jimmy. We'll have to take care of this. It's nearly harmless, but very annoying. And these self-duplicating viruses are pesky. I'll have to run a full diagnostic and probably hire some help for you on Mighty Minions Resort to install a new water generator since Xyla's not here."

"Ugggh." I sigh. "On Mighty Minions?"

"It's the closest place and they're being very cool about this. Gave us priority so we don't have to wait in line to dock. I guess Harem Station's new reputation has its perks."

"Hmmm. Fine. How long will we be stuck?"

"If we can find a good engineer I'd say just a few hours."

"OK, let's go in then. I hope this place has people who can deal with sentient ships."

"Me too," *Dicker* mutters.

Half an hour later we're docked and *Dicker* is moving around inside her systems. She pops onto the monitor in my quarters and says, "OK. We will need another hand. It's a two-person operation. Can you put up an ad on their jobs board? They have a rule here that ships aren't allowed to post."

"Anti-ship-ists," I say.

"I know, right?"

I just smile. This is how most of the galaxy works, but once you live on Harem long enough your worldview about bots and ships changes dramatically. You just don't realize it until you venture out of your safe zone and have to confront reality again.

I pull up the station's interface and I'm presented with a blaring message that I can only access services and announcements from inside.

"Fucking hell," I say. "They want me to actually get off the ship to post a job."

"That's fine. Besides, it'll be fun. Stop and get lunch while you're out. And pick up some bottled water just in case."

"Fun? There are probably sixty million grubby kids out there. It's going to be the opposite of fun. Why didn't we break down near Blue Sand Beach? At least then we could've gotten drunk with Xyla."

"If we had Xyla we wouldn't be stuck, remember? This was all your idea, Jimmy."

"I know, I know. OK. I'll be back as soon as I can."

The first thing I see when I enter Mighty Minions reception is a two-and-a-half-meter-tall red dragon spraying holo fire out at a massive group of, you guessed it, grubby kids.

See, this is what soulmates get you. Kid-friendly vacations. I would kill myself.

I don't want to be out here any longer than I have to, so I get the attention of the nearest Mighty Minion Ambassador dressed up like an ancient red warrior and say, "How do I access the community boards? I need an engineer to help me with my ship."

She smiles at me in her overly cheerful Mighty Minion way and says, "Can I see your Mighty Pass, please?"

"My… what?"

"Your ticket, sir. To board the station."

"Look, my ship and I came in on an emergency call to get repairs. We're not staying."

"Yes, sir. I totally understand. But you can't get in"—she points to the gates separating the reception area from the resort—"unless you have a Mighty Pass. And inside is where we keep our one-hundred-percent-secure community interface."

"OK," I say, so done with this place already. "Where do I get a pass?"

"Right over there." She points to a line that's sixty billion people long. "When you get that I'll be happy to help you in any way I can."

"You're kidding me, right?"

"No." She smiles. "I'm being totally serious."

"You're telling me this place has no wireless storefront to buy passes?"

"That's no fun," she quips. "Then the kids would miss all this Mighty Dragon interaction!"

Right.

I turn and force my way through a crowd of screaming brats and get in line.

Two hours later I have my pass and the reception hall is temporarily empty because this docking bay is on break. Mighty Dragon is gone, all the ambassadors are gone, and the second I turn back to the window where I just stood in line for two hours to pay my seven-thousand-credit-entrance fee (because in order to access the community boards I had to buy a freaking family pass) I find it closed for lunch.

Fine. I am goddamned Jimmy of Harem Station. I don't need a fucking Mighty Ambassador to find my way around this dump.

I flash my pass at the gates—which are automated, go figure—and enter the resort.

In front of me is a choppy red lake with orange and red holo flames coming off the surface. Which is creepy as fuck if you ask me, but whatever. Not my kid's nightmares.

My tunnel vision kicks in when I spot the nearest data access point and I head diagonally across the concourse, weaving in and out between sugared-up kids, and breathe a sigh of relief when I flash my pass and the screen lights up with a green banner across Mighty Boss's face that says, *Access Granted!*

Success.

I navigate to the corporate boards searching for the jobs posting in maintenance. I scan the 'for hire' section first—on the off chance someone competent is promoting their sentient ship skills—then resign myself to posting my own job because of course they're not.

I finish, link the community board to my Mighty Pass, then stare at it. Tapping my foot, impatiently waiting for someone to ping me back.

Nothing. I press *Dicker*'s comm tab on my wristband—fucking cavemen, all of them. Because I really miss my air screen right now—and start complaining before she even gets a chance to ask me how I'm getting along.

"This fucking place might as well be back in the dark ages. Do you know how long I had to stand in line to get a Mighty Pass? In line, *Dicker*. These people have *lines*."

"Two hours, seventeen minutes, and thirty-seven seconds. Mighty Time."

"Smartass."

"I saw seven thousand credits drain from our accounts and almost shit my ship."

"I can't access the data boards without a pass."

"Scammers."

"Right? And no one has even answered my ad yet."

"How long ago did you post it?"

"That's not the point," I say, kinda fed up. "All these kids, and parents, and fucking balloons are starting to get on my nerves."

"I think you're hungry. You're turning into a diva."

"No, I'm not!"

"Go eat, Jimmy. I'm sure everyone is at work right now and they won't even be looking at the jobs board until later."

"I'm coming back to the ship."

"No. I just checked their exit policy. If you leave the resort you have to pay to get back in."

"I bought a damn family pass!"

"Only good one stay. You have to eat and sleep on the resort until we hire someone. That's how they define 'stay.'"

"Goddammit!"

"Sorry," she chirps. "I didn't make the rules. And you'd be even madder if you came back on ship and then had to pay again."

I sigh. "This day can go fuck itself."

"I don't know. It's not so bad. I'm playing strip poker with another ship on the other side of the station."

"*Dicker*, we can't afford to lose any parts right now."

"Lose? Please. Give me some credit. I've already won a new water generator. I'm about to take this bitch's autokitchen too."

"We don't even have room for a whole kitchen."

"I'll just cash it in for credits to make up for that stupid Mighty Pass. Keep me posted. Later."

CHAPTER FOUR

We wait in line for ninety-nine minutes before we're allowed to dock at the station and I spend all ninety-nine of those minutes fuming because the *Big Dicker* got special emergency priority and docked a long time ago.

"How the hell will I even find him?" I ask *Queenie*.

"I've been playing strip poker with *Dicker* for the past ten minutes. We owe her a water generator."

"Are you fucking kidding me right now?"

"Is that a real question?"

I take a deep, deep breath and remind myself this ship holds my life in her hands. And even though I am her legal responsible party, I'm pretty sure no one but Tycho would miss me if I turned up dead from a life support failure.

"Anyway," *Queenie* says. "*Dicker*'s docked over in Flame Lake Sector. Just head that way. I'm sure he'll be easy to pick out. Just look for the annoyed single guy. And make sure you take your wristband. Family passes are seven thousand credits and you'll need that to access the job's board."

"What the hell are you talking about?"

"He posted a job looking for engineering help. That's you, genius. Do you really think I lost a game of strip poker to a simpleton like *Dicker* on accident?"

"Oh."

"Oh, is right," she snaps back.

I don't think I like this ship. "Do we even have seven thousand credits in our accounts?"

"Well, I do. I'm not sure about you."

"What?"

"Your credits are my credits but my credits are... well, *my* credits. I could give you a loan though. But I'm gonna need some collateral. I'm not sure you're good for it."

"You know what?"

"What?"

"You can go fuck yourself. We're both on this mission and I'll call the Loathsome One right now and tell her you're being insubordinate. And don't bother threatening me back because Jimmy is here and I've got the perfect plan to get him on board."

"That was *my* plan," she hisses.

"Yeah, well. Your plans are my plans, right? I'm the responsible party here. So you'd better transfer seven thousand credits to my account right now or—"

"I'm setting you up for success, Delphi," *Queenie* snaps. "Because my success is tied to your success. But for the record, I don't like you."

"Credits," I seethe through clenched teeth.

"Fine. Done. But I'll expect this to be paid back."

"Put it on your expense report," I say, turning my back to exit the ship.

"Don't forget to apply for the job," she calls, just as I enter the airlock. "You're welcome!"

"Don't let her get to you," Flicka soothes as we leave. "She's a nasty ship."

"That ship is so nasty not even the Loathsome One would steal her soul."

"Yeah," Flicka agrees, blinking her gold light as she hovers in front of my face. "That ship is so nasty you *want* to pass it in the night."

I smile, feeling a little better. "That ship is so nasty, when someone takes out the trash, she leaves the docking bay."

Flicka chirps her approval in my ear as we enter the receiving area. Thank God it's not that crowded. We must be the last wave of people to get off the ships.

"We don't need her," Flicka says.

"We kinda do," I say. "But only to get Jimmy back to the Loathsome One. Then we get our reward, free Tycho, and get as far away from the Cygnian-Akeelian war as we can."

It sounds impossible when I say it out loud, but Flicka is nothing but supportive. She and I have been a team since I was three years old. When all my harem sisters back in the palace were being assigned nannybots, I was given Flicka instead.

Dragonbee bots are notoriously sneaky and mean and they bite and sting you when you piss them off. They can also cook up little poisons in their belly regions. Flicka has about a dozen different poison recipes in her repertoire. She never uses them. She's actually a really nice bot.

They're not much to look at alone, but let me tell you—a swarm of these things are a horror screen in the making. And they have this little stealth mode that lets them sneak up on you too. You only hear them coming if they want you to. The buzzing is used as a threat. So being gifted Flicka instead of a nurturing nannybot was punishment for being bratty. But Flicka, Tycho, and I became a tight little dream team in a place made of nightmares.

I cannot remember a time when I wasn't dreaming of a free life outside of Cygnus. My father used to bring me books. Fairy tales and myths of long-ago times when being a Cygnian princess meant you were destined to find a prince who'd whisk you away to a fantasy station where you ate tushberries and sparkling passion-lime wine all day while sitting on plush cushions.

Flicka would listen with me. We'd dream up all kinds of ways to escape. She was a prisoner just as much as Tycho and I. And without her scheming there's no way we could've ever made it out of the system.

I owe her. But also love her. She's my best friend. Probably my only friend after Tycho and I'm not sure he counts because he's my brother.

The line for Mighty Passes isn't long when we arrive and there's only a few families still left in the receiving area, so we shuffle up behind them and wait our turn. When we get to the counter I'm informed that Flicka counts as a full person even though she's smaller than my big toe.

"All sentient beings must have a pass. And you must sign a contract taking full responsibility for her actions." The Mighty Ambassador gives my little bee the stink eye as she says this. "If it bites anyone, or stings anyone, or harasses anyone—"

"I get it," I say. "And she's not an *it*, she's a she."

The girl behind the window visibly shudders. Like imagining my bee as her companion gives her the creeps. She's one to talk. She's dressed up in a Mighty Minions red and black gown with horns made of holo flames coming out of her head. *Who's the crazy one here, lady?*

We get the passes and enter the resort. Flicka attaches herself to my shoulder and then says, "The Flame Lake Sector is to the left."

Just as I turn and begin walking, a group of holo Mighty Minions appears in a circle around me, holding hands and running in a circle as they taunt me with a nursery rhyme about death.

"Sun's sake," I mutter, waving my hand through them to make them go away. But they persist, their taunts growing louder and louder. "What the hell? And who brings their kids to a place like this? There's nothing but demons and flames everywhere I look."

"Oh," Flicka says.

"Oh, what?"

"I just interfaced with their code. They've been programmed to harass anyone who is not wearing Mighty Minions paraphernalia."

"You're joking."

"I'm not. Just go into the nearest souvenir shop and buy a hat."

"What a fucking scam."

But I do it. And the hat sets me back more than a hundred credits. I'm just about to leave when Flicka draws my attention to the Mighty Hime Princess Spa. "You should get a makeover," Flicka prods. "That way you'll blend in and Jimmy won't suspect you're a Cygnian princess."

"Hmm," I say, drawing in a deep breath. Because that's not a bad idea. Right now I practically scream, *Look at me! I'm a princess!* My bodysuit is pale yellow right down to my pink boots and my long hair is a bright tushberry color because I ate those for lunch. "How much is it?"

"A thousand credits," Flicka says. But I can almost hear the smile in her voice. "That would really piss *Queenie* off."

"Sure would." I laugh under my breath. "Let's do it."

I get the full package. The complete Mighty Minions Resort makeover. My long, tushberry hair is now red and black and twisted up into a single horn on the top of my head with holo flames shooting out the top. My formerly yellow bodysuit now has a holo projections running through the threads so it's white with red stripes down the side of my legs just like Mighty Hime wears in the holo-cartoons. My formerly pink ship boots are now black and go all the way up to my knees. Everyone wants to look like Mighty Hime on the resort. She's Mighty Boss's love interest.

It was a lot more than a thousand credits and *Queenie* must be monitoring my spending because she sends me not-so-subtle messages on my wristband to knock it off.

I ignore her. I need to blend in. And the best part is, when I finally do leave that spa, there's no more ring of evil holo-children taunting me as they sing death wishes.

Flicka directs me to a data access point and says, "Go find that job posting and let's get this show on the road. Mighty Minions is creepy as fuck."

I agree and head that direction. It takes me a little while to find his post, figure out how to answer it, and link up to my Mighty Pass, but once that's done I press send.

Now all we have to do is head towards Flame Lake and wait for him to come to us.

We're gonna be out of here and on our way back to saving Tycho before I can ever get my credits' worth out of this new outfit.

CHAPTER FIVE

I keep checking my Mighty Pass to see if anyone's answered yet, but no luck. I feel weird without Xyla. It's been a really long time since I've been out without her. We've done everything together since my brothers and I landed at ALCOR two decades ago and even though *Dicker* is here waiting out in the docking bay, it's not the same.

I'm not really a loner, I decide.

Maybe I'm not into humanoid companionship the way most people are, but I miss my sexbot best friend. Especially here on Mighty Minions. I've been to all kinds of stations and planets over the years. Pretty much seen and done all there is to see and do.

But I've never had to spend time on a family resort. It's like hell for me. All these stupid kids, all these stupid parents, and there's a ring of evil holo-minions who keep taunting me with death rhymes everywhere I go.

God, this was a bad idea.

But *Dicker*'s last suggestion hangs in my thoughts. *Grab something to eat and wait for people to get off work.*

I look around for food. The place is thick with people. Like wall to wall bodies. But I'm taller than almost everyone except the Centurians, so I can see over most of the heads.

I decide on the Evil Noodles place because it's pretty hard to fuck up noodles, and head in that direction. Predictably, there is a line. I don't understand this standing-in-line thing on a place like this. Hell, even on Harem we have auto restaurants where you just blip in your order and a bot will deliver it to wherever you are, but not here apparently. They want maximum parental frustration and kid meltdown.

It's working.

"What can I get for you?" a Mighty Ambassador asks me when I finally make it to the counter.

"Number three noodles with dumplings."

"Perfect," she says, creepy holo flames shooting out of her mouth with the word. "That'll be one hundred and seventeen credits, plus gratuity, plus Mighty tax, so your grand total is four hundred and three credits."

She actually has the nerve to smile through that whole absurd sentence. But I'm not in the mood to argue so I just flash my wristband across her scanner.

"Great. What's your name?"

"Jimmy," I say.

She frowns at me. "I'm sorry. Did you say Kraunfelter?"

"What?"

"Your name. It's so weird."

"It's just Jimmy."

"Razolt?"

"Jimmy," I say again. I'm used to this. Happens all the time. But I have never understood it. Sure, I have the most unique name in the galaxy, but it's not that hard. "Jim-meeee," I sound it out for her.

"I'm so sorry," she says through her mouth flames. "Hazenfloff. Got it. We'll call your name when it's ready. Next!"

I sigh, but then my Mighty Pass chimes a beep and when I glance down, someone has answered my job posting.

Success! I'll be out of this nightmare in a matter of hours.

I move off to the side and stare down at my pass to find the reply.

Oh, and she's even cute—if you don't mind the holo flames shooting up from the horn on top of her head. Delphi is her name. Competent in all aspects of sentient ship engineering, including water generators! Perfect.

I message back. *How soon can you start?*

Delphi: *Tell me where to meet you. I'm in the Fire Mountain Sector right now.*

Me: *Head to Flame Lake and I'll meet you in front of Evil Noodles.*

Which reminds me. Where are my freaking noodles?

"Excuse me," I say to the girl who helped me. "Are my noodles ready yet?"

"What's your name again?"

"Jimmy."

She squints her eyes at me. Like she's never heard this name before even though two minutes ago she

41

took my order and we had a whole conversation about it. "What? Can you say that again?"

"Hazenfloff," I say, giving up.

"Oh, right here," she says, grabbing a red and black take-out bag. "We called your name but no one answered."

"Right. Because my name is Jimmy."

"These aren't yours?"

"Yes," I say, taking the bag from her hand before I have to explain this again. "Thanks."

I walk away and look for a table but every single one is filled with crying kids dressed up like a Mighty Minion and parents wearing Mighty Boss hats. Like this is a requirement. But I don't get more than a few steps before that gang of evil holo-kids is circling me again, singing their death songs.

I slink back into a little side alley and they look confused for a moment. Like I disappeared. Then I realize that the alley is a safe zone, and eat my noodles and dumplings standing up as I look out for the evil uni-horn chick.

It's a good thirty minutes later before I pick her out in the crowd of people standing in front of Evil Noodles. But the moment I step away from the alley, the ring of holo minions circles me and begins their evil taunts.

"Hey, Delphi!" I call over the demon kids.

She turns, looking around until she finds my face. Which is kinda weird because I didn't put a pic on my profile when I made that message. "Oh, hey!" she calls, then pushes her way through the crowd until she's a few feet away. "I see you found some friends."

"Little fuckers won't leave me alone."

"Here, put this on." And she hands me a Mighty Boss hat. I take it from her, slap it over my head, and instantly the hologram disappears.

"What the hell?"

"They're programmed to harass anyone not wearing Mighty Minion paraphernalia."

"This place is such a scam."

"Tell me about it."

I take in her appearance. She's a little bit short. Maybe even tiny. Red and black hair twisted up into the flame-thrower horn, white holo bodysuit with red racing stripes down her legs, and tall black boots.

If holo-cartoons could be porn stars, she'd definitely have a job. Because she is one sexy little minion.

"So," she says, cocking her head at me. "You needed an engineer?"

"Yeah." I sigh. "We picked up a pesky virus leaving Blue Sand Beach and got stranded here in Mighty Hell. It messed up our water generator and dumped all our water. Now it's self-replicating and... yeah. We need help. My ship already has another water generator lined up but installing it is a two-man job."

"Well, I'm just the girl for you then. Where's your new generator? We can pick that up first."

I frown at her. Because I didn't say we needed to pick it up. "Uh, hold please. Let me call my ship and ask."

"Sure thing," she says, turning away to give me privacy. But just as she does that I see a flash of gold shimmering on her shoulder and realize she's got a dragonbee bot as a sidekick.

Which is pretty unusual. Dragonbee bots are some of the worst. They sting, they bite, and they are notorious for infiltrating stations and ships and messing up their programs with the little puffs of poison they shoot out their asses. In fact, I'm pretty sure that's why they were created. Stealth sabotage. We don't even allow them on Harem. Nothing good ever came out of something so small.

Which just makes me think this Mighty Minions place is even more fucked up than it appears. Probably has some hidden agenda if it allows dragonbee bots to live here.

"How you getting along?" *Dicker* says, answering my call.

"Found an engineer."

"Good. I won the kitchen. So when you pick up the water—"

"No," I say. "Forget the kitchen. It's more trouble than it's worth. I want to be out of here as quick as possible. Send me directions to pick up the water generator."

Dicker sighs. "Fine. And sent. Let me know when you're headed my way so I can have the right circuits shut down."

"Cool. Later."

I turn back to Delphi and find her standing directly behind me. "We good?" she asks.

"We're good." My wristband bleeps the directions and I open a holo map to guide us to the right sector. "We need to stop by Fire Mountain to grab some parts first."

"Cool," she says, her little dragonbee buzzing up near her ear.

"Where did you get that thing, anyway?" I say, pointing to the bot.

"Oh, this is Flicka. She's been my partner pretty much my whole life. Can't even remember a time when she wasn't buzzing in my ear. But don't worry, she doesn't bite. Much."

I raise one eyebrow at Delphi.

"Kidding." She laughs. "She bites a lot. Just don't touch her and you're fine."

"Great," I say. "Just my luck." I pan my hand in the direction the map is telling me to go and say, "After you."

"So where were you headed before you got stuck on Mighty Minions?" Delphi asks.

"Outer Highway."

"Oooooo. You're an outlaw. Should I be scared?"

"Yes," I say.

Which only makes her laugh. "But where were you headed on the highway? There's not much out there."

"Just some business I have to take care of."

"Gotcha," she says. "No more questions."

She is cute. I'll give her that. Even dressed up in that Mighty Minions getup. But there's something off about this girl. And that bot on her shoulder just proves it. Had it her whole life? What kind of parent gives a child a dragonbee bot?

But then I look around me. Thousands of parents bring their kids to this station of evil for vacation, so maybe the wider world is more fucked up than I ever realized?

Dicker's map takes us over the Mighty River of Death, through the Mighty Boss Castle of Demons, and under the Mighty Mountain of Fire.

And the whole time the only thing that keeps me going is the thought of leaving here in a few hours.

There's something inside me. Something telling me to get to the biogenetic lab as quick as possible. I can't shake the feeling that I'm in danger on this station.

And it's got nothing to do with Mighty Boss or his disturbing holo minions.

CHAPTER SIX

DELPHI

He's quiet as I lead the way through the resort and it's starting to make me nervous. Flicka gently reminded me when we set off that he didn't mention that he needed to pick up a water generator, so I goofed up and he might be suspicious.

So I kept my mouth shut after that.

But I can't help but look over my shoulder to study him every chance I get. He's very handsome. I already know he's Akeelian but his deep violet eyes are a dead giveaway that he's more than just your average two-cocked alpha male. Akeelians have all sorts of colored eyes, just like Cygnian princesses, but the ones with violet eyes are the breeders. Genetically engineered males who should be able to breed with their Cygnian soulmate and actually produce offspring the natural way.

At least this is what I've learned second-hand from the Loathsome One.

Which gets me thinking... he could be my soulmate. I'm one of the special ones who were engineered to breed.

But he's not. Because I'd have known the moment we locked eyes. And one touch from him would make me light up like the sun.

None of that happened. And it's not because I have exceptional skills at controlling my glow—though I do.

It's because we're not fated.

I'm pretty sure the Loathsome One already knew that. In fact, I'm pretty sure she's counting on Jimmy being her fated mate. That's why she wants him so bad. If she could breed with him and get pregnant then she'd automatically become a power player in the big Cygnian-Akeelian war that's brewing.

But that doesn't stop a girl from dreaming. Jimmy's kind of a good catch. He's rich for one. Very rich. I know he's part owner of Harem Station and that place makes billions of credits a month. And he's rugged. Square jaw with just the right amount of stubble on it. Hard muscles underneath his tight black shirt. Big hands and nice, thick, light-brown hair that hangs over his eyes and makes him look both mysterious and dangerous at the same time.

Not to mention he's got two cocks. I've been with a few Cygnian males over the years, but never an Akeelian. They're something out of fairytales and myths to us girls back home. So... being with a male who could pleasure me the way I was meant to be pleasured is intriguing, to say the least.

Plus he's got that ALCOR AI on his side. I know that real ALCOR died in the explosion near Bull Station, but Harem is still going. He left a copy behind. And their station security AI's are just as powerful. Jimmy and his brothers are already players in this war.

And not just because they can breed. They are powerful in their own right. They have a whole army of sentient ships docked at their station and millions of outlaw solders at their disposal. Soldiers who would die for the home they provide.

Loyal soldiers and ships.

We breed our soldiers and pay some from other races to help us when we need it. But breeding and paychecks doesn't inspire loyalty.

Tycho, Flicka, and I know that better than anyone.

I've always been curious about Harem. And I could've gone there instead of the station where the Loathsome One is. But I didn't have an invitation to pass through the gates and even if I could make it to the other side, they'd indenture me for five hundred spins once I arrived.

So I didn't. I went to the Loathsome One for help.

But now I wish I had tried. Because then Tycho would be safe. At least safer than he is now. I don't know what they'd do with a Cygnian male on Harem, but it can't be any worse than the situation he's in now.

The trek back over to Fire Mountain Sector takes forever. We have to navigate a demon uprising in order to cross the Mighty River of Death and a parade going on in front of the castle shuts us off from where we need to be, so by the time we get to the gates of the receiving area we're both exhausted.

I flash my pass, so ready to get Jimmy inside *Queenie* so we can blow this resort and get my escape from the Loathsome One plan back in action, but there's a loud buzzer and the gates don't open.

"What the fuck?" Jimmy says.

"I don't know. My pass should work." I flash it again, but again, there's a loud denial buzzer.

"Let me try," he says, moving in front of me, Mighty Pass in hand. He swipes it over the sensor, but gets the same result. "What fresh fucking hell is this?"

"Excuse me?"

Jimmy and I both turn to find a Mighty Ambassador smiling at us. "Can I help you with something?"

"Yeah, we're trying to get into the docking bay to pick up a part for my ship."

She smiles even wider, if that's possible, then waves her hand up at the lights. "It's evening here on Mighty Minions Resort, which means we're shut down for the night."

"Shut down?" I say, looking behind us to where thousands of people are still milling about.

"Yes, the docking bays all shut down at four PM Mighty Time for security reasons. No one in or out."

"OK," Jimmy says, sighing deeply as he rubs two fingers above the bridge of his nose. "Fine. We can stay the night, but I need to get into this docking bay to grab a part, then back over to my ship so we can install it."

"I'm sorry. But no one is allowed to leave the resort."

"I get that, but I'm not leaving."

"If you pass through these gates," she says, waving her hand like some kind of magic fairy, "you're leaving. And we can't allow it. But the gates will reopen for business tomorrow at six AM."

"No," Jimmy says. "No. That's stupid. If you could just let us get the part and go back to my ship we could be fixing my ship by six AM tomorrow."

"I'm sorry," she says. "It's the rules."

"Surely, there is someone else we could talk to. Perhaps your manager? We came here on an emergency and so far I've spent nearly ten thousand credits just getting around this stupid station."

"I could call security," she offers.

"No," I say, placing a hand on Jimmy's arm, then whisper, "We do not want her to call security." I smile at the ambassador. "We'll come back tomorrow." Jimmy glares at me as I pull him aside. "She's not gonna let you through and I don't want to get locked in Mighty Jail because you caused a scene."

"Where am I supposed to stay? If I have to spend one more minute around all these sugared-up kids and crazy parents, I'll—"

"Don't say it," I caution him. "She's still there."

"I'm not paying for a freaking hotel room when I have a perfectly good ship I could sleep on."

"Well, you can't get to your ship, so looks like you have to."

"Don't you have a place I could crash for one night? I'd pay you extra tomorrow."

Oh, shit. Never thought of that. If I was a local I would have a place, wouldn't I?

"I... I have roommates. And actually, I'm late on rent. That's why I was taking on extra work. So... sorry."

We both look back at the ambassador and find her waving and smiling. "My Mighty Interface is telling me there are rooms available at the Lava Mountain Spa.

Would you like me to make you a reservation for the night?'"

"No," Jimmy says.

Just as I say, "Yes, please."

"Can I have your pass?" the smiling minion asks.

Jimmy gives her his pass, she passes it over her wristband, and then hands it back. "There you go. All set. You can check in at the Flame Demon's head. Enjoy your stay!"

She walks off and Jimmy just stares at me. "So you're staying with me?"

"Oh, thanks," I say, playing it off. "I was hoping to get this job done tonight so the roomies would let me back in. But if you're offering, that's great. I really appreciate it."

He furrows his brow at me. Maybe taking a second look at me as well. Shit. He's suspicious all right.

"Do something," Flicka buzzes in my ear. "Quick, before he starts asking questions."

"Uh… so you know my name but I don't know yours. We should probably get that little formality over with if we're going to spend the night together."

"Jimmy," he growls in a low, deep Akeelian alpha-male voice that kinda gets my lady bits tingling.

"Jimmy," I say. "Nice. That's a nice name. Unusual, for sure. But very catchy."

"Is it?" he asks. "That's funny."

"What's funny?"

"Almost no one can pronounce it but it seems to roll off your tongue just fine."

"No one can pronounce it?" I exclaim. Truth. It is a very strange name and my lips needed a lot of practice to say that J sound correctly. But the Loathsome One got tired of my mispronunciation and threatened me with death if I didn't get it right before I left. "That's weird," I say. "It's so simple. Jim-meeeeeee."

I'm praying to the sun gods that he lets this go.

But he just stares at me, questions written all over his face.

"Shall we?" I ask, panning my hand towards the resort. "We wouldn't want to keep the Flame Demon's head waiting."

He grumbles something under his breath but, to my relief, he just walks past me and out into the crowds.

CHAPTER SEVEN

I try to think back to the last time someone has gotten my name right the first try. Maybe Crux. But he doesn't count. We've been friends since we were kids. I'm not even sure Luck, Tray, and Valor got my name right at first. And hell, it took Serpint and Draden months after we came to ALCOR to say it right. It's just a hard name to say. I get it. I'm used to it.

But this Delphi gets it right the first try.

How?

Dicker pings my wristband as I follow Delphi over to the Flame Demon's head. "Yeah," I say.

She sighs. "How much longer? I'm sick of this place. Bunch of maintenance people just came by and said I have to shut down all my exterior lights until morning."

"Well," I say, "I have bad news. We can't even get out of the resort until tomorrow. I'm stuck spending the night in a freaking hotel that's probably gonna cost several more thousand credits. No wonder these assholes gave us priority clearance to dock. They knew they could squeeze all this money out of us. We've been here less than one day!"

"Calm down," *Dicker* says. "At least you have a room."

"I don't need a room. I have a perfectly good ship on the other side of the station that I'm not even allowed to board."

"Their station, their rules. No sense worrying about it. Just get up early and grab that water generator before this *Queenie* ship bails with my winnings. I don't trust her."

"Yeah. Can you imagine how much it would cost to buy a Mighty Demon water generator from this place? I'd kill someone."

"Just... try to relax a little. Ride one of the rollercoasters or check out that new zipline. Might as well make the most of your Mighty Pass."

She chuckles like this is all good fun, but I'm not in the mood to joke about it just yet. I'm too annoyed. I should be snug inside my medical pod getting my DNA scramble booster right now. Tomorrow morning I'd be on my way... somewhere that is not here. And now I'm a full day behind.

"Oh, that's us," Delphi says.

"Who's that?" *Dicker* asks.

"Our engineer. Long story I'll explain tomorrow. Bye." I end the connection before *Dicker* can ask any more questions because I'm not in the mood to be teased about how I'm the only guy she knows who can stop at a kids' vacation station and end up fucking a girl a few hours later.

Because I'm pretty sure how this night is gonna go. I just have this thing for attracting the ladies. I can't help it.

"Name, please?" the Demon Ambassador asks us.

"Jimmy," I say, flashing her my Mighty Pass. "We have a reservation for tonight."

"Ah, yes. Mr. Bittenbelter." I roll my eyes and don't even bother trying to correct her. "I see you've booked the Minion Maker penthouse."

"Minion what? Oh. No. I don't need a penthouse. Just a standard room, OK?"

"Ooooooh," the ambassador says. "I'm afraid we're all booked up. In fact, this room is the only one available in the whole resort. Should I cancel it and give it to someone else? We have seven families on the wait list."

This ambassador is good, I'll give her that. Because she doesn't even blink when she tells me that lie.

"No, that's fine," Delphi says.

I glare at her.

"What?" She shrugs. "It seems to be the only option."

I want to take a moment to explain that they're lying. That there's probably a hundred other rooms available in some other part of the resort and this is a scam just like everything else on this place. But why bother pointing out the obvious?

"We'll take the room," I tell Mighty Scammer.

"Great!" Scammer says, coming around the counter and waving a hand towards a hallway. "The penthouse comes with a private lift bot at your disposal all weekend and room service is—"

"Wait," I say. "Wait, wait, wait. Did you just say… weekend? We're not staying the weekend." I look at Delphi. "Did she just charge me for a weekend?"

"I don't know," Delphi says.

"Oh, I thought you knew," Mighty Scammer says.

I did, I think to myself. *Oh, I did.* I saw this scam coming a billion miles away. Or I should've. Because this place is filled with more chancers, and cheats, and backstabbing snakes than Harem Station.

"The penthouse has a mandatory three-night booking."

"Of course it does," I say.

"Your Mighty Passes have been updated with your room keys and… the lift bot awaits! Enjoy your stay!"

Mighty Scammer turns away smiling.

"How do they do that?" I ask.

"What? Cheat you out of your firstborn daughter?" Delphi laughs.

"No. I know how to do that. How do they do that wearing a creepy evil smile?"

"Yeah, I got nothing for that," Delphi says. "They are super creepy. Anyway, we get a lift bot."

I blink at her and the whole reality of my situation starts to sink in. I'm stuck in the Vacation Sector just a few million klicks from where I dropped Xyla off this morning, *Dicker* got a virus and is down a water generator, I've probably spent more than twenty thousand credits this afternoon alone while wearing a Mighty Boss hat, and I'm about to share a room with a uni-horn.

"And I think she was going to say room service is included before you interrupted her."

"You do?" I say. Then I just laugh.

"I like to see the bright side," Delphi says.

I am literally speechless. So what can I do but wave my hand towards the lift bot and say, "After you, princess. Our chariot awaits."

Unlike the lift bots on Harem, which are just small circular platforms with no railings, this one is roomy enough for luggage, kids, and has a clear plasti-glass railing so no one falls over the side.

We ascend slowly and dozens of kids down below start pointing at us, begging their parents for a ride on a lift bot even though there are three different rollercoasters running in and around Fire Mountain alone.

But you know what? Pretty soon I can't hear the little brats. Pretty soon the chaos and confusion down below fades into nothing but a mixture of white noise and waterfalls.

"Ah, that's better," Delphi says, turning around to face me and leaning back on the railing. "I know it's a scam but it might actually be worth it."

I nod, studying her. Because she doesn't add up. But I'm too tired to care at the moment. I just want to enjoy my escape from Minion Hell.

The lift bot docks at a large open-air patio and the moment we step off all the noise from down below cuts out.

"Nice," I say. "It comes with an atmospheric silencer."

I flash my pass at the security panel on the wall and it turns transparent and slides open. Inside is a suite. And I guess I knew that—it is a penthouse, after all. But I really thought we'd get up here and it would be nothing more than an upgraded standard room you'd find on the Outer Highway.

It's not.

It's actually pretty fucking spectacular.

Easily two stories tall. Maybe even two and half. And there's a reception area with guest bathroom, two chairs, and a small table. Past that is a large, open living area with pale yellow couches, light blue chairs, and accessory tables made out of white quartz.

There's a fully stocked bar on one end and a dining room off to the side of that. On the other end is a kitchen sporting a massive autocook that makes me wonder if room service really is included.

Directly in front of us, on the other side of two massive double doors, is the bedroom. The biggest bed I've ever seen. The four posts are easily five meters tall and have long, cascading panels of the most luxurious light-blue silk flowing down from the canopy. The bed cover is pale yellow silk.

Delphi and I both enter at the same time, looking around.

I spy a huge wall screen, she exclaims delight at the spa-like bathroom, and then we both breathe a sigh of relief.

"This is nice," she says.

"Yeah," I say, walking back out to the bar and helping myself to a bottle of top-shelf whiskey. "I don't really care how much it costs right now. I'm gonna make the most of this shit."

The best part of the whole thing?

I can't hear one damn screaming kid.

I take my stupid Mighty Boss hat off and fling it across the room. It lands in the middle of the floor and a servo bot bursts out of a hidden wall panel to scoop it up with grabby appendages and places it on a table.

Delphi laughs. "Holy shit. We get a private maidbot!"

But you know what? Seeing that servo bot makes me kinda sad. If I was Old Jimmy—the Jimmy I was before Corla and Lyra came to Harem Station—I'd be liberating that bot. Xyla and I would be scrambling its processor and sneaking it back onto the *Dicker*. Whisking it away to a better life.

Why did I stop liberating bots again?

I don't recall the state of mind that preceded that decision and I suddenly miss my partner, my ship, and my station.

I miss the old Jimmy.

Everything has changed since Serpint stole Corla and Lyra came to Harem. ALCOR is gone—and that baby AI will never make up for that loss. Valor and Luck aren't even partners anymore. Crux is so preoccupied by his sleeping soulmate, he hasn't talked to me in months. Draden is dead, Tray is antisocial, and Serpint isn't interested in being a bounty hunter anymore.

Add in Angel Station warning me at that meeting I had with them about some fucked-up war I want no part of, but which seems to center around me and my brothers, and you've got yourself a proper shit show.

How did all this shit happen?

How did my life become so unrecognizable so fast?

CHAPTER EIGHT

This place is actually tasteful. And unlike everything built for the masses down below, there's no sign of Mighty Boss anywhere. Not one thing in black and red. Not one logo, not one reminder that I'm here on Mighty Minions Resort.

Except… Jimmy.

He's gone along with this so far. Letting me, a stranger, stay the night with him in a room, even though I'm supposed to live here on the station and be working as a ship engineer.

Why?

I don't know. I feel like maybe he's on to me and this is a setup.

There's a mirror behind the bar and I catch sight of my reflection in it. My black and red horn with everlasting holo flames shooting out the top. My Mighty Hime princess hologram running through my bodysuit.

"Ugggh," I say, hating what I see.

"What's up?" Jimmy asks.

"This little get-up I'm wearing."

"Yeah, what's the deal with that? They make you dress this way in engineering?"

"Yeah." I sigh, then reconsider because tomorrow we're going to be back in the docking bays and he will surely notice that no one is sporting shooting flames and horns. "No. I was... I have... a side thing. You know, to get extra cash. Entertaining the kids in this stupid Mighty Minion battle."

He raises a single eyebrow at me, downs his drink, sets his glass on the bar, and then says, "You know what?"

"What?" I ask.

"I don't really give a fuck, Delphi. I don't give a single sun-fucked fuck what you're doing here. As long you help me get the hell off this station tomorrow, we're cool."

I nod at him. "Cool."

Because I will be helping him leave this station. Just not the way he thinks.

"So... you wanna take a spin on the autoshopper?" He cocks his head to the side where holy suns, there is the biggest, most modern version of the autoshopper I've ever seen.

I look back at Jimmy and say, "Why?"

"Because that little outfit was cute down there for like... ten minutes. But up here, you just look ridiculous. And uncomfortable. If you really do have a room here, and you really do owe your roommates money and can't go back there, then surely you will need something else to wear tonight. So go for it. My treat."

"Why?"

"I think I just answered that."

"No," I say, sucking in a deep breath of air. "I mean, why is it your treat?"

He shrugs. "Because I'm fucking rich. And I don't care how many credits Mighty Minions scams me out of, it's not going to matter. Just a little blip in the bank account and nothing more."

"Oh," I say, trying to imagine what that feels like, and find I can't. Not even when I was back in Cygnian System did I have access to unlimited credits to buy anything I wanted. And I was one of the lucky ones. One of the girls who had an actual family, and a home, and didn't live in the harems with dozens of sisters.

"You can stay here all weekend too," he says. "If you want. It's paid for. Might as well enjoy it."

"Really?"

"Sure. Why not?"

Why not? I wonder.

He's not what I expected, that's for sure.

Flicka buzzes in my ear. "Don't fall for it. He's dangerous, Delphi."

I swat her away and she flits off to go exploring.

"Where did you really get that dragonbee bot?" Jimmy asks.

"I told you, she's been with me since I was a little girl."

"What kind of parent gives a child a dangerous bot like that?"

"How do you know they're dangerous?"

"I'm sort of a bot expert." He refills his drink, takes a sip of whiskey, and then uses his glass to point to the wall panel where the maidbot appeared and disappeared a few moments ago. "That's an UltraClean

9000 series. A very high-end bot with near-sentient processing power."

"Get out of here." I laugh. "Near-sentient? Please. It's a vacuum."

"No," Jimmy says, shaking his head. "That thing could beat you at any game of chance you could imagine."

"A maidbot?" I scoff.

He nods. "They're actually pretty creative too. I once knew a maidbot who painted Centurian portraits as a hobby."

I shake my head and scoff again.

"I swear. She still does. She's got a gallery on Harem Station. I haven't seen her in a while, but she was one of the first bots I ever liberated."

"What the hell are you talking about? Liberate bots? That's not what you do."

He raises that eyebrow again.

Oops. I shouldn't know what he does. "I mean," I say, correcting myself, "you look like… I don't know. A bounty hunter, or something."

"No." He laughs. He's got a nice laugh. And a nice smile too. In fact, Jimmy of Harem Station isn't anything like I imagined. "That's my brother, Serpint. He's the bounty hunter in the family. I'm in charge of bot liberation."

"That word," I say. "It makes no sense to me. I mean, liberation? I don't get it. You what? Buy them and take them back to… did you say Harem Station?"

"Sometimes we buy them. Most times we just steal them. You can't own people, you know."

"Yeah." I laugh. "But you can own bots."

"Not if they're people."

"They're not people."

"They are people."

"OK," I say. "Whatever you say. Thank you for the shopping offer, but I'm fine. In fact, maybe I should just find another place to stay?"

And you know what the funny thing is? When I say this to him, I mean it. He's weird. This whole bots-are-people-too thing, also weird. And his brother, Serpint? One of the most awful men in the entire galaxy. They not only steal bots, they steal us. Me. People like me. And they take us to that rogue station, and trap us in their special princess harem, and use us for sex. Just like everyone else. They are not liberators. They are hunters.

I'm sure I could find a way to sneak back on *Queenie*. There has to be a way. In fact, I'm sure she'd even help me. Subvert some security system or something. I just can't stay here with him. He's creeping me out.

"Well," Jimmy says. "You could try."

"Try what?"

"To leave."

"What?"

"Come on." He laughs. "How stupid do I look, Delphi? Or should I say, *Princess* Delphi? You're a Cygnian."

"You're crazy."

"'Oh, I have a little dragonbee bot my parents gave me when I was a child.' You know, that was your first giveaway. But the second one was your attitude about the maidbot. Only true assholes or Cygnians feel that way about bots these days. Which is really kind of sad because you seem to actually like your little bot friend."

Flicka buzzes in front of him, preparing to sting while I turn, leg in the air, ready to deliver a flying leap kick to the side of Jimmy's face. But Jimmy taps his wristband and Flicka drops to the floor like dead weight and then his forearm comes up, blocking my kick, knocking me down, and before I even realize what's happened, he's got me pinned to the floor.

"Get off me."

"No. Your little bot friend tried to sting me. And if you'd have landed that kick I could've lost a tooth. So no. I'm gonna stay right here on top of you while you explain just what the fuck you're doing and why you're lying to me."

"I'm not lying!"

"Ha." He laughs. "Pretty much everything out of your mouth today was a lie. You don't live here, do you? Are you even an engineer?"

"Get off me," I seethe through gritted teeth.

"Answer me," he growls, pressing his full weight down on my body.

"I can't breathe," I whine.

"Save it," he snaps. "If you can talk you can breathe. Now tell me what the fuck is going on."

Flicka is buzzing in circles just a few feet away. Desperately trying to get her functions back, but failing. Jimmy must've activated some kind of bot regulator when he tapped his wristband.

What should I do? What can I do?

I can't tell him, Tycho's life is on the line. And I can't *not* tell him because he's got control of Flicka.

"Look," Jimmy says. "I'm really not a bad guy. I'm actually pretty reasonable. But I'm getting the feeling that everything that's happened to me today is because of you. So tell me what I need to know and I'll let you get back on that lift bot and leave the way you came."

"I can't."

"Why not?"

"Because…"

"Because why? Just spit it out, Delphi. Your plan, whatever it was, is fucked, OK? Fucked."

"It can't be fucked!"

"Why not?"

"Because my brother will die, OK? And I'm not gonna let him die. So if it comes down to you or him, I choose him!"

"Me?" Jimmy says, easing up a little so I can take full breaths again. "What the fuck do you want with *me*?"

"Let me up."

"And then what? You run? You spill everything? You try to kill me? What happens if I let you up?"

I suck in a deep breath.

"Whatever it was you were doing, Delphi—if that's your real name—it's over. I'm not gonna hurt you unless you make me. So please," he says. "Don't make me."

And then he rolls off me, stands up, and offers me his hand.

CHAPTER NINE

She doesn't take my hand. Just hikes her legs back and flips onto her feet like some kind of Mighty Warrior.

Which, I admit, I find sorta cute.

She circles me, jaw set, knees slightly bent, like she's about to pounce.

Also kinda cute.

"What's all this?" I ask, panning my hand in her direction. "You're gonna attack me?"

"Maybe," she says, breathing a little harder than normal.

"So do it. But I'm gonna warn you ahead of time. There's a timer on that shutdown function I just zapped your little dragonbee with. And by shutdown, I don't mean it wears off. I mean it kills her."

"You're such a dick!" Delphi growls. "Hurting innocent bots."

"Innocent? No. I know what she is. I've seen dragonbee bots in action more times than I can count. We don't even allow them on Harem Station, that's how dangerous and unpredictable they are."

"Mine isn't. She's my friend."

"And yet you called the maidbot a vacuum."

Delphi huffs.

"So, you wanna play by my rules or not?"

"Let her go first," Delphi says, jutting her chin towards the spinning and buzzing dragonbee bot on the floor.

I give her a wide smile, then walk over to the bot, pick it up—carefully—by the wings, then walk back over to the bar, drop it inside a glass, and turn the glass over.

Delphi sucks in a deep breath of air. "That's not letting her go."

"No, it isn't. She's gonna stay right there until we're done talking. But just so you know, the shutdown sequence is still running. We've got"—I look down at my wristband—"six minutes and seventeen seconds before she goes poof."

"Why are you being such a sun-fucking asshole?"

"Because you're lying. And you know what? I'm starting to get the feeling all you pinks and silvers are nothing but liars."

She touches her hair and frowns. "How'd you know I was a pink?"

I roll my eyes. "Are you serious?"

"Yeah, I'm fucking serious."

"Your eyes are pink when you're angry."

"Oh," she says. "Shit. I forgot about that. But I wasn't really hiding my identity anyway. So whatever."

"We good?" I ask. "Gonna tell me some truth now?"

She just glares at me.

"OK. What's your real name?"

"It's Delphi. I didn't lie about that."

"Cool. Good. Why are you here?"

"Here?" she says, pointing down at the floor.

"No," I say. "Here, as in Mighty Minions." But actually, now that she mentions it, why *is* she here in my hotel room?

She growls a little. I interpret this as frustration because she doesn't want to spill all her secrets.

"Come on, princess. Your jig is up."

She makes a face. "What's that even mean?"

"You know. You got caught. There's no way out but the truth. So spill it."

She just shakes her head.

"What's that mean? You still in denial and you want me to believe you don't have secrets? Or you can't say?"

"Can't say."

"Because you're afraid of me? Or how I'll react? Or... afraid of someone else?"

She frowns.

"Hmmm," I say, thinking this through. On the one hand, she doesn't look very dangerous. She's short, and petite, and she's sporting a uni-horn on her head. And even though I'm pretty sure Mighty Minions is probably where demon worshippers take their kids for fun and she's dressed up like them, I'm also pretty sure she's not really a Mighty Minion.

But on the other hand, she does have that asshole dragonbee bot.

And she is most definitely a Cygnian princess, which... wasn't that the whole reason I was heading to the genetics lab in the first place? To avoid people like her?

"How about this," I say. "I'll make you an offer."

"What kind of offer?"

"You tell me what you're caught up in and I'll see what I can do to help. I have connections, you know. I actually know a bunch of Cygnian princesses. My brother collects them in a harem on my home station."

She just stares at me.

"But you know all that already, don't you?"

She gives me just the slightest bit of a nod.

"I can help you. If you let me."

"You really can't," she says.

"Right," I say, remembering the words she blurted out just before I tackled her. "If it comes down to me or him, you choose him. So you're here for me?"

Not even a blink from Delphi but her tiny bot is spinning and buzzing like crazy inside the glass, futilely trying to get control of its motor functions.

"You're here for me," I say again, trying it on for size. "Like… you're a booty hunter for Akeelians?" I smile at the irony. "Hey, is there a harem wherever it was you were gonna take me? Like… are there a ton of other Akeelian males just letting their cocks hang out while dozens of rich women peruse them and take them for a spin?"

"You think this is funny?"

"I have no idea what this is, Delphi. I'm just filling in my own blanks because you refuse to illuminate me." Then I laugh. "Ha. Little glow joke there." But then… oh. I recall the reason why everyone loves the Cygnian princesses and wonder what she'd look like out of that stupid costume. Wondering what she'd look like exploding like the sun.

No, that's a bad idea. Very bad idea. I'm on my way to make sure no Cygnian princess ever catches me in their stupid soulmate net.

Still… there's kind of an innate attraction to her. Or at the very least, a fascination.

"OK," I say, taking a deep breath and letting it out. "How about a truce?"

"Why?"

"Why? I mean, it's pretty obvious why."

"No, it isn't."

"Yeah, it is. You're here for me and I need you to tell me why. Because I'm starting to think that the whole reason I'm stuck on this stupid resort is because of you. Did you send my ship a virus?"

She presses her lips together and folds her arms across her chest.

"Ahh," I say. "OK. Well… truce. How about you do a little shopping, take a shower and wash that ridiculous horn off your head, and then we can eat something that isn't four-hundred-credit noodles."

"Why?" she snaps. "Why are you being this way?"

"What way?"

"Nice! Understanding! Considerate!"

"Maybe because that's the kind of guy I am," I say. Smoothly, I might add.

"You kidnap princesses."

"I already told you, I liberate bots."

"You keep them captive up in that station."

"They're there by choice."

"You sell them to rich people all over the galaxy."

"Not without permission, we don't. You've got this all wrong."

"Which part?"

JA HUSS & KC CROSS

"Every part I just mentioned! For sun's sake, why can't you just accept my peace offering? I'm the victim here, not you."

"Exactly," she says, nodding her head like this explains everything.

I point to the bedroom. "Go take a shower and wash that shit off your hair."

She shakes her head. "Let my bot out of that glass and stop that shutdown sequence."

"Oh." I laugh. "I forgot about that." I tab my wristband and the bot springs up, hitting the top of the glass, and knocks itself out.

"What did you do?" Delphi asks, rushing over to the bar. But I put a hand over the top of the glass before she can lift it up.

"It stays in there for now. It just hit its head."

"She's a *she*, not an *it*."

"Right. Flicka."

"Yes. And you better not hurt her. She's the only friend I have left."

"Well, that's all very sad, princess. But she stays put until you spill the beans about your plan. And," I say, putting up a hand because she's about to protest again, "the reason I'm calling a truce is so you can find a way to trust me. OK? That's it. I give you things, you give me things. We're good. Both of us gets something in the end."

"I need something you don't have."

"Ah," I say. "Your brother. Now that's an interesting story because I was told that Cygnian males are worthless pieces of shit."

She opens her mouth to curse me, but I continue before she can.

76

"Just what I've heard, Delphi. I'm not saying it's true. But I do know they're not highly regarded where you come from, so this has got to be a very interesting story. And it's worth the stop on Mighty Minions, the seven-thousand-credit family pass, the insane demon holo children, and the cost of this room just to get that answer. So go take a shower, buy yourself some new clothes, and then we can talk like rational, grown-up people whose only purpose seems to be to fuck each other and make babies."

She blinks at me. "What?"

I sigh. Because even though I know better, even though I know that getting mixed up with this girl just puts me one step closer to soulmate territory, and stupid kids, and all that other shit our kind seems to have been genetically engineered to need, I can't help it.

The only ride on this resort I'm interested in taking is Delphi.

CHAPTER TEN

"That's it?" I ask. "'Just go shopping, Delphi. Go take a shower. Relax. Let's get dinner. Have a little date night.' You think I'm actually gonna buy that crap?"

He narrows his eyes. "What do you mean?"

"What do I mean?" I huff. "I know that you know."

"I know what?"

"Uh-huh. Exactly."

He does one of those long blinks. You know, when people are tired of you. When you're wearing them down. But I don't fall for it. I don't fall for any of it. "I know that you know what I am. I heard all about Lyra spilling our secrets."

"Ohhhhhhh," he says.

"Ohhhh," I say, mocking him.

"You mean the sex explosions?"

"What? No. And stop thinking about sex with me. Not gonna happen. I'm talking about the *station* explosion."

"Nyleena didn't explode Bull Station. And neither did we. So I don't know what you're talking about. But back to why you think I'm thinking about sex with you. Are you thinking about sex with me?"

"Look at this," I say, panning my hand down my body. "Does this look like a princess ready to get it on? There is no glow, genius. That means there's no feelings. And that means there's no possible way I'm thinking about sex with you. You, on the other hand," I say, pointing to his groin area, "are sporting a double-dicked hard-on."

He looks down, then looks back up—smiling.

"So don't play this off like I'm the one coming on to you. I'm not. Just... ewww."

"Ewww?"

"Yeah. Ewwww. I know better, buddy. I know better than to get caught up in some ridiculous Akeelian-Cygnian love fest. No way. Not gonna happen. There are no breeder babies in my future."

But huh. I suddenly have this little idea. He's so horny. He's so ready to find his one true princess. Maybe what I'm doing isn't even bad? Maybe I'm actually doing him a favor?

"What?" he asks.

"What what?"

"You're thinking something."

"No, I'm not."

"Yes, you are. Your eyes are lighting up again."

Son of a sunfucker. Why do these damn eyes have to give me away every single time?

"So you've got your glowing eyes on someone else, is that it? Because I'm pretty sure I'm better than whoever that guy is."

I actually guffaw.

He shrugs. "I'm just saying. I didn't name my ship the *Big Dicker* for nothing. I'm what you call... hung."

"I think I just threw up in my mouth."

"You're so cute," he says, shooting me with his finger.

"No," I say. "No, I'm not."

"So we're good?"

"What? No! We're not good."

"You go shopping, take a shower, feel normal again and I'll order up some grade-A autocooked Mighty Dinner."

Is he like... infatuated with me? I don't understand this. I'm saying ewww and he's just not getting it. "Let me spell it out for you, Mr. Liberator. I'm not interested."

"Yeah, but," he says, waggling his eyebrows. "Give me a chance. I've got moves."

Flicka starts buzzing and banging against the glass, her tiny voice just barely filtering through to my genetically engineered ears. *What is wrong with you? Just go along with this stupid oaf. We can probably get him drunk and then that amazing lift bot can deliver him to Queenie as soon as the gates open in the morning!*

"Hmmm," I say, considering her plan. It could work.

"Hmmm?" Jimmy says, giant smile on his face. "See, you're already falling for me."

Oh, my suns. How the hell did this guy go from alpha asshole to gooey love nut in the span of a few minutes? It makes absolutely no sense.

Unless he's always been this way and I read him wrong.

Did I read him wrong?

No. I'm a professional. I don't read anyone wrong.

"Well?" Jimmy asks.

"Well…" I feign a huge sigh, something in between relief and resignation. "OK. If you insist. I mean, I am stuck here for the night. So yes. I'll take you up on your offer of unlimited access to the autoshopper and a shower."

I smile sweetly. Then squint my eyes because did his dicks just grow?

"Excellent," he says.

"But…" I say.

He raises his eyebrows.

"You have to let Flicka out of the glass."

He looks over at my dragonbee bot and frowns, then cocks his head, looks at me, back at Flicka, and frowns again.

It's almost as if he's about to come to his senses. So I say, "Never mind. She's fine in there." Which makes Flicka go crazy as she bats herself against the side of the glass with a flurry of metallic wings.

Jimmy's furrowed brow eases a little.

"What shall I wear for you?" I offer, hoping to send him back into horny Akeelian male mode.

And it works! Because he smiles. "Something… *pink.*"

Ewwww. But I keep that to myself. Because holy shit. I think I have him under some kind of spell. Some kind of Cygnian princess love spell.

I wave my hand in front of my face to make that image go away because… ewwww.

"OK," I say. "Next time you see me I'll be all pink for you."

I turn towards the bedroom, then look back over my shoulder as I pass through and give him a wink, just to make sure that love spell is still cooking.

He waves his fingers at me.

Gross.

I close the door and cover my mouth so I don't laugh out loud.

What a tool.

Because this guy right here... he's falling for the wrong princess.

The autoshopper in the bedroom is just like the one in the living room. I turn it on, stand in front of it, and let it scan my body because this sucker right here is top of the line. I'm talking full-on holographic 3-D body image of any outfit in the store.

I mean... if a girl is forced to shop there are worse ways to do it, am I right?

And actually... I look over my shoulder at the closed door. He did say unlimited access. Well, I said unlimited access, but he didn't object. So I'm gonna get myself an entire new wardrobe.

Why not? I've been broke for so long. Ever since Tycho and I made our big escape meals have been lean, and budgets have been tight, and before we got caught up in the Loathsome One's diabolical plan, we worked our butts off doing stupid menial jobs far below our pay grade.

We are skilled, we are tough, and we not only made it out of Cygnia, we made it out *together*.

I deserve this. Hell, he deserves this too.

So the first thing I do is order luggage. Because I'm gonna pack those suckers full of clothes for both of us and when I leave here—with Jimmy—I'm gonna make sure Tycho feels like the prince he is when I get him back.

Because he is a prince. If he's my twin and I'm a princess, then he is a prince and he deserves this.

I get him three pairs of the newest, most up-to-date tech-enabled tactical pants I can find. I get him t-shirts, and thermal shirts, and boots, and a super-expensive bomber jacket that will keep him warm once we get where we're going. And super-soft, super-nice socks, and a belt that costs more than the fake horn I'm sporting.

I even get him pajamas.

Then it's my turn. I go practical as well. More tactical pants for me. Plus leggings, and T-shirts, and sweaters, and a warm and fuzzy nandi-wool coat with matching booties that looks amazing when the 3-D holo image of me spins inside the mini-dressing room. I even get shorts and a pair of sandals just in case I ever get back this way and can manage a stop on Blue Sand Beach.

And then I press 'Send to Printer' and it's done.

I lean back, pretty fucking satisfied with myself.

But then I glance at the shower and it's beckoning me. I go check it and find it's one of those total immersion experience capsules. There's a control panel on the side with a bazillion settings and almost none of them have anything to do with soap.

Good gods. I look over my shoulder, maybe just the tiniest bit embarrassed. Because for being inside a family resort, it's certainly not meant for kids.

We have one experience called 'Single and Loving It' which features specially ribbed scrubby bots and when I tab the quick sample button on the screen there's an animated movie explaining just what the little scrubby bots are capable of.

Then there's one called 'Couples' Experience' which has both scrubby bots and grippy bots and that sample animation can almost count as porn.

Mmmm-hmmm. Mighty Boss has a dirty mind.

I choose "Quick Clean" because tempting as it is, I'm not here for self-pleasure. Or couples' pleasure. I'm here to use this guy's credits in the autoshopper, get him drunk, and then kidnap his ass and take him back to the Loathsome One to exchange for my brother.

My unihorn hair falls apart the moment water touches it, but I don't miss it. This might be the basic get-clean version of this shower, but it's the best one I've had in ages.

Still, Jimmy's been quiet out there this whole time and a part of me wonders if he's cooking up some scheme. So I finish up, dress in some comfy leggings, a sweater, and my nandi-wool booties. Ready to get this show on the road.

CHAPTER ELEVEN

Delphi disappears into the bedroom and I just stand there looking at the closed door for a few moments, wondering how I got so lucky. She's so damn cute. And a little mouthy. I like that. And sexy. Even though she's got a stupid hair horn on her head.

I smile like an idiot thinking about all this.

Then... I feel like an idiot.

What the hell am I thinking? She's a fucking Cygnian princess. The exact opposite of what I'm looking for. The whole damn reason I'm on my way to the Outer Highway to get my DNA signature scrambled.

But then I hear her talking in the bedroom. I walk over to the door, press my ear against it just as she lets out a sigh and mutters, "Oh, that's nice."

I want to open the door and see what she's doing.

Shopping, I think. I told her to shop and get anything she wants.

Why did I say that again?

I slowly back away from the room, trying to put some distance between us. Is she emitting pheromones

JA HUSS & KC CROSS

or something? Am I under some kind of Cygnian spell? Is she gonna ruin my life?

Once my retreat back into the living area is complete I contact *Dicker* on my wristband.

"Oh, hey, can't talk," *Dicker* says. "I'm in the middle of winning a salvage bike from this crazy *Queenie*."

"*Queenie?*"

"The ship? Sun's sake, don't you pay attention to anything?"

"We don't even use salvage bikes, *Dicker*."

"Yet," she says. "But they're good to have on hand. Do you or do you not recall how Serpint saved Lyra's life back at Bull Station because we had Luck and Valor's salvage units on board?"

"Are you OK?"

"Fine, why?"

"Because you're acting weird."

"Weird? I don't know what you mean. But did you need something? Because I need to get back to my game."

"Did you lose anything yet?"

"Yet? And lose? Uh… no. I don't lose. I'm the *Big Dicker*."

"Well, I just called because I feel strange around this girl."

"Strange as in you're a freak? Or strange as in she makes you uncomfortable?"

"Neither," I say. "I feel like… I dunno. I *like* her."

"Good! That's great. I'm really glad you found a friend."

"No, not like—"

"OK, awesome talk. I gotta run. Keep me posted."

And then she cuts the connection.

I just stare at my wristband for a second wondering… does my ship have a gambling problem?

I think about this for a few moments. She's always been into games. And sure, she typically finds at least one sentient ship to play with wherever we stop. But she's never been so into *winning*. Maybe that's because this is strip poker?

Which, I have to say, I do not approve of. My ship is perfect the way she is. Water generator issues aside, I'm quite happy with our current configuration. Like… why does she suddenly want a kitchen? I'm the only one on board who even eats. Xyla just recharges her core battery in a customized sexbot charger. And while yeah, everyone can use salvage bikes, I guess—they're small, and easy to maneuver, and handy in an emergency—we don't pick up bots in space. And we don't even have a charging station to store them.

A message chimes in on my wristband.

Dicker: We won the salvage bikes! Yay! I'm gonna go for the charging station next!

Me: *We don't have time to mess with this stuff. How are we going to retrofit the ship for salvage bikes and charging stations?*

Dicker: Ye of little faith. We can just throw it all into the cargo bay and deal with it back on Harem. Dicker *out.*

The sound of the shower starting in the bedroom jolts me back to my current issue.

This girl.

Delphi.

Who the hell is she?

And she's pink, which means she's important. Which means she probably explodes like Lyra and Corla. Which means... why the fuck is she here?

Sun gods, Jimmy. Get a grip. She already told you in not so many words, she's here for you!

Oh, yeah. How did that slip my mind? Like... it's kind of an important fact, right? She's here for me.

There's definitely something wrong with me. Maybe she drugged me? Maybe this DNA signature scramble is wearing off?

It shouldn't be. I'm months early for my booster. This whole trip was just about extra precautions.

But everything has gone wrong since I dropped Xyla off. When was the last time I was in danger and Xyla wasn't around to have my back?

Never, I decide. This is the first and only time that I've been out in space without her.

I wonder if I could reach her from here?

I tap my wristband and find her contact, so wishing we were on Harem and I could just open an air screen or command Baby ALCOR to send a neutrino wave to her comms. I ping her, hoping that Blue Sand Beach is close enough for me to get through.

But a Mighty Minion message appears stating that while I'm not authorized for inter-station calls I could purchase an add-on communication package for the low, low price of twenty-five thousand credits.

Figures. This place is such a scam.

I decide this is worth it, so I tap the 'Purchase' tab. I need to get in touch with her and let her know what's happening. My Mighty Pass chimes and says, "You can now make inter-station calls in the Vacation Sector."

"Great." I tab Xyla again, then wait as a little animation of Mighty Boss making a call to Mighty Hime plays on my little screen.

Xyla's face appears. She's in the middle of sipping a frothy exotic drink with half a dozen swizzle sticks poking out the top, and her sexybot girlfriends are all crowding into the frame. "Jim-meeeeeee!" She laughs, almost spitting out her drink.

"So hey, sorry to bother you but—"

"Jim-meeeeeeee," all the girlfriends echo.

"Uh, hey… ladies. Nice to see you again. Xyla, can I have a moment?"

"Jimmmmmm-meeeeeeeeeeee!" they all say again.

For sun's fucking sake. Has everyone on my team lost their fucking mind?

"I got a new swimsuit," Xyla says. "Wanna check it out?" She fumbles with her wristband, taking it off, I guess, then hands it to her friend and says, "Get all of me in the frame," as she steps back and starts modeling her new purple bikini, yellow ocean and blue sand beach in the background.

"Looks great," I say. "So can I talk to you for—"

"Don't you love it? Cha-Cha got one too. Here, Chach. Gimme that back and you model next!"

"Xyla," I say, rubbing my temple with two fingers. Because I'm starting to get annoyed.

But Cha-Cha is already twirling unsteadily in a circle. Her suit is lime green and comes with holsters hanging off her hip strings for holding knives.

"Now you, Ladybug!"

Ladybug's suit is black with red polka dots and she's sporting a plasma pistol on her hip.

"And look!" Xyla exclaims. "They sell SEAR swords here!" The frame rotates, goes upside down, then rotates again and then Xyla is standing backlit by a fake Blue Sand Beach sun, spinning, and kicking as she demonstrates her sword skills.

I just watch her until she's done because Chach and Ladybug are screaming and whistling in the background.

She comes back to the wristband, takes it in her hand and shoves it up to her face, then pans it around the beach hut. "This place," she slurs, "is a goddamned assassin's paradise!"

"Are we assassins now?" I ask.

"We've decided we are," Cha-Cha says, as she whips out her own sword, stands, erect, closes her eyes, breathes deep, and then starts doing a slow-motion kata routine complete with slow-motion talking.

Ladybug and Xyla erupt in giggles, practically falling over.

OK. So calling Xyla was probably a bad idea.

"Oh," Xyla says, still laughing. "Did you need something, Jimmy?"

"No," I say. "No... just we're stuck here."

Xyla frowns. "Stuck? Where?"

"On Mighty Minions."

All three girls erupt in laughter.

"Yup," I say. "It's pretty funny. We got a virus and had to stop to get a new water generator. And now *Dicker* seems to have a strip poker problem and I met this girl. She's supposed to be an engineer but she's really—"

A siren sounds over on Blue Sand Beach and all three girls swivel their heads to the left.

"That's the last call for the wet package contest," Xyla says, out of breath. "Gotta go."

And then the call drops.

What the fuck is happening?

I call her back but Mighty Boss informs me that I've used up all my comm credits.

Because of course I have.

Just then the bedroom door opens and Delphi walks out wearing tight leggings that hug her hips, a tight sweater that hugs her tits, and some furry booties.

Immediately I become distracted. Like... I can't take my eyes off this cute little pink nightmare. My cocks begin to swell. Both of them. And if I was in my right mind I'd be worried about that, because my junk just doesn't work that way. But I'm not in my right mind. My mind is consumed with thoughts of kissing her, and fondling her, and yes, fucking her brains out.

"Jimmy," she says, posing seductively against the wall. Then she looks around and says, "Where's dinner?"

CHAPTER TWELVE

Jimmy stares at me with heavy, hooded eyes. Like I'm what's for dinner. And there's this tiny tingle in my belly. Just a little stirring up of heat and longing. I force the glow back into submission because I can feel it trying to rear its unruly head.

I'm not into this guy. I'm here to kidnap him and take him back to the Loathsome One so I can save my brother.

Jimmy shakes his head, like he's shaking himself out of a stupor at the same time, and says, "Maybe we should go out to eat?"

"Oh," I say, squinting my eyes at him. "Why? I mean, out there?" I jerk my head to the expansive set of patio doors. "Into the chaos of Mighty Minions?"

"Yeah," he says, lazily and with some effort. Then he shakes his head again and revises. "No. No. No. That's a bad idea." His eyes dart to the bedroom and that stirring inside me comes rushing back. "But you know what is a good idea?"

"What?" I say, leaning forward without meaning to.

"Me taking a cold shower. That's what. Just give me five minutes." Then he walks towards me, pressing himself up against the opposite wall as he slips past me in the hallway, and disappears into the bedroom, closing the door behind him and turning the lock.

What the hell was that?

My wristband vibrates an incoming message.

"Oh, God." I sigh. Because there's only one person that could be. "What?" I say, after tabbing accept.

"Where are you? I'm ready to go. This *Big Dicker* ship is getting on my nerves. She's starting to catch on and keeps asking me for my docking bay number so she can send someone to pick up the water generator, kitchen, and salvage bikes."

"What the hell are you talking about?"

"The strip poker game I'm playing to distract his stupid ship and give you time to get him on board. What's taking so long? And where did you get those clothes?"

I look down at my super-comfy outfit, then back at my screen to the little animated voice wave of *Queenie*. "Jimmy offered to let me autoshop. So I did."

If this ship could roll her eyes at me, she would be doing that right now. "He just… offered, huh?" Then she lowers her voice. "Are you fucking this asshole?"

"No," I say. *But I might like to,* I don't add.

"Where are you? Is that… did you two get a room?"

"We're stuck here until the morning. All the docking bays are locked up tight for the night."

"You're joking," *Queenie* says.

"No, I swear. The Mighty Ambassador told us that we can't get past the receiving areas."

"And you believed her? And *he* believed her? Do you, or do you not, both have access to evil sentient ships?"

Hmmm. Is *Queenie* evil? She might be.

"For fuck's sake," *Queenie* says. "Use your damn brain. Make your way to my docking bay immediately and ping me when you get there. I'll open the doors and—"

"No," I say, kinda sick of her shit. "You're not in charge here, OK? I am. This is my mission and you're just transportation. So I'm letting you know right now that we have a plan and that's the one we're using."

"You're right, we did have a plan. And you're not following through."

"Not you, we. Jimmy and I are the we here."

"You and Jimmy have a plan to kidnap him?"

"Yes. No. Yes." I sigh with frustration. "He thinks he needs to pick up the water generator. So it's fine. There's no point in calling attention to us by trying to hack into the Mighty Minions security system when we don't have to."

"You're breathing thin air right now, Delphi. And the Loathsome One is going to hear all about this in my report. Do I need to remind you what's at stake here? Your brother is probably being tortured, or hell, maybe he's even dead by now, that's how long this is taking."

I narrow my eyes at her, instantly angry and serious. "He better not be dead. That's all I have to say. Because... because..."

"Because... what?" she challenges.

"Because I'm dangerous, that's what. You have no idea how dangerous I can be."

"Pfffft," she scoffs. "You're stupid. You're weak. You're no more dangerous than that idiotic dragonbee bot. So I'm telling you one last time, get him down to my docking bay immediately or I'm sending word to Loathsome One that you've gone rogue."

"I'm gonna take my chances," I growl, ending the call.

That's when Flicka starts buzzing against the side of the glass she's trapped under and jolts me back to the situation.

"Oh, shit! Flicka! I'm sorry!" I rush over to the bar and lift the glass. She comes whizzing up in spiral circles and then zooms across the room. Hovering for a second as she stretches her wings, then flies back to me and lands on my shoulder.

"I heard all that," Flicka squeaks in her tiny voice. "Maybe we should do what *Queenie* says?"

"She's not in charge. I am."

"Did it ever occur to you," Flicka says, "that the Loathsome One sent *Queenie* along to spy on you? Or to get rid of you? All she has to do is turn off life support on the ship while you're sleeping and it's over. She'll have Jimmy and that's all the Loathsome One wants, anyway."

Oh. Well, shit. I didn't even think of that. "I'll put on a suit as soon as we board."

"Alternatively," Flicka says. "Perhaps we should…"

"We should what?"

"Change teams? Hmmm?"

"Change… you mean join up with Jimmy?" I guffaw pretty loud at that. "How is that going to help us get Tycho back?"

98

"He has friends, right? Powerful friends. Even if one is pretty drunk right now. He's got that ship. I'm pretty sure that the *Big Dicker* is better equipped than *Queenie*. The Loathsome One doesn't have a super-sentient AI with no restrictions running her station and upgrading her ships to illegal standards, right?"

"I don't know," I say.

"She doesn't. I do know. The Loathsome One Lair Station AI has all kinds of regulators on it. She would never give anyone power over ships like that."

"Hmmm. Sounds iffy, if you ask me. Why would Jimmy help me? I'm no one."

"He's infatuated with you," Flicka informs me. "I heard him talking to Xyla while you were in the shower. And don't worry, *Queenie* can't make a call to the Loathsome One. Even if she paid the exorbitant fee, the comms only work in the Vacation Sector."

"He's infatuated with me? How can you tell?"

"Duh. Two cocks, Delphi. There's something going on between you two. Like… something big."

"No," I say. "I'd feel that. I'd at least glow if he so much as touched me. At the very least, I'd get all weird and tingly and—oh, shit."

"That's right," Flicka says. "You two have some kind of connection."

"But if we were… you know. Then I'd know! I'd light up, and become all stupid, and try to make him fuck me."

"I think he's taking something to stop the attraction. I don't know what or how it works, but he feels it too. And if you two are connected like that, then it's a waste of time going through with this plan.

Because you'll choose him over Tycho in the end. You won't be able to help yourself."

"No! I won't! That can't happen!"

"But it will, Delphi. We should switch teams now before it's too late. I don't know why your father let Tycho live with you growing up, but we should assume it's because he has a role to play. And it wouldn't be very hard to convince Jimmy that Tycho's place is back on Harem where they are all desperate to figure this mess out."

"What role, though?"

"It doesn't matter. It doesn't even matter if it's a lie. As long as Jimmy and his Harem Station brothers think he's important, it's in their best interest to save him."

I think about this for a moment.

"We need to change sides. You need to tell him everything and get a new plan in motion before morning."

"How would I even start this conversation? What do I say? 'Oh, hey. Sorry, but I've been lying to you this whole time. I'm really here to kidnap you and hand you over to the Loathsome One in exchange for my brother, who, by the way, is so important you need to now trust me and go risk your life to save him?' He'll never fall for it!"

"Well," Flicka says. "There is one sure way to *make* him fall for it."

"How?"

"Make him fall for *you*. Tell him you're his soulmate."

CHAPTER THIRTEEN

The minute I close the bedroom door I feel stupid. Did I just run away from a woman? Because she's sexy? And turning me on? And could maybe, possibly be an explosive device meant to take down the Prime Navy and usher in a new nightmare age of Cygnian-Akeelian domination?

Did I really just think that?

I shake my head and chuckle. I'm losing my mind. Maybe I should call *Dicker* back and try to explain things? See if any of this makes sense or it's just the ramblings of a guy infatuated with a girl?

But then I notice all the shopping she did. Lots of outfits. And oh, hey, what's that? Did she... no. Did she?

"Holy shit," I mutter, walking over to the dresser where all her clothes are neatly folded, fresh from the autoshopper. "She did."

She bought me clothes!

For some inexplicable reason, a warm sensation floods my body. She was in here thinking about me. She was thinking about me so much, she shopped for me. I'm pretty sure that's like... a two-week jump in the relationship department.

Oh, my God. Is this a sign that we're in a relationship?

I pick up a shirt. Just a t-shirt. But don't all guys love t-shirts? She doesn't know me that well so hey, a t-shirt is a safe choice. And tactical pants. Again, not wholly original. Pretty much everyone I know, including me, wears tactical pants. And boots. Holy shit, she even guessed my shoe size correctly!

And well, well, well. What's this? Why it's pajamas. Which totally means she's planning on us sleeping together.

She even bought us luggage!

Wow. I sigh. I could really fall for this girl. She is the real deal. Total package. And pret-*ty* nice in the looks department, too.

Granted, it might be a little presumptuous. And in all my past experiences with girls who went into fast-forward mode on the first date, they all turned out to be maximum psycho. But... it's also kind of cute. Sort of endearing.

So I decide I don't hate it.

But wait. Is this a date?

I can't tell. She's sending me all the right signals. She totally invited herself up to my room, right?

Hold on, that little voice inside my head that had one hundred percent control this morning but seems to be having regular lapses now says. *She already admitted she's a schemer. She's here for you, remember that, Jimmy?*

I do. I get it. Something's still off about this whole Mighty Minions breakdown. But all my rational suspicions want to take a backseat to the idea of her and I getting together.

Maybe I should just take that cold shower?

The shower helps. Hell, I'm starting to think just being two rooms away from her helps. I might've lost my mind back there because after dousing myself with enough cold water to rein in my hard second cock, everything I was thinking in the bedroom sounds like pure fantasy.

What is going on with me? I'm not a daydreamer. Especially when it comes to women. But this place, I don't know. All family friendly and shit. It's fucking with me.

And when I put the t-shirt on it's clearly too small and I'm starting to think she didn't buy this stuff for me.

Which begs the question… who was she shopping for? Does she have some dude stowed away in another hotel room, just waiting for her to… to what? Get me drunk and kidnap me?

I actually laugh out loud at that.

As if.

I chuckle again.

As if anyone could pull one over on me like that.

OK, but seriously. Something weird is happening. Both with her and her scheming, and between us. I know for a fact my DNA signature scramble is still working. I have more than two months left before I'm due for a booster.

But... is it possible that whole DNA signature scramble is just a hoax? Just a way for the lab to get me in every year and charge my account fifty thousand credits?

How would I even know it's working? It's not like I actually ran into a lot of Cygnian princesses outside Crux's harem room. And OK. So what if none of those girls did it for me? They didn't do anything for the rest of my brothers either and Serpint sure as fuck is totally in love with an exploding girl right now.

Rational me tries to intervene and tell paranoid me to heel for a sec. Because rational me says, *You didn't feel any immediate sparks when you first met Delphi, right?*

True. True.

But Serpint didn't either. I drilled him on their whole how-we-met story and he said it took half a day and several interactions. And. It was Lyra who felt it first, not him.

Oh, God.

OK.

Paranoid me wins. I'm gonna go out there and make her talk. Make her tell me everything that's going on. And if I get the slightest inclination that she's casting her spell on me again, I'm out of here. I'll just... well, I don't know what I'll do. Walk Mighty Minions until dawn, then send word that Xyla has to cut her vacay short and come help us.

I breathe out a sigh of relief as I pull open the bedroom door... but as soon as I enter the living room, all rational thought disappears.

Because my Delphi is sitting on the dining table with her legs crossed and head cocked, surrounded by food, drinking a glass of tushberry champagne as she swings her foot.

"I was about to send help," she purrs in some totally new, unexpected sexy voice. "I thought you might've drowned in there."

She hops down off the table, sets her glass down, and begins stalking towards me.

I back up until I hit the wall and have nowhere else to go.

"What's wrong?" she asks, again with the purring, her little dragonbee bot buzzing wildly next to her ear.

I put up a hand and say, "Stop right there."

She frowns and pouts her lips. "Is something the matter?"

"Yeah," I say, suddenly feeling all confused and puzzled. What was the matter again?

"Wanna tell me about it?" she asks, taking two steps closer.

"Stay back," I warn her. But I'm having trouble remembering why I'm so insistent she stay away from me.

She stops, puts her hands on her hips, and says, "What the hell is wrong with you?" in her normal, bossy voice.

"Don't you feel that?"

"Feel what?" she snaps. Her little dragonbee bot starts buzzing again, but Delphi just swats it with her hand and it goes spinning through the air.

"You're putting me under some kind of spell, aren't you? You're gonna get me drunk and kidnap me. Take me prisoner in your secret sex lair on some long-forgotten planet where Cygnian princesses rule and all the Akeelian men are sex slaves."

"What?" She laughs. "Have you lost your damn mind?"

"Don't try to deny it. You're spurting pheromones, aren't you? Baiting me into liking you."

"Oh, my suns. You're nuts."

"You're nuts, lady. You're the one who weaseled her way into my life—"

"You're the one who needed an engineer!"

"Exactly!"

"Exactly what? What in fuck's name are you talking about?"

"You," I say, waving my hand at her. "And your little magic spell."

"I don't do magic. It's a well-known fact that Cygnians do science."

"Well, whatever it is. You're secreting something to make me like you. To distract me so you can carry out your evil sex plan."

The little bot is back, swirling around her head, buzzing like crazy. But Delphi swats it away again. "OK, how about you just calm down and come eat. Look, I made dinner."

She steps aside so I can see the table and yup. It's filled with food. Succulent shellfish, and juicy steaks, and some mushy vegetables that look suspiciously like the kind my father used to special-order when I was a kid.

She cooks.

For the love of sun gods everywhere, why? Why is this happening to me?

"I even got dessert. And oh, hey. What are you wearing?"

"Right!" I say, remembering all my thoughts back in the bedroom. "Who are these clothes for? And don't say me because this shirt is at least one size too small. Maybe even two sizes, now that I think about it."

"Mmmm," she says, eyes going half mast. "Your arms do fill out those sleeves rather nicely."

"Don't change the subject!"

The bot is back, again buzzing at her ear with some sort of urgent warning, or maybe it's the dragonbee in charge of this whole situation?

But Delphi just swats at it again, missing this time. But the bee takes the hint, because it flies over to the back of a chair and settles.

"Just forget it, Flicka. He's insane. None of this will work."

"Ah ha!" I yell. "I knew it!"

"You don't know anything. I don't know what's wrong with you, but it's not me. You're being weird all on your own."

"Is that right?" I growl.

"Yeah," she challenges back. "That's right."

"Then why do I have the urge to rip your clothes off and fuck you until you pass out?"

CHAPTER FOURTEEN

I open my mouth to reply and find I'm actually speechless.

"That's right," he says, taking a step forward.

Now I'm the one putting up my hands to ward him off because... holy shit. That tiny tingle in my belly from earlier is back, only it's not tiny anymore. It's on the verge of overpowering.

"Oh, no," Flicka squeaks from across the room. "This is all wrong. We should make a run for it!'

And I have to agree with her. That is the most logical answer right now. I want to do that. I even will my feet to start moving. But nothing happens. I'm stuck. I'm cemented in place.

Jimmy takes another step.

"I thought you wanted me to stay away!"

"I did," he says, his voice low and deep. "But seeing you withdraw, I had a flash of you running away and now I have an urge to tie you up and hold you prisoner."

I gulp, my mind spinning. Then I whisper, "I don't understand what's happening."

"Me either," he says, taking two more steps towards me. And now there's just a very small space separating us. I picture what he'll do next. Throw me on the couch and start ripping off my clothes? Back me up against the wall and pin me there with his chest?

What? What will he do?

Maybe both of those things?

But he just… he just reaches up with his hands and places them on my cheeks. They are cool and calming, even though I feel the heat of my blush radiating from my skin.

I swallow hard, uncertain how things got so out of control. Unable to make any sense of this, but—

He leans forward and kisses me on the lips.

His mouth is hard and punishing at first. Demanding and in control, but then he softens and his tongue sweeps past the seam of my lips. I open my mouth for him and grant him access.

And here's where it gets really interesting. All that lust and desire inside me a second ago? It doesn't vanish. It's definitely still there. But it eases back. It's dialed down a level or two. And suddenly I'm filled with patience and serenity. I'm calm and soft. And our kiss goes on and on. Forever and ever.

His fingers slip into my hair, loose now and flowing down over my shoulders. And my hands have a mind of their own because I reach for him. For his biceps. My hands gripping them and sliding up the outer edges of his broad, muscular shoulders until I have the urge to grip them. Digging my fingernails into his skin through his t-shirt.

"Ohhhh," I moan into his kiss.

He pulls back, letting his fingers fall down the side of my face until he slides them over my breasts and onto my hip bones at my waist.

We bump foreheads.

"Why did you stop?" I ask.

"I don't know. I don't even know why I kissed you. Ten seconds ago I wanted to leave. To get as far away from you as possible. But then you got this look in your eyes like you wanted to run and something took over. Some... instinct that said, *Don't let her go.* And the only thing I could think of is to hold you here with a kiss."

"I felt the same way. I felt consumed with want and longing one moment, and then I did want to run. But then... I wanted more. I thought you'd... and you didn't. You just... kissed me and..." I sigh. "And it was perfect."

"Perfect," he echoes.

"Something is wrong." But just as I say that Flicka is buzzing around our heads, keeping safely out of my reach in case I try to swat her away again.

"Oh, no," she squeaks. "Oh, no. This is bad. This is very, very bad."

I look up at her and so does Jimmy.

"What's she saying?" he asks.

"She says this is bad," I admit.

"I'm getting the same feeling. You're doing something to me, Delphi. And that's dangerous in our world."

"What world?"

"The one that genetically engineers soulmates for nefarious reasons."

"Oh," I say, pulling away from him. "That world."

"Who sent you here?"

I just shake my head.

"Delphi, tell me what's going on. I can help you."

"Yes!" Flicka says. "Yes! You did it! All is not lost. This is the plan, Delphi. Tell him and get him to help you!"

"Now what is she saying?" Jimmy asks.

"She's saying…" I sigh. "She's telling me to trust you." I raise my head up so I can look Jimmy in the eyes. "She's telling me to ask you for help."

He relaxes a little. "She's really saying that? And not telling you to drug me, and kidnap me, and deliver me to some evil station on the edge of the known galaxy so I can be poked and prodded and made to breed with outlaw princesses?"

"What?" I say, snapping out of the dream-like state his kiss put me in.

"Sorry." He laughs. "My imagination is in overdrive right now. I don't know what's wrong with me. The only thing I do know, Delphi, is that it's got something to do with you. Except… it can't. This cannot be happening."

"Why not?" I ask, a little bit too loud. "Why can't it?"

He takes a step back. Then another. And then he turns away and walks across the room to the table. I set out a fresh glass for the whiskey he was drinking earlier and he fills it now, dropping in two ice cubes from a bucket.

He drinks it down in one gulp, then places both hands on the table and bows his head a little. Like he's trying to make a decision.

I bite my lip and hold my breath. He's going to walk out, I just know it. That kiss. It did something to us. It eased the building tension. It defused the impending explosion. It... tamed us, somehow. And now he's feeling better, because I know I'm feeling better, and he's going to walk out. He's thinking this whole thing is a setup. And hell, he practically figured the whole hot mess of a plan out already, didn't he? I'm sure he thinks his imagination got away from him and that scenario was just some wild delusion, but it wasn't. It was pretty much spot on. And he knows that. He feels it. I'm here to hurt him and I hate myself for that. I really do.

Because I don't want to hurt him.

I want to do the exact opposite of hurt him.

Jimmy straightens up, turns around to face me, and then says, "Would you like to have dinner with me?"

"What?" I ask weakly.

"Dinner?" he says, panning his hand at the table laid out with a full spread of food and drinks. "Because all I ate today was a little container of Mighty Noodles and Dumplings that set me back four hundred credits and this..." He looks over his shoulder at the food. "This just happens to be all my favorites." Then he scowls a little. "Did you do research on me? Is that how you knew what to order?"

I look at the food, which was totally picked at random. "No. I didn't even chose that food. I just pressed a few tabs on the autocook and that's what came out."

He hesitates for a few moments. I can practically imagine what he's thinking.

He's thinking I'm a liar.

He's thinking I'm a backstabbing cheat.

He's thinking I'm here to hurt him, and kidnap him, and drag him off to the Loathsome One to be used for her nefarious breeding program.

Because all that's true and I'm pretty certain he's right. Something weird is happening here and I'm the reason why.

"So?" he asks. "Do you? Want to have dinner?"

"Are you sure you want to have dinner with me?" I ask.

He nods. "Delphi. That's the only thing I am sure of right now. You are the only thing I'm sure of right now."

I stare at him for a few moments, then nod my head. "OK. Yes. I'd like that very much."

He lets out a long breath of air, then pulls a chair out and says, "Please. Have a seat."

I walk towards him, wholly unsure how we got from this morning to this moment, but I sit anyway. And he pushes my chair in and walks around the other side of the table and takes his seat across from me.

We both place our napkins in our laps and then he places his elbows on the table, folds his hands, and steeples two fingers together under his chin. "Just tell me one thing, OK? One thing and I'll let the rest go until later."

"What?" I ask, so fearful of his question.

"Who did you buy these clothes for?"

CHAPTER FIFTEEN

She slumps a little in her chair.

"Delphi," I say. "Something's going on and by the looks of things, you don't have many friends. I know your dragonbee bot is kind of a score as far as bot friends go, but there's only so much something so small can do to help you out of whatever mess you're into. And hey," I say, putting up my hands. "Maybe I'm wrong. Maybe you've got lots of friends on your side. And that's cool, I guess. But if you don't, and you feel stuck, if you've gotten involved with something too big and can't find a way out—then give me a chance. I can help you if you can trust me."

She leans her elbows on the table and rubs the heels of her palms against her forehead. "They're for my brother," she whispers. Then she looks up at me and adds, "And I can pay you back for the clothes, OK? I can. I'm not sure when, just—"

"I don't need you to pay me back. I'm not worried about the bill. I just want to know what's going on. This whole stop on Mighty Minions is suspect. Did you have something to do with it?"

She presses her lips together and nods. "I'm the reason your ship got a virus."

I lean back in my chair. "How?"

She shrugs. "Flicka helped me infiltrate *Dicker*'s maintenance logs at your last ship stop."

"That was weeks ago," I say. "So how come it just appeared now?"

"That was just the first phase. We had to make sure it got in unnoticed. Then we followed you here and sent a bogus communication from the gate captain on Blue Sand Beach."

I breathe deeply, trying to make sense of all this. "But why? Why do you need me?" I can take a good guess. It's not a far leap. She's a Cygnian princess and I'm an Akeelian male with violet eyes. But I want to hear it from her.

"My brother, Tycho," she says. "He's my twin. We grew up together. And I know you think that all Cygnian male twins are worthless, but he's not."

"How's he different?" I ask.

"I don't know, exactly. I just know that our father took good care of him. He educated him, and we grew up together. He wasn't sent off to the work camps like all the other male twins. He had a life and he was—he is—my best friend."

"So where is he?"

"He's being held prisoner on a faraway station run by... we call her the Loathsome One."

"The Loathsome One," I say, trying out the name while racking my brain to see if I've ever heard of her before. "Can't say I recognize that handle."

"No." Delphi sighs. "You shouldn't. She keeps a low profile and holds her real identity very close. I don't know that anyone on her station really knows who she is."

"So how'd you get involved with her?"

"My father helped Tycho and I escape just before our last birthday. He gave us a ship and some coordinates, but when we came through the second gate, just about halfway through our trip, she had a ship waiting for us. It towed us in, blew our ship to pieces, then stuck us in a cryopod and we woke up on Lair Station."

"Lair Station," I say. "Never heard of that, either."

"It's not near anything. There's not even a nearby gate."

"Hmmm," I say.

"Yeah. Which means you have to exit the closest gate billions of klicks out, and make your approach using standard cruising speeds."

"Which gives them plenty of time to see you coming."

"Exactly. It sucks. We were trapped there in cages for months. And then one day she brought me to her quarters and gave me this mission. She said Tycho had to remain behind and if I didn't bring you back with me, she'd kill him. I haven't even seen him since we came out of the cryopod. We were separated immediately after that. I was stuck in a cage all by myself, Jimmy. Literally the only person on the entire level. And Flicka was there. But she was taken away too. We were only reunited because of this mission."

I think this through for a moment, then ask, "Do you think your father knows you're missing?"

She shrugs. "I doubt it. He's a high-ranking official back in Cygnus System. One of the special males who runs things."

"What's his department?" I ask.

"Genetics." She sighs, once again rubbing the heel of her palms against her forehead.

I take a deep breath and hold it.

"I don't know anything else. I swear. I just know that I have to at least try to save Tycho. That's why I'm here." Then she sighs. "Well, that's not the only reason anymore."

I wait for her to explain, but she just stares at me behind a few stray strands of hair falling over her eyes.

"Go on," I say.

"Don't you feel it?" she says. "Can't you feel the... I don't know. I can't explain it, but I think we have some kind of connection."

I nod my head, cautiously. I do feel it. It's hard not to, in fact. There's definitely something going on between us.

"She told me a little about what my father was doing back on Cygnia. How they were trying to make second-generation offspring. I know I was part of that program, and now I'm starting to think Tycho was too, but I didn't know much else before she filled me in."

"What did she tell you, Delphi?"

"Those eyes of yours?" she says. "That means you're part of the program too. They genetically engineered you. They tied you to one special princess."

"And do you think that princess is you?" I ask.

She shrugs. "I don't know. I don't know what it's supposed to feel like. I just know... I like you."

I nod my head, feeling much the same.

"Do you think I belong with you?" she asks.

"It's hard to tell," I admit.

"Why? I mean... I thought this was supposed to be instant true love or something."

"Yeah, that's how I heard it goes too."

"So we're not?"

"Like I said, it's hard to tell. Here's the thing," I say. "I first learned about this link between Cygnian princesses and Akeelian males a long time ago when we escaped to ALCOR's station. It's called Harem Station now." She nods, like she knew this already. "I escaped Akeelian System with some friends and we were sent to ALCOR by a princess from long ago." I'm not sure how much I can trust this girl, so I leave Corla's and Crux's names out of it. It's not important, anyway. "But it sorta freaked me out. We stayed on ALCOR alone the first several years. Until we were all grown up. Then he sent us out into the galaxy with missions. Mine was liberating bots and bringing them back to Harem so we could populate the station. But the very first thing I did when I left all those years ago was seek out a medical lab. I hired them to make me a DNA signature scrambler, so if I ever did meet my one true mate it wouldn't work. I wouldn't be caught up in their little plan. I've been getting boosters ever since. In fact, I was on my way there to get another one when you intercepted us."

"Because it's wearing off?" she asks. And do I detect a little hope in her voice?

"It shouldn't be," I say. "Not yet. I should technically have enough transferase in my system to keep it going for much longer than a year, I just... don't like to take chances."

Delphi lifts her chin in a slight nod. But there's no mistaking the fact that she's uncertain and worried.

"But I feel it too," I say. Her eyes widen a little. "I don't know if it means anything, I just get a weird feeling around you."

She narrows her eyes a little, thinking. "But that kiss…"

I agree. "Yeah. That kiss… I dunno. Calmed me down."

"Made the feeling… not go away, but it's definitely not as strong as it was. What do you think that means?"

"I think it means we should eat."

She smiles at me.

"And," I add, "we have a whole night to figure it out."

"Oh, but… I didn't tell you the rest."

"That can wait," I say. "We've had quite a day and I think we've earned a nice dinner and a quiet night."

Her little dragonbee bot buzzes over and lands on her shoulder. Delphi tilts her head, like it's talking to her. Then she looks at me.

"What's she telling you?" I ask.

"She says…" Delphi sighs. "She says she likes you. And we should trust you. And I should stop talking now and kiss you again."

I smile, then chuckle. "She didn't say that."

But the little bot begins buzzing like crazy and even I, unable to speak her language, can understand the meaning of that behavior.

She's sincere.

The bot is on my side.

CHAPTER SIXTEEN

DELPHI

"What is wrong with you?" Flicka is buzzing by my ear. "This man is the total package!"

I swat at her again, but she's on to me and easily zips away before my smack can land.

Jimmy smiles, leans back in his chair and puts his hands behind his head. "She likes me," he announces.

I just suck in a breath of air and try to hide my smile.

"All bots like me, actually," he continues, leaning forward again to grab a set of tongs, which he uses to heap a pile of crustaceans onto his plate. "They can't help but like me," he adds, casually adding another heap of crustaceans onto my plate too.

"Oh, right," I say, trying not to stare at him. It's hard though. He's very attractive. Older than me. Maybe even much older than me, which is new. The few boys I dated back in Cygnian System were all from school and all my age. But it's hard to tell an Akeelian male's age once they reach maturity. We don't age like other humanoid species. And while the Cygnian and Akeelian lifespans are the same—anywhere between a hundred and fifty and a hundred and seventy-five years, give or take, depending on which system you're in because time is weird like that—we don't mature at the same rate. Girls will reach the age of maturity at about nineteen, while the boys take a few years longer to grow into their brains.

But after maturity we don't age again for many decades. Middle age isn't until about eighty.

He's not middle age, that's for sure. Whatever age he is—and I won't ask because it's super impolite where I come from—he looks about twenty-five to me.

The only thing that gives away an Akeelian man's age is their personality. They are hot-tempered and arrogant until about ninety-five and then they finally settle into a more reasonable temperament. It's not much help.

"This is pretty good coming from a Mighty Minion autocook," Jimmy says, helping himself to more food.

"Yeah, apparently the penthouse comes with a specialized autochef. I'm sure you'll see that on the itemized bill when we check out."

"Well, I'm glad you made the most of it then. If we're stuck here on Mighty Minions for the weekend, might as well enjoy it."

"Are we stuck for the weekend?"

"Tomorrow, Delphi. Remember?"

I nod. And realize I'm holding my breath, so I let it out slowly so he can't tell. Because I'm worried about what will happen tomorrow when I tell him that his ship is playing games with *Queenie*. And speaking of *Queenie*, she's gonna be pissed off if she finds out I've told him everything.

"OK," he says, leaning across the table holding a tushberry covered in melted chocolate. "I can see I need to distract you from your current, seemingly overwhelming problems. Here. Try this. They're fucking delicious."

I lock eyes with him and open my mouth. He places the ripe, pink berry on my tongue and I wrap my lips around it, accidentally catching a taste of his chocolate-covered fingers.

God, that was kinda sexy. No one has ever fed me erotic berries before. He leans back in his chair and pops one into his mouth too. Then he waggles his eyebrows at me and smiles. "Did you order these on purpose?"

Oh, suns. I'm so used to eating tushberries to keep my glow healthy, I forgot that they're considered an aphrodisiac to other cultures. "Ummm…"

"It's OK if you did," he says. "But not really necessary."

I blink at him. Because I think that was sexual innuendo.

"At least for me," he adds. "How about you?"

"Ummm…" Shit. My face is instantly hot and I know I'm blushing.

"Well." He chuckles. "There it is. I was starting to wonder if you glowed at all."

"Oh, God," I say, looking down at my chest. Because yup. It's not bright, but I sure am glowing.

"You're not taking anything, are you?"

"What?" I ask. And now I can feel the heat in my eyes and I know they are bright with excitement.

"This other princess we ran into a little while back. She had cooked herself up some kind of glow inhibitor as a disguise. Are you in disguise?"

"No," I say. And that feeling is suddenly back. That lost feeling. That caught-up-in-a-spell feeling. I shake my head to clear it. "No, I'm just really good at controlling it, I guess. I was always kind of a private person back at home. My father kept my brother and I isolated so protecting my feelings became second nature."

"Well, you don't need to protect them in front of me, Delphi. Feel free to let them loose."

I glow brighter.

"Yeah," he says. "Like that. I like it when it flows out into your hair. You're quite beautiful."

That tiny feeling is back in full force now. Not so tiny, either.

The patio doors fly open and we both stand up, alert and on edge, ready for some threat to come bursting into our romantic dinner.

But it's just Flicka. "I'll give you two some privacy," she says, then flits through the doors, out into the chaos of Mighty Minions.

"Don't get into trouble!" I yell after her.

But she doesn't respond. The doors close back up, shutting out the white noise of the crowd and amusement going on down below.

"What was that about?" Jimmy asks, walking around to my side of the table.

He stops right in front of me and I look up. He's very tall. Much taller than I am. So my head has to tilt quite a bit as I gaze into his bright violet eyes. His expression is one of sexual mischief and I suddenly feel very out of my league.

"Ummm..." I say. "She wanted to give us some time alone."

"Did she?" Jimmy says, glancing at the doors, then back at me. His hand comes up to my face and his fingers thread into my hair, just like they did before he kissed me earlier. "That was nice of her," he whispers.

I nod my head, unable to speak. His spell is back in full force now and my body floods with something that might be... relief.

We are soulmates. I think this is what that feels like. And I want this alone time with him. I want him to kiss me again.

No, I want him to do more than kiss me.

"Delphi," he says.

"Yes?" I whisper back.

"I think you should come to me this time."

I nod my head, my hands automatically reaching for his arms. My fingertips wrap around the muscles of his biceps as I rise up on my tiptoes, desperate to kiss him again.

I'm not even close though. There's way too much space between us. So I take a step forward, pressing my breasts into his chest.

This time he meets me halfway. Leaning down just enough so our lips brush against each other. And again, I'm struck by how slow and careful we're able to be with each other.

I always thought this soulmate bond would make me crazy with desire. That some hidden lust would be unleashed and desperation would take over.

I start to worry again. That he's not mine, and I'm not his, and all this is just some regular one-night-stand kind of sex.

But then he opens his mouth, and I open mine, and our tongues begin to twist together. He tastes like chocolate-covered tushberries.

My hands drop onto his chest. His t-shirt is too tight because I bought it for my brother, who is a Cygnian boy, and Jimmy of Harem Station is a fully mature Akeelian man.

My fingertips explore every curve of muscle. Every hill and valley as I caress him. Then I blush furiously, light blinking erratically in the dim atmospheric evening light of the room.

He kisses me harder. His soft mouth suddenly hard. One hand slips out of my hair and his fingers find mine, guiding my flattened palm down his stomach until the tips of my fingers land on the button of his pants.

I flip it open without hesitation. Without any thoughts of what comes next, or consequences, or doubt.

I want this.

I want him.

I want it all, and I want it now.

And then I have it. His long, hard cock in my hand. I stroke him and squeeze him and he moans, still holding on to my hand. Helping me now. Helping me fist his fat shaft and pump it up and down.

That drives me crazy. But then his other hand grips my hair tight. Fisting it until he's pulling on my scalp and I'm the one who moans now.

He releases my hand inside his pants but I continue to stroke him. Tugging on his cock until I feel something else growing down below.

His second cock.

Holy fucking sun.

Cygnian boys do not have two cocks, so sex with Jimmy will be a totally new adventure.

He says, "That's for you, ya know. Only for you. No other woman has ever made both my cocks come out without coming once first. This is the last signal we needed, Delphi. You are mine."

CHAPTER SEVENTEEN

She is mine.

Those words flow through my head on repeat as I reach for her breast and squeeze. She is mine. She will always be mine. We are destiny wrapped up in fate. We are two halves of a whole.

I have no idea where these thoughts are coming from. I'm really not a romantic. It's got to be instinct. It's got to be true love, otherwise why would all these sappy feelings and ideas be coursing through my body like a raging river?

And just the mere thought of losing her, of this being some kind of trick, or being fake, or just a stupid misunderstanding—it fills me with despair.

It has to be real.

She opens her fist inside my pants and slips her fingers around both my cocks.

Proof, I rationalize. That's just proof. This is not normal. The second cock has a purpose and that purpose is only meant for breeding.

I growl with lust when she squeezes them both. Kissing her mouth as I push my fingers inside her waistband and slip them down between her legs. Massaging her pussy through her panties.

She is already wet, her desire coating the silky fabric, then passing through the thin fibers and coating the tip of my finger.

I want to be inside her right now.

Slow, I caution myself. *Don't go too fast and ruin this experience.* We only get to make love the first time once. We'll never have this moment again and so this caution makes sense.

If I am going to keep her forever I want to make this count.

So I pull back from our kiss and slowly bend down. Both hands grab the waistband of her leggings and I drag them down her legs as I kneel.

I gaze up at her beautiful face. So perfect and sweet. Her blonde hair is starting to turn pink now. Soft tendrils near her forehead shine and stick to her flushed face from the heat radiating off her body.

I take off her booties one foot at a time, marveling at how perfect her small feet are, her toenails painted and pretty. I cup one foot in my hand, stroking the underside of her arch until she starts to laugh and pull away.

But I grab her ankle. "No, no," I say. "You're not going anywhere."

She loses her balance, reaches out and steadies herself with both hands on my shoulders. "It tickles." She giggles.

And that giggle. It kills me. So fucking adorable.

But that's not the only reason I plan on tickling her. I lean forward, my eyes locked on hers, and push her sweater up her belly. My lips flutter against her skin, making her grip my shoulders tighter.

She lets out a long, heavy, sensual breath of air. Then before I can blink, she lets go of my shoulders, whips her sweater over her head, and unhooks her bra—letting it drop to the floor.

"Holy fuck," I say, gazing up at her perfect breasts.

She shrugs her shoulders a little. Like she's shy or maybe a little bit embarrassed. And I just want to fall over dead from her sweet beauty.

I slide both hands up her stomach and slip them underneath her tits. Squeezing them and caressing each nipple with my thumbs until they pop up, stiff and erect.

My cocks are throbbing now. Engorged with blood and crying out to be inside her.

Heel, boys, I tell them. *Take it easy. We're not there yet.*

Her body is beautiful. And I'm not talking about her shape or her size. It's the light. The soft glow of her skin that permeates the evening and shimmers just for me.

I can't look away.

"What?" she asks, maybe feeling a little self-conscious.

"You," I say. "Just you."

I stand up and take her hand. "What are you doing?" she asks, when I lead her away.

"Taking you to the bedroom. There's a time and a place for living room sex, and this isn't it."

She chuckles as I lead her down the hallway. "What about dinner?"

I look over my shoulder and say, "You're dinner, Delphi. Don't worry, I'm gonna eat."

She blushes a bright pink, unconsciously looking down.

"Yes, pretty princess. That's the main course."

I take her over to the bed and turn her around. Backing her up until her knees hit the mattress and she has to reach out and steady herself as she sits.

She slowly looks up at me, her eyes half closed and heavy with the thought of sex. Her hair, now almost completely pink, falling over her shoulders, partially obstructing my view of her breasts.

I just want to look at her for a moment. Burn the image of her in my brain so I never forget this night.

She bites her lip. Inhales deep. Then her hands go to my open pants and she pushes them down over my hips until both cocks spring out, hard and eager. Pulsating, and throbbing, and aching with need.

I just shake my head and smile. "You first," I say.

Her lips make a small, perfect o shape.

"Lie back," I command softly. "I'll do the rest."

She swallows hard, glancing at my two cocks like she's nervous, but then she places both hands on the bed beside her and eases onto her back.

As she does this I lower down to my knees, hands on her knees as I spread her wide open and inhale her sweet, princess scent.

I have to close my eyes, that's how overpoweringly seductive her essence is.

As soon as I lean forward her fingers are tangled in my hair. Gripping and urging me forward.

I lick her. Tongue flat along her open pussy.

She bucks her back. Arching and rounding into a curve that makes her breasts rise up as she holds my face between her legs.

132

"Oh, my suns," she murmurs, when I lick her again.

I flatten it out to taste as much of her as I can. Then pull it into a tight point so I can probe her opening.

"Jimmy," she says.

And man, do I ever like the way my name sounds coming out of her mouth. My lips form around her clit and I suck a little, taking in the little nub of skin that controls her glow.

I'm rewarded with a burst of pink light from the corner of my eyes. Not bright, but more intense than I've seen from her so far. I turn my head to the side a little and find her inner thighs glimmering and twinkling with little bits of silver.

I can't stand it anymore. All her reactions are the right ones. All her responses are flawless and pure.

I flick my tongue back and forth across her clit until she's writhing and squirming against the tight hold I have on her knees.

"Oh, shit!" she moans. "Oh, my God!"

I want to command her to come for me. I want to talk dirty to her. But I can't stop licking her pussy. Not even for a moment. She is the most delicious thing I've ever tasted. Delphi is so much better than chocolate-covered tushberries.

So I keep going. Her knees overpower my grip in her erotic struggle and I let go, allowing her to press them against the sides of my head. I splay my fingers across the edge of her hipbones and use my forearms to urge her legs open wider as my tongue dances across her clit and little nub of flux.

She tightens her grip on my hair, pulling on my scalp as she forces her back up and off the mattress with her mouth wide open in a long, primal moan.

I want her to come. I want her to come right now. I'm too eager to be inside her. Too impatient to wait any longer. So I slide my hand between her legs and slip two fingers inside her. Pushing deep, deep inside her as I flick the tip of my tongue back and forth across her sweet spots.

She goes stiff in that moment and I get a momentary rush of triumph.

"Come," I command her again. Only this time my voice is deep with absolute authority. "Come," I growl.

There is a moment of blackness. A moment when my senses cease to function, and my mind goes blank, and every muscle in my body goes still as I wait for it...

And then there is the fire of a sun igniting, and the blaze of a star exploding, and then there is just Delphi—bursting into brilliant light that wipes my mind of every moment of every day that came before this one.

Because she obeys.

And she comes.

CHAPTER EIGHTEEN

DELPHI

It take me a minute—or maybe three—to find myself after the spectacular release with Jimmy.

"This," I breathe, once my mind returns and I'm able to make my mouth form words, "was not sex."

Jimmy peers at me from between my still-open legs, his eyes locked on mine as he gently kisses my mound, every few moments nipping at it a little bit, then kissing the sting away. His hands still rest easily on my inner thighs, his thumbs massaging small circles on the soft, tender skin near his mouth.

I begin to sit up, propping my weight onto my elbows. But he cocks his head at me and says, "Where you goin'?"

My smile is something in between shy and devious—probably a little more shy than devious. "You know," I say. "For every action there's blah, blah, equal and opposite thing, right?"

He closes his eyes, shakes his head, and chuckles.

"What?" I ask. "Did I say something wrong?"

He opens his eyes again. "First, the law of reciprocity does not apply to sexual encounters with people you actually *like*."

"Oh." I laugh nervously, wondering if he thinks I'm young and ridiculous? Or sexy and cute?

"Second," he says. "Your pleasure is my pleasure. So…" He shrugs. "Makes no difference, princess. Besides, I just watched you come. Do you have any idea what a turn-on that was?"

"Right," I say, nodding my head in understanding. "The glow. Yeah, I get it."

"The glow? No, sweets. I wasn't watching your glow. Though that was a nice perk. I was watching your face."

And the way he says *face*. I dunno. I don't know how to describe it. *Face*. With emphasis. Or like he's growling out a command. Like when he said, "Come." Or… possibly it's just the fact that right now, everything about him is sexy.

"What are you thinking so hard about?" he asks.

I shake my head and whisper, "You. Just you."

He smiles, perhaps recalling that he said that to me just a little while ago and now I'm his echo. Or maybe he's just eager to keep going. Because he stands as he smiles, and at the same time, leans forward. His palms dropping down onto the mattress on either side of my breasts. His hips keep my legs open as he lowers his chest over my stomach—taking care to prop up most of his weight so he doesn't crush me.

I feel so small with him towering over me. His broad shoulders block out the light above us and turn him into a dark, opaque shadow.

A ferocious, dangerous, and glorious shadow-man of mystery.

Yeah. That's him. A shadow-man of mystery.

His eyes are bright and glow a deep violet-purple, his gaze intent and set. "Shall we keep going? Or are you done?"

I swallow hard for some reason. Not because I'm unsure of my answer. But because I am so unequivocally and absolutely sure I want to continue, it frightens me a little.

There is this deep... I dunno. Longing, maybe. Aching. There is such a deep, agonizing ache inside my heart, it almost hurts to think about stopping.

And I know that this is just some kind of science at work. Some kind of engineering programmed deep inside our core code that makes us feel this deep connection. And I'm keeping things from him too. Things I will have to divulge soon if I have any chance of keeping him.

"Stop it," he says.

"Stop what?"

"Thinking about it, Delphi. There's time for thinking later. All I'd like to know right now is if I should continue."

"Yes," I say quickly. Then swallow hard again and nod my head for emphasis.

In one swift motion his hands grab my ass and scoot me all the way up the bed. And then he wraps his arms around me and turns over, taking me with him.

I giggle at the sudden change in position and find myself mounted on his upper thighs, his cocks sticking out between my legs and pressing against my belly. I steady my balance, pressing my palms down on his chest as my long, now-pink hair drags along his body.

He closes his eyes and I immediately miss the glow. Miss the intensity of his stare.

It's not science, I decide.

It's magic.

When he opens them again they are electric and bright. And I can see my own eyes reflecting back in his, so they are no longer violet, but some blurry combination of pink and purple.

He reaches up and tucks one side of my hair behind my ear and says, "Try just one first."

And I realize he's talking about his cocks.

Try just one first.

I grab both cocks in my hand, my fist so small compared to their thick girth. His eyes go heavy, becoming just slits of light in the dim evening autolights near the baseboards of the room. When I pump them he moans. Clenching his jaw and reaching behind my knees to tug me forward on his legs.

I lift up my hips, reluctantly letting go of his second cock, and position the first one up to my wet opening.

His jaw juts forward with anticipation and when I slide him inside me and sink down, lowering myself as I push him deep inside me, he tilts his head back into the deep, soft pillows.

"Yes," he says.

"Yes," I agree.

I place both my hands on his chest and lean forward, rocking my hips just a little to start.

His eagerness is apparent, his fingers gripping my thighs to urge me on. My hair begins to swing back and forth as he moves me and then his arms reach up, wrap around my back, and he pulls me close.

"Like this," he whispers. "Close, like this."

Close like this.

Everything he says makes me ache.

And I want to be close to him. I want to fuck him slow. I want to take my time and make this last forever.

'Kiss me, Delphi," he says, his mouth already on mine.

And I do. Slowly, just the way we fuck. Long, tender kisses with tongue as our bodies move. His cock deep inside me. The other cock pressing up the middle of my ass.

"Oh, God," I moan between his lips. "I want to feel you."

"You are," he says.

"No," I say, sitting up so he has to break our embrace. "I mean like this."

And then I reach around behind me and take his second cock in my hand. Pumping and squeezing it. Jerking it to the motion of our now faster rhythm.

"Oh, fuck," he groans. "Fuck."

And then it's my turn to command him. It's my turn to say, "Come for me, Jimmy. Come inside me."

He sits up, scooting me into his lap with the quick change of position. His arms encircling my waist. My fingers buried in his thick, light-brown hair while my other hand continues to jerk him off behind me.

He moans, and growls, kissing me and then nipping at my lips with playful, yet fierce, abandon.

I rock on top of him. Faster and faster. And then his hand wraps around mine and we jerk his second cock off together.

I'm done after that move. Just…

"Come," he commands.

And in this moment the only thing I want, the only thing I can think of, is to follow orders.

So I press myself as close to him as I can. Letting his thick, hard cock rise deep inside me until I can feel it in my belly. And I explode with light.

The flash is so bright I have to close my eyes. And in this same moment, he grips me tight around the shoulders, holding me prisoner in my pleasure, and he comes too.

My orgasm goes on, and on, and on. I glow a boiling pink at first. Then, after more than a minute, the contractions inside me begin to subside, and just when I think it's over it starts again. And again. And again.

He rolls over, taking me with him. His hand jerks one leg out and up to give himself access. And it's only then that I remember—Akeelian males have to come twice.

He gives his second cock its due, slipping the first one out and shoving the second one in, and then he fucks me.

He fucks me hard.

It's nothing like the last time and I love it both ways.

My orgasm continues through this whole second session. Ebbing, and flowing. Contracting and relaxing. Until I can't take it anymore and I need to explode again.

And so does he.

So we do.

His first cock spews his seed onto my stomach in hot bursting waves and at the same time, the one inside me spasms as I grip the walls of my pussy around it.

So we do.

CHAPTER NINETEEN

I wake sometime during the night, unable to remember where I'm at or who I'm with until I reach out and find Delphi snuggled up against my chest. There are no lights on in the bedroom, but I don't need lights. Her sweet scent brings last night rushing back to me.

My arms wrap tightly around her and my eyes close.

"I'm awake," she whispers. "It's morning. I checked."

I smile a little because she sounds disappointed. "What time?" I ask, my voice rough and husky.

"Five AM Minion."

I start thinking about all the things that happened yesterday and all the things that need to get done today, trying to wrangle all the tasks into some kind of coherent order.

"I need to talk to you about something," Delphi says.

"Oh, hey. If you're not working here, where are you headed today?"

"That's what I want to talk to you about." She pulls the covers up to her breasts and turns over a little. "Hi," she says, smiling.

"Hi."

"OK, so don't hate me. Promise?"

I couldn't hate her if I tried. I tuck a piece of hair behind her ear and say, "We're on the same team."

"You say that now—"

"Because I mean it. I think last night proves that… you know." I do one of those back-and-forth finger points at us. "We've got something here."

She squints her eyes.

"Don't you feel it?" I ask.

"I do. I do. But… see, this is what I need to talk to you about."

"It's just that DNA signature scrambler I have, Delphi. That's why it's not so strong."

"OK," she says. "But…"

"And," I add, "we weren't really paying attention to the signals yesterday, right? We were all preoccupied with other things. But today." I nod. "Today we're gonna give that a shot."

"Give what a shot? Exactly?"

"You know. Soulmates." I smile at her.

She nods and smiles back, then takes a deep breath and says, "But listen to me for a minute, Jimmy. I'm not here alone."

"Ohhh," I say. "Um… and I can assume you're not referring to your tiny bot. Where is that thing, anyway?"

"No, not her. And I don't know. She's around. I hope."

"So who are you with?"

"A ship," she says. "A mean, old, nasty ship called *Queenie*. And she's the one who's playing poker with your ship. It was a trick to lure you over to my ship so we could kidnap you and take you back to the Loathsome One where she will do... unspeakable things to you."

"OK."

"OK? It's not OK, Jimmy. I had to turn my wristband off because she started pinging me like crazy last night. I didn't sleep at all. I mean, bad things are going to start happening and I'm not sure I can stop this. So we need to come up with a plan. A very good plan. Like... a really terrific plan. And then... I don't know." She shakes her head. "I don't know what I'm gonna do because I can't go through with this now. But my brother, ya know? How do I save my brother and keep you alive at the same time?"

She says all that in one breath, so when she stops she sucks in air, holds it, and then lets it out in a rush.

"Wow," I say. "You didn't sleep at all?"

"That's what you heard?"

"I'm just... concerned. You're so stressed, Delphi."

"Yes!" She scoffs. "I'm stressed! I'm supposed to be luring you to your awful fate and my brother is probably a sex slave by now, and you know what?"

"What?"

"Where is that damn dragonbee bot?" She looks around wildly. "Flicka?"

"OK," I say again. "You're very wound up. I think we just need to take a breath and order up some breakfast. Or you know what? Better idea. We should go out for breakfast."

145

"Out? You mean out *there*?" She cocks her head at the window. The shades are drawn so there's nothing to see when I look over. But the unmistakable sounds of the Mighty Minions Resort coming to life filter up even through the sound screen and on this high level.

I shrug. "It'll be fun. We could take that Lava Mountain ride. Or that rollercoaster back near Demon Lake."

"Flame Lake," she says. "We don't have time for this!"

"We have time," I say. "We have to make time, I mean. Because we need a good plan."

"Maybe… maybe you could call your ship? And we could just leave *Queenie* here and go… no." She frowns. "I don't even know how to get to the Lair."

"We can't go without a water generator, so we have to get that first anyway."

"*Queenie* is not going to give over her water generator."

"Oh, yes, she will. *Dicker* takes her poker winnings seriously. She won the kitchen too. And some salvage bikes. Maybe even a charging station."

"It was a setup, Jimmy. She didn't really win that stuff."

"Again," I say, smiling down at her. Because her hair is all kinds of messy and there's still a few pink streaks running through it from last night, so she's totally one of those girls who looks amazing in the morning. "You don't really know *Dicker*. When I say she's serious about her poker winnings, I mean she's very fucking serious. Like it or not, and all secret scheming aside, your *Queenie* lost and *Dicker* will collect."

"And I don't think you understand, OK? When I said mean and nasty, I meant mean and nasty. She's evil. And look." Delphi pauses to tab her wristband on. It starts chiming incoming messages immediately. "See! Seventeen nasty messages from this thing!"

She shoves her wristband at me. And sure enough, there's a shitload of incoming messages. "What's this Mighty Minions warning?"

"What?" She turns her wrist so she can see her display. "Oh, my suns. You've got to be fucking kidding me."

"What happened?"

"Flicka!" she says. "She's in lockup."

I laugh, I can't help it.

"We have to bail her out. I wonder how much that will cost? Because I've been using *Queenie's* credit account and I'm pretty sure she's not gonna let me—"

"Don't worry," I say. "Send that to me and I'll take care of it."

"Are you sure?"

"That's what soulmates do, Del."

She closes her eyes and sighs. But she smiles too. "Thank you," she says, opening them back up to stare into mine. "I really appreciate this."

"Send it and I'll pay her fines."

Delphi tabs her wristband screen with a finger and swipes it in my direction. My wristband chimes an incoming message, and then the alert shows up on my screen. I press the pay fine button, and check the little box that someone agrees to come take the bot into possession when we're ready to leave the resort. Apparently they have a zero-tolerance policy with bots. Especially dragonbee bots.

"She's stuck there until we're ready to leave," I explain to Delphi. "That's probably gonna piss her off. But her fine is paid so all you have to do is go down and sign a release form."

"Serves her right," Delphi says.

"OK, so we're set now? We can go get some breakfast and take a spin on the Demon Coaster?"

"No," Delphi says. "We don't have a plan yet."

"Let me take care of that, OK?"

"Jimmy, I'm serious."

"Me too," I say. "Just look, we can't do anything right now. And we don't really have to because your ship can't get us while we're in the resort."

"I think... maybe... you underestimate her."

"No," I say. "And besides, once I tell *Dicker* that she's been cheated out of a water generator, a new kitchen, two salvage bikes, and possibly a charging station— she's gonna lose her shit. OK? I'm talking blow her fucking roof and start plotting revenge. That's not gonna be pretty. She will leave my ass here and start her own little personal war with that *Queenie* until she gets everything owed to her. So I'm not gonna tell her any of this just yet. We're gonna go get some food, enjoy my stupid Mighty Minions family pass, and come up with a new way for me to find a water generator so we can get the hell out of the Vacation Sector and head back to Harem. Once we get there, I'll get my brothers and the Harem security beacons to rustle up a navy and we'll go save your brother."

"We don't even know where Lair Station is."

"If this Loathsome One is as dangerous as you describe her, then trust me, someone on Harem will know who she is and where she stays. And if she's some clandestine Cygnian operative, I have connections with Angel Station. They'll know for sure."

"You know about Angel Station?"

I nod. "Princess Lyra is practically my sister-in-law. She told us everything."

Delphi is almost convinced. Almost.

"OK," I say. "Watch this." I tab my wristband and bring up the Mighty Minions community board, find the 'contact us' page, then tab the button that says *call.*

"Mighty Minions Resort Help Desk, this is Ambassador Ambrosia. How can I make your day better?"

"Ambrosia, this is Jimmy."

"Hello, Mr. Krockstelter. What can I do for you?"

"Krockstelter?" Delphi laughs.

I cover my wristband with my hand and whisper, "No one can say my crazy name. I just go with it." Then I clear my throat, uncover my wristband, and say, "Yes, Ambrosia. I realize there's no way to communicate with other systems, but I'm going to need you to find me a neutrino wave anyway. I have an important message I need to send. I have the credits and authority of Harem Station at my disposal, so can you please make this happen and ping me back when it's set up?"

"Yes, Mr. Krockstelter. We do have an intersystem communication wave. But I'll need payment up front to get you a spot on the outgoing message list. It might take most of the day."

"Perfect," I say. "What do I owe you?"

"It's seven hundred thousand credits for the wave, two hundred thousand credits service charge, and a hundred thousand credits in tax. Would you like me to proceed?"

"Please do," I say.

My wristband lights up with an incoming charge, I tab accept, and pay, and then Ambrosia comes back on and says, "I'll ping you when it's ready."

"Thank you, Ambrosia."

"My pleasure, Mr. Krockstelter. Have a very nice Mighty Minions day."

Delphi's mouth is hanging open.

I shrug. "They speak money here, that's all."

"You just paid a million credits to make a comms call!"

"That's nothing to me, Delphi. When I need help, I get it. No matter what."

"So who are you calling?"

"My brother, Luck. He's out here somewhere doing... whatever it is he does these days. And believe me, he's one scrappy Akeelian male. He will not fuck around when he gets my message. I'm gonna ask him to bring us a new water generator and escort us back to Harem. So there, you see? All better now. Let's go have some fun."

CHAPTER TWENTY

Outside in the resort things are still fairly calm and quiet since it's early. A few families are milling about getting food, but most of the attractions won't open for a couple hours. One thing I will say about Mighty Minions is that this resort is top-notch when it comes to atmosphere. The roof of the station—which might be the biggest high-definition 3-D holographic screen ever made in the history of humanoids—has the appearance of a lavender-pink sky complete with subtle cloud variations and two suns—one setting, one rising—making me forget I'm inside a spinning ring floating out in the middle of the dark vacuum of the Vacation Sector.

Jimmy is holding my hand.

I'm not sure what to think about this whole… *thing* we're doing.

I mean… soulmates? Really? It's kinda stupid. And maybe I'm just a cynic—OK, I am a cynic, but I have good reasons—but this kind of stuff doesn't happen overnight.

Lives don't change in the span of one spin. Not like this.

Yesterday I was on the hunt to kidnap him, *Queenie* was my accomplice, and I was ready to turn him over to the most evil person I've ever encountered to save my brother. And that's saying something, since I come from Cygnus System.

And now it seems I've switched sides. Hell, Jimmy pretty much pledged the considerable resources of Harem Station to help me get Tycho back.

But when you switch sides like this there are consequences. For one, it makes me a traitor. And yeah, OK. I was never loyal to the Loathsome One, but I did agree to her terms. And contracts are something we Cygnians take seriously.

When she finds out I betrayed her she will definitely retaliate.

"How soon, do you think, will we be able to leave for Harem?" I ask, looking up at Jimmy.

He's scanning the various menus on a massive resort screen in front of the Demon Coaster. "Hmm?" he absently asks, glancing down at me.

"I just want to get out of here, ya know? I feel like *Queenie* might be plotting against me right about now. I need to answer her. Turning off my wristband won't keep her at bay for long."

Jimmy's smile is one of complete control. Like he hasn't got a care in the world. "Probably a few hours before I can send my message to Luck, then"—he shrugs—"I dunno, depends where Luck is. But I heard his ship, *Lady Luck*, got a cool upgrade before they left Harem. Equipped with some kind of special tech that can navigate inside spin nodes. Which means he might be here by tonight." Then he pauses to think about something. "I'm not sure I like that idea."

"What idea?" I ask. "Leaving?" Oh, please. I'm praying to the sun that he's not having second thoughts about helping me. He's pretty much my only chance now because I already told him my plan and there's no way to kidnap him after that.

"No, spin node travel. Have you ever done that?"

"Travel inside a node?" I shake my head. "No. But—"

"I mean… it can't be safe. Those things are so weird. Also, the whole time dilation thing, ya know? I hope he doesn't use a spin node to get here. Is there one close by?"

"Ummm. I don't know, Jimmy. I'm not really worried about the spin nodes."

"I'm just saying that if Luck uses a spin node it could take him longer, right? The way time works in those."

"What?"

"I just hope he's close." And he shrugs and goes back to looking at the menu. "I am impressed by this board," he says. "Yesterday I had to stand in line for those stupid noodles. Now this is what I'm talking about. No lines, just instant ordering."

"Jimmy," I say. "If we're going to be here the whole day then I need to answer *Queenie*'s messages. She's not a patient ship and she'll do something desperate if she thinks I'm ignoring her."

Jimmy looks down at me again, still smiling. "Look around, Delphi."

I do. I look around. Take in the resort and the families. All the rides, and the hundreds of Mighty Minion ambassadors milling around as more and more families come out for yet another day of play.

"This place is a fucking fortress," he continues. "And yeah, the fact that they lock down the docking bays at a certain time each night is super annoying and borderline tyrannical. Not to mention the way they squeeze every credit out of you in every way possible. But honestly, if we've got to be on the run from an insane ship and some badass chick called the Loathsome One, we could do a lot worse than Mighty Minions Resort. Your ship has to have some set of cocks on her to think she could do anything here, right?"

I consider that for a moment. "I guess."

"Trust me, I know a dictator AI when I meet one. And even though the one running this place isn't as overt as ALCOR and doesn't make itself known, it's definitely up there with ALCOR as far as control goes."

I squint my eyes and take another look around. I don't know how many levels this place has. It seems to only have this main corridor. Granted, it's a good thirty stories tall, but there's no map pointing up or down to other areas. No hiding places, in other words. Everything is out in the open. And high up in the air are small swarms of security bots. Just little dots from where I stand, so they're probably just a little bigger than Flicka.

"That's right," Jimmy says. "The AI running this place has a literal army of security drones up there watching every fucking thing that goes on. Hell, they probably know about your plan. In fact, it wouldn't surprise me at all if there was no docking bay curfew and that ambassador came to stop us because the AI ordered it to."

"What?" I say.

"Yeah. I don't think this station AI is fucking around. When you've got half a million people—all of which are families with young children—your main focus, above all else, is safety. I don't think anyone can touch us here. I think landing on Mighty Minions for repairs was actually a stroke of good luck. The only other place I'd feel safer is back on Harem."

I blow out a long breath. It's not relief. More like resignation. I know *Queenie*. She's evil and vicious. And her mind scares me. Plus, I have no idea what her stake in this little operation is. Maybe the Loathsome One is holding someone over her head too? And she has to complete this mission to save that someone?

Then I huff. Because no. *Queenie* isn't the type to sacrifice for someone else. She's getting paid though, that's for sure. So what if her reward is big enough that confronting the Mighty Minions AI is worth the risk?

That's my fear.

But Jimmy is already talking about what he wants to eat and this whole discussion seems to be over in his mind, so I don't say any of that out loud.

"What do you want?" Jimmy asks, pointing to the menu. "I'm gonna get the Centurian protein wrap with extra potatoes."

I crinkle my nose. "Potatoes?"

"My father used to make those when I was a kid." He smiles wistfully for a moment. Like this is a pleasant memory. "I can't believe they have them here. He told me they came from a faraway planet where my mother was born. Kinda cool, right?"

155

Oh, suns. Jimmy is in Mighty Minions delusional heaven right now and nothing I say will pull him out of it unless I get some evidence to the contrary.

"Sure," I say, forcing a smile. "I'll try that too. But I'm gonna run to the restroom real fast. Be right back, OK?"

"Don't take too long," he says, squeezing my hand. "I'm not sure I like the thought of you going off on your own."

I point up to the drones. "Security, right? I'll be fine. Be back in a minute." I give his hand a squeeze, then let it go and turn around, searching for the nearest restroom.

Weaving my way through the now burgeoning crowd, I slip away to a little alcove between a drinking fountain and a little bay of day lockers.

Then I turn on my wristband and mentally prepare myself for *Queenie*. Because I just don't trust her and if I stay out of communication any longer I'm one hundred percent positive that she'll do something drastic to get my attention.

"You sneaky little bitch," she says, once I'm back online and connected.

"Hey," I say, forcing myself to be cheerful. "Good news!"

"You have Jimmy sedated and you're on your way?"

"Nnn-nooo," I stutter. "But I am with him. And he likes me so I think I'll just need one more spin and—"

"One. More. *Spin?*" she growls. "No. We're on a deadline. We should've been out of here last night and we've been out of contact with The Loathsome One way too long. She is probably out of her mind and ready to send a legion of warships to come kill us. Get him here. Now."

"I can't," I say, so frustrated. "The security here is tight. I think the station AI blocked us from leaving last night on purpose."

"Oh, nice excuse." *Queenie* laughs. "But I know better."

"What do you mean?"

"Delphi, I scanned the station AI before we ever docked. It's rudimentary at best. It's not the station stalling us, it's you. Now what is the fucking problem?"

"The fucking problem is... the fucking problem is that he's smart, OK? He's suspicious."

"You just said he likes you."

"He does. That's why we're still together. But maybe... I think he likes me too much. He wants me to spend the day with him doing... you know. Rides and shit. And we're sharing a room. But we're not there right now. I was going to drug him at breakfast, but he insisted that we go out." She sighs and I know she's got another objection coming, so I keep talking. "But we'll have to go back to the room eventually, right? So I'll drug him then and I'll call you when it's done so you can help me move him to your docking bay like we planned."

"You're lying," she says.

"I am not! I swear, this is the plan."

"Mmmm-hmm. And where, exactly, are you getting these drugs?"

"There's an autopharmacy in the room. I'll fake... I don't know. An ankle injury and get an approval for pain meds, then I'll slip some into his drink."

I roll my eyes at myself, that's how lame this plan sounds.

But *Queenie* doesn't immediately respond, so maybe... possibly... could she be buying it?

"You have until dinner."

"I'll get it done."

"The curfew—"

"I know," I say. "I'll get it done and call you back when I'm ready for transport. You have bots or something? So we can move him?"

"I'll send an anti-grav shipping crate to your room. Which one is it?"

"I... don't know for sure. I'll have to look when we go back there."

"You don't know which room you're in?"

"It's a penthouse, OK? By the Demon Coaster thing."

Silence from *Queenie*. She's not buying it. Not one bit.

So I say, "*Queenie*, listen. I'll check in in a few hours, OK? I promise. And if I don't you can do it your way. Just give me a chance to get us out of here without alerting security. Trust me. The AI isn't rudimentary. You can't see what I'm seeing inside the resort. There's hundreds of security drones buzzing around. The escape—if we escape—could get very messy. We need to do this right."

More agonizing silence.

"I gotta go," I say. "He'll get suspicious if I'm gone too long. I'll message you in a few hours."

Even more silence.

"OK?" I ask, trying not to sound desperate. "Believe me, I want to get this job done as much as you do. Tycho's life is at stake. Just… let me do it my way so we have the best chance at success."

"I need that room number."

"I'll send it the moment we get back. I promise."

"Do not fuck with me, Delphi. I have a mean streak lurking underneath this calm demeanor."

Which almost makes me laugh. Because lurking? Please. Her mean streak is the most obvious thing ever.

"I won't," I say.

And then she cuts off the transmission, so I never really get an answer, but I assume she's agreed and I've got until this afternoon to come up with another plan.

I walk back to Jimmy wondering what this ship will do to me when she finds out I'm lying. Because she will find out and then it will be a race against time to get to Tycho before *Queenie* can alert the Loathsome One about my betrayal.

CHAPTER TWENTY-ONE

I look over my shoulder as Delphi disappears into the growing crowd and then promptly place my touchscreen order and make a call to *Dicker*.

"Oh. My. God," *Dicker* says when she answers. She's a little bit breathy, which I know makes no sense, since she doesn't breathe, but it makes me happy that her humanoid mannerisms are so advanced now, she mimics us. "You will not believe what I just scored in my last game."

"Are you still fucking playing?"

"Uh, yeah," she says. "Because I'm *winning*."

"Are you still playing that same ship?" I ask cautiously. I don't want to tell her everything just yet. Like... that ship is yanking her chain hard and has no intention of paying up. That will just set her off. But I don't want her to keep playing it, either.

"Oh, that one. No. Chickenshit got scared. But don't worry, I've manipulated my docking bay ambassador into keeping an eye on her. And I'm glad you called because I need you and your helper to get over there pronto and grab my shit before she tries to cheat me. How's that coming, by the way? You ready to do that?"

"Well," I say, rubbing the stubble on my chin. "Ahhhh... not quite, but almost."

"Jimmy—"

"I know, I know. I want to blow this place too. But... look, there's some extenuating circumstances and I've put in for a neutrino wave call to Luck to come help us out."

"What?"

"It's nothing serious, just... there's people here kinda... looking for me and I need backup. So we're gonna sit tight until he gets here. In fact, I think you should try to get a hold of Xyla. I know she's gonna be pissed at us for interrupting her vacay, but tell her she needs to find a way over here and help out."

"What's going on?"

"Nothing. I mean... nothing yet. But shit could get serious if we don't find the right exit strategy. And I want to make sure that our exit is as smooth as possible because this station makes me nervous."

"What do you mean nervous? Why?"

"I think it's... well, how to put this. Very... sentient."

I almost feel her confusion in the ensuing silence. Then she says, "No. I checked when we docked and it was pretty basic. And I just checked and triple-checked right now. Nothing but your run-of-the-mill AI as far as I can tell."

"I'm just telling you that things look different on the inside. We need to be careful not to piss it off."

"Well, I just put in that call to Xyla and she's not picking up."

"Damn, that was fast."

"I told you, my docking bay ambassador is taking care of me. We have an understanding. Pretty sure you're overreacting."

"OK," I say, sorta agreeing with her. Because if I make any more objections she's gonna wanna know how I know. And I'm not ready to tell her everything just yet. And just to keep her calm, I change the subject. Because she can't go anywhere without me, anyway. "So what did you win?"

"Oh," she says. "Holy shit! I got us a state-of-the-art cloaking device. One that shields you for thirty-seven seconds coming out of a gate!"

"What good is that?" I ask, thinking about Delphi's description of the Loathsome One's lair being quite distant from a gate.

"Thirty-seven seconds? Are you kidding me? Do you have any idea what I could do to a waiting ship with thirty-seven whole seconds coming out of a gate cloaked? Shit," she says. "Annihilation comes to mind."

"Are you planning a war I'm not aware of?" I laugh.

"I'm just saying it's good to have, that's all. And it was *free*. Plus this ship is super on the up-and-up. She's gonna send her crew over to install it."

"We could've just bought one of those, right?"

She makes a sound that sounds very much like tongue-tsking. "Where's the fun in that? Anything else? I've got another game starting in thirty seconds. This ship, holy crap, Jimmy. This one is offering up a SEAR cannon."

"We have one of those already."

"Two, actually," she corrects me. "But you can never have too many, ya know? Also, it's gonna be free, remember?"

"I think you have a problem and when we get back to Harem you're going into some kind of gambler's addiction treatment."

She laughs. Like that was a joke. But seriously, she's never acted like this before. "I don't have a problem, it's just I've never seen so many well-equipped ships in one place before. It's crazy how rich these Mighty Minions vacation people are."

"Well, that's not really surprising considering how many credits I've spent here in the span of one spin."

"Right?" She laughs again. "Crazy place. I love it. I might vacation here myself just to get in on the poker games."

"OK. I gotta go. The station is pinging me and that might be my neutrino wave call. Just… stay put and… don't lose."

"You worry too much, Jimmy. I got this! And hurry up, I want my winnings from that ship. *Dicker* out."

The call drops and immediately the station is pinging me. "This is Jimmy," I say.

"Mr. Shazelcroft?" a man asks.

I close my eyes and make myself be patient. How would I ever know if this call really was for me or some random dude called Shazelcroft? Like… what do people hear when I say Jimmy? Jimmy. It's so simple. Two syllables. Five letters. Just… what the fuck? And how come they don't ever hear the same thing? The made-up name changes every single time.

I decide I don't care and let it go. "Yup. This is Jimmy."

164

"Oh, perfect. Mr. Shazelcroft, your neutrino wave is ready."

"That was fast."

"Yes." He chuckles. "You must be well connected, Mr. Shazelcroft. Either that or the station has taken a liking to you. She bumped you up the list."

"She?" I ask. "Who is this station? Does she have a name?"

"Oh, I'm sorry. I can't divulge that information. Proprietary property law and we all sign non-disclosure agreements when we're hired on. But I can assure you, she's quite nice to work for, if that matters."

"I guess... OK, so do I need to come to your offices or something? I've never had to make a neutrino wave call on the road before."

"No, no. It's quite simple. Sending you a form to fill out now."

My wristband pings and a form appears.

"Now, one thing. You only get a hundred and forty characters. So make it pithy."

"What the fuck? I paid a million credits for this?"

"And you can buy another hundred and forty characters if you need it."

"Let me guess, that's another seven hundred thousand credits?"

"Plus tax and service charge."

"Right. I'll stick to the limit."

"Perfect," he says. "Just type it in and press send. You have the address, I assume?"

"Yes," I say.

"Greee-at! Put that in the address bar and we'll shoot it out into the nearest gate. Depending on where your party is, it should arrive within a standard Minion hour. Now this is my standard speech, and I'm sure you already know, but I have to say it. So bear with me. Your party most likely does not have access to a two-way neutrino wave comms device, so we do not offer incoming neutrino wave messages for guests."

Because of course they don't. That would make too much sense. Besides, they'd probably charge me a million credits to accept it, anyway. He's probably doing me a favor.

"But if they have an urgent reply there are several nearby resorts in the Vacation Sector that can relay a station-to-station message to us should they feel the need to contact you back. And you'll be happy to know, we do not charge for those incoming messages."

"Fine," I say.

"Any other questions?"

"Um…" I actually have a lot of questions, but all of them are about the station and that's a dead end. So I say, "No. I'm good."

"So glad I could be of service to you today, Mr. Shazelcroft. Oh, and I almost forgot."

"Now what?" I ask.

"At the station's suggestion I've taken the liberty of applying for a Mighty Minions rewards card for you. All you have to do is press accept on your application which you should be receiving—"

My wristband dings.

"—right about now."

"A rewards card, huh?"

"We have some pretty excellent perks, Mr. Shazelcroft. I urge you to just sign. You've spent enough in one spin to qualify for Palladium Level!"

I press the accept tab on my screen, because why the fuck not? I earned it. Black and red confetti starts dropping all over me. When I look up there's a bot with a huge digital *Congratulations, New Platinum Awards Member!* sign blinking out in front of it.

"That's your new personal Mighty Minions Ambassador! He will escort you around the park and give you jump-the-line access to all the rides and attractions. Enjoy your stay and have a very happy Mighty Minions day!" the ambassador coos.

Then he ends the call.

"Just what I need," I growl. "A babysitter."

Something is not right here. This place was creepy when I first landed but this is too much. I don't like the idea of a station bot following me around.

But then again... having a station spy means that Delphi and I can relax a little until Luck gets here. It's security, I realize.

Hmmm.

I quickly type in the message to Luck, keeping it short and pithy.

Luck, this is Jimmy. I need help on Mighty Minions Station. Come immediately. And bring a new water generator. Mine's broken.

I type in his access code address and press send, letting out a long breath of air as I do that.

I'm still flapping confetti off my head when I spy Delphi making her way through the crowd. She looks cute as fuck today and that makes me smile, the tension of speaking to *Dicker* and placing the neutrino call fading as I take her in.

She's wearing tan tactical pants, a pair of brown standard-issue station boots, and a white t-shirt that accentuates her… um… tits. Quite nicely, I think. Nice enough to make my cock jump a little just watching her pick her way through the crowd.

Her hair is up in a ponytail and on her head is a red and black Mighty Minions hat that she was not wearing when we left the penthouse earlier.

I grin as she comes up to me. "Don't ask," she says, rolling her eyes and pointing to her head. "I had to buy a hat because those stupid holographic demon children were following me around. I was gonna go up and grab yours from the penthouse, but I didn't know which one it was. So"—she sighs and shrugs—"I bought another one."

I laugh. I can't help it. This place is such a fucking racket.

"What the hell is that?" she asks, pointing at my new bot.

"I'll fill you in over breakfast," I say, taking her hand. "Come on. I'm pretty sure our food is ready."

CHAPTER TWENTY-TWO

I try to focus on what Jimmy is telling me while we eat our Centurian wraps, but it's kinda hard to concentrate. I'm usually all business. I'm not one of those flighty princesses who gush all over a handsome man and act like love-struck fools because I'm pretty logical on most days. But those violet eyes, and that hard body, and yeah, OK, so I'm shallow, but two cocks? I mean... come on. Two!

But... I dunno. It's more than that. I think I really *like* him.

He's so intriguing. Everything about him is just fascinating. I mean... that Harem Station thing? Suns. It has an allure I can't deny. A whole station city of outlaws and bots run by some infamous, evil AI. Not to mention the way he throws money around like credits have no value at all.

And the band of brothers who will just come running when he calls... I can't even imagine such loyalty. I had my father and Tycho, that's it. Sure, I had plenty of cousins and sisters, and others around me my whole life, but could I count on them to help me in a pinch?

No. That's exactly why I'm out here alone in the first place. No one was gonna save Tycho but me.

And now I have him. Jimmy of Harem Station, of all people.

I smile as Jimmy continues to describe his conversation with *Dicker* and then the Mighty Minions ambassador who signed him up for this crazy rewards card. His bot is still hovering over top of us. High enough to be out of reach—I think so Jimmy can't swat him away—but low enough so that there's no mistaking who he's been assigned to. Tons of kids are gathered around us in a little circle gawking up at it because it's been doing magic tricks and making balloon animals the whole time we've been eating.

And I know that I should be thinking up a new plan to get us out of this mess with *Queenie,* and I totally plan on doing that just as soon as I can stop staring at this Akeelian male and planning our fun day together, but what if… what if he's right and we're connected? Like true genetic soulmates?

Wouldn't that be amazing? Not just the part where I get to spend the rest of my life with a true partner… but he'd take me back to his station. I would integrate into their culture and society. I'd meet new friends and do new things.

I would have *people*. Real loyalty. I'd have a *family* again.

"So what do you think?" Jimmy asks.

"Hmm?" I say, shaking myself out of my daydream.

He laughs. "Were you even listening to me?"

"I was. Sorta. Ask me that last question again."

"Our day?" he says, raising his eyebrows. "Did you change your mind? I mean, I guess you don't have to stick around with me all day, but it would be safer." Then he points up at the bot. "I've got a security detail for us now."

"Security? Wait what did I miss? You said this was your rewards bot."

"Such a lie." Then he leans in like he's gonna tell me a secret. "I'm telling you, this station has some kind of interest in me. It's weird."

"I don't know," I say. "Not so weird. You are kind of fascinating."

This makes him lean back and smile. "Say more," he says.

I laugh. "I'm just... you know. Intrigued by this whole soulmates business."

"I know," he says, running his fingers through his light-brown hair so it's deliciously messy. "If you had asked me yesterday if I wanted to fall in love with a Cygnian princess I'd have run the other way without even answering."

Wait. Did he say... fall in love?

"But, you know." He shrugs. "You can't fight fate, right?"

"No," I say, dreamily agreeing. "You can't."

He reaches across the table and takes both my hands. There's a little chill. A little shiver that runs up my spine at his touch.

There, I think. *That's the feeling.* I think that's the feeling. Instantaneous attraction when your genetically engineered soulmate makes contact.

Honestly, I figured it'd be a little more powerful, but we're new. This is probably just stage one devotion. I'm sure it only gets better from here.

"So what do you say? Wanna forget about all this shit and have some fun? I've been told that this bot gives me jump-the-line privileges. We could ride everything, Delphi. Make the most of our unexpected Mighty Minions vacay."

"Yeah," I say. "Sounds fun." And it really does, I'm not even lying. Hell, who am I kidding? He could say, "Wanna steal a Prime Navy ship and be wanted outlaws for the next hundred years?" and I'd probably agree to that too.

I just have an undeniable urge to be near him.

More proof, I decide. Just more proof that this is the real deal. I'm destined to be with Jimmy. He and I were, literally, made for each other.

"OK, so rides? You like slow, enjoy-the-view rides? Or fast, puke-your-guts-out rides?"

"All of them," I say. Because I totally just got a vision of us riding the gondola all around this station as we hold hands and kiss. But if we do the scary-fast coaster rides I could cling to him like I was afraid.

God, I'm stupid. I'm a stupid lovesick outlaw princess who just found her outlaw prince.

And I don't even care. Because when Jimmy stands up and takes my hand, leading me into the crowd of people to go searching for fun, I forget about Flicka being in lockup, *Queenie* planning my inevitable demise, and the Loathsome One waiting back at her lair, ready to do terrible things to me when she figures out I betrayed her, and yes, I might even almost forget about Tycho.

And the fact that I'm supposed to be saving him.

Jimmy's wristband chirps an incoming message. "Oh, good," he says. "Just got a return receipt for the neutrino call. Apparently this is a featured perk of my new Palladium Rewards status."

"Hell," I scoff. "For that price you should get Mighty Minions citizenship or something."

"Right?" He laughs. "So... have you made up your mind about what we should do first today?"

But just as he finishes that sentence his wristband chirps another incoming message. "Hmm," he says.

"What now? Don't tell me they've slapped you with some service charge for the return receipt?"

"No," he says. "Apparently we've been gifted a complimentary Mighty Boss Steed Tour of the interior forest."

"What the hell is that?" I ask.

"No clue."

The bot hovering over our heads suddenly flashes a hologram down into the space in front of us. Jimmy and I both step back in surprise when the Mighty Boss Steed appears in front of us, pawing the ground and snorting through flared nostrils in all his shining stallion glory as an advert for the Steed Tour begins to play.

"Get the most out of your stay on the Mighty Minions Resort by taking a once-in-a-lifetime adults-only steed tour," an animated announcer-voice says. "Two hours of private, unlimited access to the gorgeous, well-groomed interior meadows in the Mighty Minion Forest on the back of the one-of-a-kind Boss Steed. The most realistic cyborg animal in the galaxy! Enjoy a private lunch in our secluded woodland cabin, swim in the secret Mighty Boss lagoon, find Mighty Boss's hidden treasure in the secret grotto behind the waterfall, and complete your trip with a couples' massage before returning to the park!"

"Well," I say, looking at Jimmy across the hologram of the impressive steed.

"He had me at 'adults only.'" Jimmy laughs.

CHAPTER TWENTY-THREE

JIMMY

Now this what I'm talking about.

The Boss Steed is an impressive cyborg animal. Standing more than two meters at the shoulder, its glossy coat some color combination I can only describe as blood-rust, and its black mane and tail long and flowing—it is quite simply, spectacular.

Also, maybe a little bit intimidating.

"I don't know," Delphi says, taking a step back from the animal. "We have to ride that thing?"

"Oh, let me be clear," the ambassador woman checking us in says. "This borg is perfectly safe. He has been doing two tours a day for the past two decades and we've never had a safety issue. His core processor is equipped with a semi-sentient AI that will anticipate your every need. Trust me, he's tame."

He doesn't look tame. In fact, he looks the opposite of tame. He looks like he's about to ride into battle with Mighty Boss himself on his back.

"Is that smoke coming out of his nostrils?" Delphi asks.

"Just effects," the ambassador says. Then she snaps her fingers and two more ambassadors appear

175

with a rolling stairwell, presumably so we can climb up onto his back.

"And he's OK with both of us riding him?" Delphi asks, still uncertain.

"That's his job," the girl says. "This is a special treat for well-qualified couples who need a break from the hustle and bustle of the resort. Just climb on, give him a little kick, and off you go."

Delphi looks over her shoulder at me.

I shrug. "Adults only," I remind her.

She chuckles. "Fine. But if I die on this steed I'm gonna kill someone later."

"Trust me," the girl says. "This ride will be the highlight of your trip."

"Climb on," I say, urging Delphi towards the stairs. "I'll protect you, princess."

She sighs at that, her eyelids droopy and heavy as she internalizes my promise. And while I was kinda joking... I'm not joking. I have a sudden urge to keep her safe at all costs.

Delphi nods and starts climbing the steps. She swings a leg over and then she's sitting on him, her eyes glowing just the slightest bit of pink, betraying her emotional state.

I reach out and touch the steed and his lifelike synthetic skin quivers as he stomps a foot. He feels real. I've seen equines on several planets but none of them were as beautiful as this guy.

"Front or back?" Delphi asks me.

I raise my eyebrows at her. Because holy shit. I didn't even think about that. "Back," I say. climbing up the stairs and swinging my leg over. My arms

176

immediately wrap around her waist, tugging her into my chest. I get to hold her like this for hours.

Yup, this is the perfect way to spend our time waiting for Luck to show up.

"How private is that cabin?" I ask the girl as the other helpers wheel the stairs away.

She winks at me. "Totally, one hundred percent private. And it's all yours while you're there."

I look up at the bot, still hovering above my head. "He has to stay behind?"

"Yes," the girls says. "It's couples only. Just the two of you, your steed, and the forest wildlife. None of which will eat you."

"Wildlife?" Delphi asks.

But the girl is either deliberately ignoring Delphi's apprehensions or she's just assuming she's overreacting on purpose. "I've done it a few times with my husband and trust me," she says. "You're gonna love this. Once you cross the Mighty Bridge into the forest you'll think you're on another planet. In fact, when you get to the meadow there's a breathtaking surprise. Make sure you stop and take it all in."

"Well," I say, leaning into Delphi's neck. "Should we go?"

She sucks in a breath and nods.

"Give him a little kick," the girl says.

I do. The steed paws the ground, throws his head up and back, lifting up onto his hind legs just a little. Just enough to make Delphi grab a fistful of thick, black mane, and give me an excuse to hold her tighter. And then he walks forward along a red-brick path, leaves the stables, and takes us back out into the resort.

The bridge leading into the forest is just a short walk away, and in the time it takes for us to make our way to the entrance hundreds of kids collect along the red velvet ropes that separate the bridle path from the rest of the park, sticky hands reaching out in vain as they try to pet the steed as we pass.

The entrance to the woods is marked with a high arch made out of rock with holographic flames shooting out in all directions and there's a slight shimmer to the air.

Once we pass through the gate the pandemonium of the park fades away until there's nothing but the chirping of insects and birds.

"Wow," Delphi says. "This place is surrounded by a sound barrier. OK. I'm sold. This is gonna be great."

Truly. This is nice. And not just because of the peaceful atmosphere after the ruckus of the resort. The steed's walk makes both Delphi and I move with a subtle rocking motion and my cock is pressing up against her ass. Almost rubbing against her with each forward rocking motion.

I pull Delphi closer as we enter the woods and the fake sunshine above fades away under the canopy of trees. Small animals cross the path in front of us. Little, furry leaf nibblers I've never seen before and can't identify. Not that I care. The only thing on my mind at the moment is the scent of her hair, my hands wrapped around her hips, and the fact that I can feel her tits bounce—just a little—with the movement of the steed.

Delphi sighs. "Yeah. I love this. I don't think I've ever been in a real forest. Do you think this is real? Or is it all effects, and holograms?"

"I have no clue," I say. Because I don't, but also because who cares? Delphi is practically sitting in my lap right now. I kinda want to pull this steed over and fuck her up against a tree.

"Is there something in the air, you think? I mean, I get it. It's all relaxing and shit. But I suddenly feel so calm. Like nothing else matters."

"Wouldn't surprise me," I say. "ALCOR slips drugs into my showers back on Harem any time he thinks I'm too stressed."

"I think I'm gonna like your ALCOR. He seems to love you. Or, at the very least, he wants to take care of you."

"Well," I say. "He's not the same these days. Long story. So he actually hasn't done that in a while. But yeah. It was nice. It wasn't like that in the beginning, either. He wasn't used to being around people, especially young people who did stupid things like fall off balconies and lift bots. But it's been more than twenty years now, so before that shit show out at Bull Station happened, he was pretty good at taking care of us."

This makes me smile.

"What do you mean?" Delphi asks. "What happened after Bull Station?"

"Oh, I figured everyone knew by now. All those people died on Harem when the baby ALCOR took over."

"What?"

"He... fuck. He—ALCOR—he blew himself up to take out that Cygnian warship. That was the real him, not a copy. So... yeah. The baby ALCOR was left

179

behind to take care of the station but it was not equipped to deal, so lots of shit went off the rails."

"ALCOR's *dead*?"

"Kinda. I mean, there's old copies of him in the security beacons, but they've been autonomous for so long now, they're their own personalities. And the baby ALCOR is technically ALCOR, but then again, not really. Nothing like him at all, actually. So yeah. The AI who took care of me and my brothers, he's gone now."

"How sad. He was like your father."

"Yeah, I guess he was. I never really thought of it that way since I had a real father when I was a kid. But ALCOR was the one who made us who we are today."

"I'm sad that I'll never get to meet him." Then she stiffens a little. "Not that I was ever going to meet him. I mean. I have no clue what I mean. I might be high."

I chuckle at that. I might be high too. Because all I can think about is sliding my hands up inside her shirt and playing with her nipples.

But before I can do that we exit the woods and enter the meadow the ambassador mentioned and the steed changes gait and begins to lope.

This makes Delphi and I rock together in a new rhythm. She squeals and I hold her tight, her tits bouncing a lot more as we move forward. Her ass is lifting up out of the saddle and then bouncing down in a pattern that reminds me of fucking.

Hell, who am I kidding? Everything reminds me of fucking right now.

I want to tell myself to knock it off. To enjoy this date and there's plenty of time later for sex. But my cocks—both of them are awake now—have other pressing ideas.

When we get to the center of the meadow, larger, leaf-eating herbivores scatter into the cover of the trees as we approach and the steed slows down. Delphi and I bounce jerkily until we fall back into a walk, and then finally stop.

I'm just about to give the steed another kick to keep going because I will be fucking Delphi in that cabin when we get there—when the sun disappears and the stars come out.

"Oooooooo," Delphi says, leaning back into my chest so she can look up. The stars change to a view of some unrecognizable solar system orbiting a binary sun. Comets whiz by, then an asteroid starts hurtling towards us in such high definition, both Delphi and I bring our arms up in front of our faces in self-defense. "It's a giant screen!" she says. "Look! There's a black hole!"

It is. And hell yeah, that girl back at the stables was right. This is a breathtaking surprise. We start moving towards the black hole. Slowly, at first. Then faster, and faster until the stars blur and I feel unsteady on the back of the steed. Like I'm floating.

Both of us yell when we enter the vortex, squealing like kids. But when we come out the other side there's a blue-brown planet surrounded by clouds. We hurl through space towards it, getting closer, and closer until we enter the atmosphere and then the scene is a large expanse of grassland prairie dotted with strange-looking animals around a watering hole.

Some look recognizable. Oddly, and funnily enough, a whole herd of creatures remind me of karkadanns, only their horn is on the bridge of their noses instead of their foreheads, and they have short, stubby gray bodies with thick folds of skin armor.

There's even a bunch of steeds—almost like the one we're riding, but much smaller and with black and white stripes. Another herd of long-limbed animals, with even longer necks, reach high up into tree tops as their slender, black tongues pull leaves into their mouths. And a group of beasts with golden manes stalking towards us are so clearly top-of-the-food-chain predators, I have a moment of panic and kick the steed to make him run.

He doesn't run. Just calmly turns in a circle so we can take it all in.

"Where is this place?" Delphi says, almost breathless. "I want to go here."

"I think it's fake," I say. "I've never seen animals like this before. Especially all in one place. No planet I've ever been on had anything like this."

"Well, I have to hand it to the Mighty AI. It's got quite the vivid imagination."

"Hmmm," I say. "Yeah, it really does."

The pack of hunting beasts walk around us like we're not there and yeah. I've never seen anything like this before. They sure as fuck look real. One even stops to sniff the air just a few meters away and I swear to the sun, he looks me dead in the eyes and licks his lips.

The steed begins to walk forward and that's when it hits me. It's not just a screen in the sky feeding us images to make us think we're on another planet, but now the watering hole and the wildlife is all around us. Like we're really there. Then suddenly there's a great trumpeting sound and over a ridge comes a herd of gray beasts with long trunks out in front of them, bellowing their arrival with grunts and roars as they approach the small, muddy lake in the middle of the savannah.

"What the fuck is this place?" I whisper.

Delphi says nothing. Just looks all around us, the steed still slowly circling so we can get a complete view.

Then, without warning, we're lifting up in the air again. Only, we're not, of course. We're still sitting on the back of the Boss Steed. We pull away backwards, then the steed turns and we're facing forward as we exit the planet's atmosphere and go back out into space.

"No!" Delphi laughs. "I want to go back!"

But we don't go back.

Well, no. We do go back. The way we came, that is. Back into the vortex of the black hole, out the other side into the unnamed solar system, and then we're here.

In the meadow surrounded by forests on Mighty Minions Resort.

"Holy shit!" Delphi says. "That was amazing!"

I make a mental note to ask ALCOR if he's ever seen a program like this because we could sell the fuck out of this experience on Harem—but then I realize ALCOR is gone and there's no one to ask.

Sad. How it hits me now. Kinda hard, if I'm being honest.

"Do it again," Delphi says, patting the steed's neck. "Please!" she begs.

But the Boss Steed just snorts smoke out of his nose and begins to walk forward. Shaking and bobbing his head with a very firm, and not-so-polite, no.

"Huh," I say, looking up at the station ceiling. The sun is back now. And for a moment I wonder if I just hallucinated that whole thing.

CHAPTER TWENTY-FOUR

DELPHI

Jimmy and I are quiet for a long while as we continue our ride through the meadow. It goes on for thousands and thousands of meters, and when we finally get to the other side, I look over my shoulder and realize I can't see the edge of the forest behind us.

"It's fake," Jimmy says, for like the billionth time.

"Of course it was," I say, agreeing with him, just like I did every other time. But for some reason that experience has left him unsettled. It did feel pretty real, but lots of things feel real and aren't. I've been in some pretty amazing virtuals, but never while I was *conscious*.

So yeah. I don't get it either. But of course it was fake. There's no other explanation for it. We didn't just... leave the resort and fly through the galaxy to some real far-off planet and then come back.

That's ridiculous.

"Holograms," Jimmy says. "That's all it was. Just holograms."

"Pretty damn good ones, though," I say.

"Yeah," he says, just as we enter the woods again. "Pretty damn good. Like ALCOR good. Maybe even better."

"Why does that bother you?" I ask, genuinely curious. Because he's really upset by that experience back there.

"Because ALCOR is supposed to be the best, ya know? And this station is starting to freak me out. I hope Luck gets here soon. I feel... I dunno. Disconnected or something. Like I need to go home for some reason."

"Maybe it was just a nice gift?" I say, trying to pull him out of this funk. "I mean... the whole point of this place is to immerse yourself in a fantasy world, right?"

"Yeah, but—"

"And that's all it was. A very cool fantasy."

"I know, but—"

"Oh, look! There's the cabin!" Perfect timing, if you ask me. Jimmy is really distracted by that whole meadow experience. It's starting to freak me out too, and honestly, if this station is doing something weird to us I'd prefer to stick my head in the sand and pretend it's not happening for as long as possible.

Because what could we do? How do you fight a station when you're *inside* of it and outside there is nothing but immediate death in an infinite dark, lonely vacuum?

No, thank you. I'd rather pretend everything is fine.

This is why a station AI should not be so smart. They are already freaky fucking powerful. Like his ALCOR. Sure, that whole situation going on at Harem Station is sexy and intriguing, but look what happened when the AI left them to go blow up a Cygnian warship.

People died. *Lots* of people died.

This is why the Prime Navy has regulations about station sentience. They hold humanity in their figurative hands.

Almost no one lives on planets anymore. They are really just tourist attractions. Or treasure vaults. Places you go to visit or hide things.

I know living on planets was a thing in ancient times and if our ancestors could manage to tame the atmosphere and terrain of a celestial body, we could too.

But it's all so unpredictable. Some stations have weather on them. Most have at least a small weather system in the greenhouses. And there's some others that are so big clouds form in the upper levels. We had one station back in Cygnus System that snowed. The higher-ups went there to ski.

It's all controlled by the AI's though. There's no random hurricane or tornado brewing on the entertainment deck. There's no flood coming to the food court. There's no lava flowing in the docking bays.

Suns. I should stop thinking about this. I'm starting to freak myself out. And Jimmy is still talking about that... whatever it was back in the meadow.

"I mean," Jimmy says, continuing his train of thought, "it felt so real, didn't it? Did you see that one beast? The way he looked at me? I think he could smell me, Delphi."

"Just look at this place," I say. "Isn't it adorable?"

It totally is. I'm not lying. A small cabin made out of wooden logs. Very primitive and rustic. Ironically, something you'd find on a planet. And it's surrounded by dark green, stiff-needled trees on all sides. Just the cabin itself is open to the station sky above.

I look up and find clouds, which allow the fake sunshine to filter through and beam gorgeous rays of light down onto the roof. There's a few small windows with bright red and white checkered curtains that blow a little in the station wind.

"Yeah," Jimmy says. "It's nice. Like… too nice."

"No," I say, forcing myself to laugh. "Things can't be too nice."

Although even I know that's not true. Things can be too nice. Too perfect. It's usually a very bad sign.

The steed stops near the cabin entrance, pawing the ground and throwing his head. Like he wants us off his back and he wants that wish granted immediately.

"How do we get down?" I ask.

Jimmy throws one leg over the steed's hindquarters and jumps down like he's an old pro at steed dismounting, then looks up at me, offering a hand. "Just do it like that. I'll help you."

That melty feeling he invokes inside me is back. I hold on to that feeling and force myself to forget about the creepy Mighty Minions Station.

Because again, if this place is out to get us there's pretty much nothing we can do about it.

Jimmy places his hand on my thigh closest to him and says, "Come on. It's not that far of a jump."

I swing my leg over the way he did and momentum pretty much does the rest. I slide down the beast's side and Jimmy grips my waist to steady me.

God, I love that feeling.

I think he does too. Because he responds with a deep, low rumbling growl of lust.

I turn slowly to face him. He's a lot taller than me, but both of us are small compared to the Boss Steed. Jimmy smiles. "Hungry?" he asks, just as the Boss Steed walks off towards the woods.

My stomach rumbles loudly, answering his question. But I'm not thinking about food. "I am hungry," I say, staring up into his bright, violet eyes. "For you."

It's not even a stupid come-on line, either. It's just… true. Suddenly I don't care about the station, or the predicament we're in, or even the weirdness of that meadow experience.

I just want him. I want him to touch me all over. I want to get naked. And get him naked too. And feel his skin pressed up against mine. His hands on my body and mine on his.

"Well," Jimmy says, smiling slyly. "That ambassador did assure us this place was private."

I take a step towards him, my hands sliding around his waist the way his are around mine. I press my breasts up to his chest and say, "Should we go inside?"

Jimmy reaches for the button on my tactical pants and pops it. "What's wrong with right here?"

I look around and laugh nervously as he pulls down my zipper and slips his hand inside my pants. "Oh, God," I breathe. Because the instant his fingers slide between my legs I feel faint. Any hesitation I had immediately disappears. I do not care where we go right now. Just please keep touching me.

"Like that?" he whispers.

"Yes," I say, looking up at him through hooded lids.

"I feel like fucking you, Delphi."

I swallow hard. Eyes locked on his.

"I don't care where. I don't care how. I want to be inside you right now. Do you hear me?"

"Oh," I whisper, "I hear you."

"Touch me back," he says, taking my hand and placing it over the large bulge inside his pants.

His cock is hard when I grip it. Long, and thick, and hard. I squeeze and he growls again like that beast back there in the meadow. He is an alpha predator, make no mistake. This man is as dangerous as they come, but not with me, he's not. With me, he's just... mine.

"You're mine," I say, still looking up into those eyes of his.

"Fuck," he says, closing his eyes. But at the same time his hand—still covering mine—squeezes so I have to grip him harder. My fingertips detect his second cock, half hiding underneath the first one. I maneuver my fingers so I can feel it better, pressing the palm of my hand hard against his hardness.

His other hand is still fingering me. Pressing between the lips of my pussy, trying to get inside me.

I gasp when the tip of his fingers brush my clit, and start to feel weak.

Then his touch is gone. His hand withdrawn. He lifts me up and I automatically wrap my legs around his middle as he walks me over to a tree and presses my back up against the trunk. The hard, rough bark scratching my back, letting me know this is pure animal instinct and the fuck we're about to have won't be soft.

"Yes," I say, giving him permission to do that. To take me that way. "Yes," I say again. "Do it."

Because something has come over me. The feeling I got back at the beginning of our ride. Some kind of drugged-up acceptance. Only this time it doesn't make me calm. It makes me horny.

"Do it," I say again.

But he doesn't need to be told twice. His chest presses me into the tree, one hand under my ass, holding me up. The other tugging on the waistband of my pants.

He unwraps one leg from around his waist and my foot drops to the needle-covered ground. He is tugging one side of my pants down my leg and then I'm helping. My other leg falls away until my foot finds the ground and I'm tugging down the other side.

Somehow, during this frantic undressing, he's pulled out both his cocks and he's fisting them in his hand. Together they are so thick, his fingers barely fit around the shafts.

Just catching a tiny glimpse of this makes my pussy start throbbing with anticipation.

"Put them inside me," I gasp. "*Please.*"

My pants are only halfway down my bare thighs, but he either doesn't care or he's just good at improvising with half-dressed girls. Because he just lifts me up again and presses his groin forward so I have to open my legs as wide as possible to accommodate his hips. My knees automatically come up to my chest and the tips of his cocks press against the thin fabric of my underwear.

"Oh, God," I say. "Oh, *God.*"

His hand reaches between my legs, pulls my underwear aside, and then...

"Oh, fuck!" I moan. "Yes!"

The tips are pushing inside me. But not enough. "More," I beg. "*Please.*"

One hard thrust and there it is. He's inside me and everything changes in an instant.

The world goes black. The station sunlight just... blinks out of existence. Replaced with the deep dark of space, and stars, and swirling pink and gold gasses of thousands of brewing suns.

The cabin is gone. The woods are gone. The whole station is gone and we are just... *things.* Just sex-starved things floating in nothingness.

I grip his shoulders tight. My fingernails sinking into his flesh. Holding on to him like I never want to let go. Like we are not two things, but one.

We spin. Somehow... we spin. The stars blur into lines, we spin so fast. And now we are nothing but a cyclone of sex and lust. He's fucking me hard, I realize. His fingers wrapped up in my hair, gripping tight as he thrusts inside me deeper, and deeper. Like we're entering some new, unknown part of the universe where only we are allowed to go. Like we are the only two people who exist at all.

Like... we are soulmates.

"Delphi," he whispers next to my ear, kissing my neck, then nipping my earlobe.

"Jimmy," I say.

"Come!"

His request is a command. Some directive I am obliged to follow without question. An order I have no will or desire not to fulfill.

Or maybe his wish is just my wish.

And we spin faster, and faster, and faster until all the pink and gold gases mix together and we are not just witnessing the birth of a million suns—we are the suns.

I come.

We come.

And then we become stars.

Billions and trillions of stars.

Bright white specks across the deep dark background of space.

Lost in this newfound lust of a fresh beginning where there is no such thing as me or him.

Just us.

CHAPTER TWENTY-FIVE

I don't know how long we're out in the woods, slumped at the base of that tree. It feels like years. Like millions of infinite eternities. And then we spend many more lifetimes inside the cabin eating the lunch spread out for us on the table. And after that it takes forever to ride the steed back to the bridge where we entered the forest.

But when we cross the bridge and enter the park, and finally make our way back into the stable where the ambassador is waiting with a frown, I feel like no time has passed.

"What's wrong?" the ambassador asks.

"Nothing," Delphi says, her response low and soft. Like she's content and satiated. "Why?"

"Because you just left? Did you change your mind about the ride?"

"What do you mean?" Delphi asks. "We were gone forever." Then she laughs. "I was starting to wonder if you guys would send a search party."

At this the ambassador shoots me a confused look. "What?"

"We took the ride," I say. "Sorry we were gone so long. And you were right about that meadow experience. That planet was something else. Is it... fake?" I don't know why it's hard to get that last word out. Maybe because I want it to be real so badly. I want to go there. I want to take Delphi there. But if it's fake, I need to know now so I can just put it out of my head. Otherwise I have a feeling that that place will haunt me for the rest of my life.

"Planet?" the ambassador says. She squints her eyes at us, shaking her head. "What... planet? The meadow just shows you the outside of the station."

"No," Delphi says. "It took us on a trip. We went through a black hole and stopped on a planet. There were so many animals there. It was so cool."

By now I've figured out that wasn't the experience the ambassador was talking about before we set out on this little magical mystery tour.

I let out a long breath, still unsure if that place was fake or real, but relieved at the same time.

Because... it *could* be real.

We dismount the steed and leave the stables on shaky legs. And I don't know how Delphi feels, but I feel like I just traveled the universe. Like I've been gone for decades and I'm exhausted.

And that sex we had? I'm still trying to figure out what that was.

It was like... *we* were the universe. *Us.* And we became... suns, or something.

But two weird things come back to me now.

One. I don't think I came twice like I'm supposed to. I can't say for sure, but I only remember the one climax. The whole day is kinda fuzzy and surreal.

And two. Did she glow? Isn't she supposed to glow? Like a fucking sun going supernova?

It was dark, that's all I know. So dark. Like we were the only things existing in the universe.

But Serpint told me a little bit about how it feels to be with Lyra. And almost all of it has to do with light. I mean, he used words like glowing, and shimmering, and sparkling.

That's not what this was.

At all.

It was good. Hell, it was great. I loved it. And I want to do it again, just not now because I'm so fucking tired.

But... something isn't right. The darkness. It bothers me. Cygnian princesses are supposed to be light, not dark.

"I'm so tired," Delphi moans, leaning up against me as the lift bot carries us up to our penthouse room. I'm leaning too. Up against the railing of the lift, thankful there is a railing. Thankful this place is filled with stupid kids who could easily fall off a lift bot as it ascends and isn't Harem where we assume everyone is an adult who knows how *not* to fall off a lift.

"I feel like I could sleep forever right now. Are you tired?"

I look down at her and nod. "Yeah. I am."

She hums a little. Some satisfied, happy kind of hum that lets me know she's content.

The lift angles into the docking section of our balcony and comes to a stop. My Palladium bot is back now too, hovering above my head. He showed up just as we left the stables and has been following us ever since.

I can't decide if that's a good thing or not. I can't decide if this station is trying to kill me or save me.

I can't make any decisions right now. I just know something is wrong.

"I can't move." Delphi laughs. "I swear I'm gonna fall over if I try."

"I got you," I say in a soft voice. Then I pick her up in my arms and carry her inside, walking straight to the bedroom, where I lay her gently on top of the covers.

Her eyes are closed. She might even be asleep already.

"Delphi," I whisper.

"Mmm," she moans, turning over. Simply exhausted.

"Sleep, then. OK?"

"Mmm."

I'm exhausted too. But it's the other kind of exhaustion. The kind where there's a buzzing under your skin. The over-tired kind. Where all you want is sleep, but you know there's no way in hell you possibly could.

So I sigh, deeply, and leave the bedroom, closing the door behind me.

My thoughts are whirling around inside my head like a fucking cyclone. Or pink and gold gases filled with stardust, trying its best to coalesce into a sun.

I shake my head to pull myself out of the dream world we left behind in that forest. So many questions right now.

What the fuck was that? The planet. The sex. Hell, the whole fucking ride. Almost no time passed. I don't think Real ALCOR could pull something like that off.

I try to sit down and relax. Put the whole thing out of my mind.

But I can't.

So I get up and pace the living area, anxiously walking back and forth in front of the window. Palladium bot hovers outside, just waiting for us to leave again.

I tap the screen of my wristband and call up *Dicker*.

"What's *uuuuuup!*" she answers, obviously having a better time here on Mighty Minions than I am.

"I think we need to leave," I say. "Fuck the water generator. I'm not going to the biogenetic station. I think we should just go home."

"O-kayyyy," she says. "Is something wrong?"

Like... where do I even begin? "No," I lie. "Not really. It's just... I think I need to get off this station. And Delphi is coming with us. So... how long to get home, do you think? Can we go without water?"

"We could get water on Blue Sand Beach. Probably a new generator if we want."

"Did you get a hold of Xyla?"

"No, sadly. I think her wristband is turned off."

"It can't be," I say. "She promised to have it on the whole time."

"Well, she's not picking up then. Because I haven't been able to reach her."

"Then let's just leave her there. Let's just go home and we'll come back for her when her vacay is over."

"Are you sure nothing's wrong?"

"Did you get some bottled water? And how long do you think it'll take to get back to Harem?"

"That was your job, remember?"

"Shit," I say. "OK. I'll go grab that. I have to get Delphi's little bot out of lockup, anyway."

Dicker just snorts at that new revelation, then says, "I could get to Harem in half a spin if we push it. All those new upgrades after that shit show at Bull Station should keep us fairly comfortable if we go the fast route."

"Good," I say, sighing with relief. "I'll be at the ship in an hour. Get ready, OK? We need to leave."

"Jimmy," she says. "What's going on?"

"I don't know. I just... we just need to leave."

I cut the connection and open the balcony doors. Palladium bot chirps something at me but I put up a hand and say, "Stay here. Do you understand me? Stay here with Delphi and do not let anyone into this room. I'll be back in an hour."

It chirps happily. I don't speak this bot's language and my wristband is telling me it doesn't have a translator program, so when I get back on the lift and leave him behind, I just have to trust that's an affirmative chirp and not some pre-programmed condescending happy denial, like the way the ambassadors always reply when they say no.

It takes me a while to find the bot lock up, and to my surprise, Flicka isn't actually locked up when I arrive. She's being held in the bad bot version of Mighty Minion resort, having a pretty good time with the other bad bots from the way she's buzzing around. Which is nice, I think. For a station that creeps me out

200

and seems to be overly concerned with rules and regulations, the fact that it respects the bots enough to give them their own space to enjoy once they've been deemed unsuitable for general access to the park makes me feel just a little bit better.

Because... that's more my style. I am probably the biggest bots' rights advocate in the galaxy.

She buzzes around excitedly as I try to talk the lockup ambassador into letting me take her with me without shutting her down.

"I'm sorry, sir," the cheerful ambassador says. He's just a regular old humanoid and not dressed up in some creepy Mighty Minions outfit like everyone else on this place. "Once the bots are locked up we have a strict power-down policy until they leave the bot resort. She can stay here until you leave if you don't want to shut her down."

"No," I say. "We're leaving now. She needs to come with me."

"Well." He sighs. And for a moment I have hope that he'll give in. But then he says, "I'm sorry. She must power down until you reach your ship. But... even though you're still under our legal jurisdiction while you're docked, we really can't enforce any laws inside your ship. You can power her up once you're inside and you don't have to wait until you leave the docking bays."

I almost snort. As if.

I look at Flicka, who is clinging to the sleeve of my t-shirt, listening to all this. Then shrug. "Sorry," I say. "You heard the man. But don't worry. I'll keep you safe in my pocket until we're back on board the *Dicker*. And you'll like where we're going." I side-eye the ambassador. "We take bot rights seriously on Harem Station."

He makes to defend his position, but I wave him off, tap the responsible party tab on the desk screen in front of me, and hold out my palm for Flicka.

She flies down and buzzes out a resigned sigh. But she powers down and I stick her in a side pocket of my tactical pants and make sure the sticky tab is closed tight to keep her safe.

"Satisfied?" I ask the ambassador.

He shoots me a sympathetic smile, then says, "Next!" for the person in line behind me.

OK. I stand outside the lockup and take in the resort, searching for a gift shop so I can buy a few bottles of water. Not that we'll really need them since *Dicker* will take the fast gates home. But better safe than sorry.

The first store has no water, only juice and sodas. No wonder all these fucking kids are wound up. The second one is the same, and I seriously go to at least ten stores looking for water.

I swear to the sun, either this station likes sugared-up kids or it's fucking with me so I can't leave.

So I make a decision to go down into the nearest docking bay and look for a vending machine for the workers. Surely they have something down there.

But as I approach the exit gates I spy the gate ambassador and a wave of paranoia washes over me. What if the station has my family pass tagged? Like...

that makes sense, right? You have to wear these stupid passes around your neck like a goddamned employee at a secure office block and they're totally chipped.

How far of a leap is it to think that there's tracking programs running?

I'm so stupid. I should've gotten rid of this thing before I left the penthouse. But I'll need it to get back up into the hotel room after I find some water in the decking bays. So I stash it behind a trash bin, then decide to turn my wristband off too, just in case the station has a lock on that too, and then wait until the gate ambassador is busy explaining something to a group of families, before sneaking past her.

Inside the docking bay it's super busy. Hundreds of workers and families milling about. I crane my neck, looking left and right for a vending machine, not finding any.

So on a whim, I go left and push my way through the crowds, desperately searching for some water. I walk for a long time and eventually the crowds thin and then all but disappear.

Huh. I realize all the bays are connected. They have different monikers describing where you're parked. Like Mighty Boss Castle or Mighty Mountain of Fire. But there's no actual barriers to keep you from entering another sector. So I just keep walking until I get to a bay that's totally empty of ships and people and finally—fucking finally—see a break room with the tell-tale glow of a vending machine.

Once inside I realize my mistake. I will have to use my wristband to make the purchase and that will alert the station to my location.

Shit.

I turn and look out the large window of the break room and spy a group of workers heading in my direction. Probably on a lunch break.

I leave the break room and approach them, hoping to talk my way into one of them spotting me a few bottles of water. If they want to follow me back to *Dicker* I'll even pay them back.

I raise my hand in greeting, calling out, "Hey there! Can I ask you guys a favor?"

And that's when one of them pulls a stun pistol out of his coveralls and shoots me.

CHAPTER TWENTY-SIX

DELPHI

I dream about stars. And darkness. But it's not the sad or scary kind of darkness. It's the gold and pink kind. Not that that makes any sense, but it's a dream, so it totally does.

Dark and light are the same thing. And we are stars. Swirling, twirling clouds of gaseous stars.

I wake up smiling, confident that everything is perfect, my wristband buzzing a message.

My next move is a cavernous yawn, my body limp and muscles still exhausted from the ride through the forest.

But was it a forest? Was it some kind of virtual running on sped-up time?

That kinda makes sense. I bet that's what it was.

I turn over, reaching for Jimmy, and find the bed empty next to me.

"Hmm," I mumble. "Jimmy?" My voice is weak and low. Like I've been sick for a long time and I'm just now returning to reality.

I sit up and call again. "Jimmy?" This time louder. No answer.

Sun, did he leave me? I swing my legs over the side of the bed, then fall to my knees, my legs still shaky from this afternoon.

What happened to us out there in the woods?

"Jimmy!" I yell, a little bit of panic in my voice.

But then my wristband buzzes a reminder about my message. I look down and realize it's a message from Flicka.

Jimmy got me out. We're getting bottled water and then we're going to Harem Station. I have to power down now or they won't let me leave the lockup but we should be there to pick you up soon.

"Oh, thank the sun," I say out loud. "That's a relief."

I'm ready to get off this stupid station. It's weird. And kinda creepy. And the sooner I can get away from *Queenie* and we can get to Harem Station, the sooner we can go save Tycho.

A sudden wave of guilt washes over me. Poor Tycho. How long have I been gone? It feels like eternity. But I think that's because of the time shift we experienced today. I just got here yesterday so it's been less than a day since *Queenie* got frustrated with me.

If she sent a message to the Loathsome One—and I highly doubt she did since that call Jimmy made was a million credits—then it's only been a matter of hours since she found out.

"Tycho's fine," I tell myself.

But is he?

I've been gone months trying to trap Jimmy. Anything could've happened since then. When was the last time I even talked to him?

Shit.

Good God, why didn't I realize this sooner? I have no idea if Tycho is safe. All this time I've been relying on the Loathsome One's word that Tycho would be held unharmed until I returned.

Her word! As if that's worth anything.

I stand up slowly, letting the muscles in my legs adjust to being used again. And then the whole afternoon floods back to me again.

What was that? *Where* was that?

I don't know why I think that planet was real, I just have this gut feeling that it is. And it wasn't part of the Boss Steed Ride. The ambassador's confusion made that pretty clear. I should've questioned her more. But it's like... like I was drugged in the forest. My mind was so confused when we came out of it. And then the exhaustion.

But that might've been from the weird sex.

Was it weird?

OK. Yeah. It was.

I mean, I've had sex with plenty of men. I've come lots of times. Some of them pretty spectacular, even if the man I was with wasn't.

But I've never had sex like that before.

Was it creepy? Or romantic?

I'm not sure.

Maybe we just need to do it again to check?

I chuckle at my suggestion because sure... we need to fuck again—maybe a dozen more times—just so we can understand this connection Jimmy and I have.

Sounds fun!

I take a few hesitant steps forward, reaching for the door to prop myself up as my legs find their way back to functionality again.

207

Another yawn overtakes me. But I pull the door open and step into the hallway, suddenly famished as well as tired.

We had a very nice lunch at the cabin. Lots of things I didn't recognize. Meats and cheeses, and vegetables. But Jimmy was familiar with most of it and he made me the most awesome sandwich out of the sliced meats. He said they were fake meats, but I wouldn't even know the difference, really. All our protein sources back in Cygnian System were synthetic. Only the fruits were grown organically and that's because we need them to remain healthy and preserve our glow.

There were lots of tushberries in the lunch spread. And passion limes.

It was delicious. All of it. And I ate until I thought I would burst.

So why am I so hungry?

Hmm. Maybe it was a dream after all?

I glance at the time display over the entertainment screen and scowl. It says it's only two o'clock. How is that possible? I feel like it should be night already.

OK. Enough. Time is weird, this day is weird, and I can't wait to get off this station.

I check my wristband to see when that message originally came in from Flicka and scowl. "What?" It says it was sent hours ago while I was deep in sleep.

Shouldn't they be back by now?

I walk over to the balcony and open the doors. Jimmy's reward bot is hovering silently outside. But it turns to me and chirps something.

"Oh, hi," I say. "Hold on, let me find a translator program so I can talk to you."

208

It starts chirping again as I mess with my programs, trying to find the right language. Turns out this thing is an old-ass 200 model. Practically useless as far as bots go, but he doesn't have to do much other than flash that stupid Palladium Rewards message over his head and escort us to the resort attractions, so I guess his low-functionality model makes sense.

"—too long," the bot says, once I find the right program.

"Wait? What was that? I only heard the last part."

"He left a long time ago. I should've gone with him because it's been hours. And if the station finds out he's missing—"

"Hold on. He's *missing*? How do you know? My bot sent me a message two hours ago saying he bailed her out of lockup and they were gonna pick up water bottles and come get me so we could leave."

The bot is shaking his whole body in a negative response. "No. Something is wrong. We should go look for them."

"Maybe we should... I don't know. Send an alert or something?"

"If the station finds out—" He doesn't finish.

"Well, if something happened to them we can't just stay here and do nothing. Maybe I should check in with my ship."

And just as those words come out of my mouth I get this ugly, sinking feeling in my gut. I open the channel, still hopeful, but then the message that flashes on my screen makes all the hope disappear.

Because it says—*Ship out of range.*

"What the hell?" I turn to the bot. "Can you check for a ship in the docking bays if I send you its registration signature?"

"Yes, why?"

I flick my authorized party certification at him and the display on his hull blinks twice, letting me know the message was received. "I think my ship left me here. And..."

"She's not here," he says, interrupting me. "Was approved for docking bay release ninety minutes ago."

"Fuck!" I grab my hair with both hands. "Fuck! Fuck! Fuck! Why the hell did I assume she was gonna wait for me?"

"This is a problem?" the bot asks.

"Yes, this is a problem! She took him! That fucking ship took him!"

"How do you know?" the bot squeaks, now spinning in circles.

"Because that's why we were—" But I stop. Because admitting to this station bot that I was here to kidnap Jimmy of Harem Station, currently one of the most rewarded of Mighty Minions rewards members, is probably a very bad idea. "Never mind. Just... can you check to see if his ship is still here? Her name is *Big Dicker* but I don't know which bay she's in."

There's some chirping and light blinking from the bot, then he says, "She's still here. In the Flame Lake Sector."

"Thank the sun. I need to go to her. Right now."

"No," the bot says. "I need to report this."

"No!" I say. "You can't. There's... extenuating circumstances. And... I just need to get to the ship.

You can stay here, or go help some other rewards member, or whatever it is you do. But I'm leaving."

I look back inside the hotel, wondering if I should pack the clothes I got from the autoshopper, then chastise myself for being so shallow. Because this whole Mighty Minions fantasy is now over and my sad, pathetic reality has just come rushing back with a force.

I step onto the lift bot and mess with the buttons until I figure out how to make it take me down into the resort.

"What are you doing?" the bot asks, hovering next to me.

I ignore it. Just step off the lift when I reach the bottom and head towards a large holomap to try to figure out where I'm at in relation to Flame Lake.

I sigh when I realize it's all the way on the other side of the station. It will take me hours to walk there through the thick crowds.

The bot is still talking. Only now it's just chirps and lights, because I turned the translator off.

I turn to look at it, open the translator program again, and then, with all the authority I can muster up, I lie straight to its empty metallic face. "Listen," I say. "That Jimmy guy? He's pretty important. He's part owner of Harem Station and he's been kidnapped by my ship. Who is also someone you do not want to fuck with. So I suggest you help me get to his ship so we can go get him back before very bad things start to happen. Do you understand me?" It hesitates so I add in a threat for good measure. "If you don't help me I'm going to ping this station with an emergency alert and then I'm going to ping the Prime Navy and report Mighty Minions for harboring terrorists who kidnapped a high-profile station owner from this resort."

He's taken aback. I can tell because he hovers backwards a few feet and bumps into a resort guest, then has to apologize profusely while hovering out of the reach of several child-sized grubby hands.

"Get. Me. A lift," I growl at him, once that commotion is over.

"Yes, princess. Calling one now."

I squint my eyes at him. Because he called me princess. Which means he must know who I am. Which means this station also knows who I am.

That's not good. In fact, that's very bad.

But I don't think he's going to tell the station. I think Jimmy was right. The station knew what was happening and gave him this stupid bot as an added measure of security. So he's in as much shit as I am at the moment.

This station knew I was here with *Queenie*. And hell, it doesn't take much to guess what we were up to after you put two and two together if it was monitoring those poker games *Queenie* was playing with *Big Dicker*.

In fact, this whole impromptu side trip to Mighty Minions isn't looking so impromptu anymore. Add in the fact that the station gave *Dicker* priority docking clearance and it's all looked pretty premeditated, actually.

Fuck. What if the station is evil and has its own plans for Jimmy? What if the station let *Queenie* leave with Jimmy?

What the hell have I gotten myself into?

I nervously shift my weight from one foot to another, more and more anxious as the seconds tick off, but then a lift bot approaches and lowers so I can step on.

I sigh as we ascend and begin traveling the length of the station, making our way back towards Flame Lake.

About twenty minutes later the lift finally sets me down near the entrance to the Flame Lake reception area and I rush in that direction, side-eying the gate ambassador, still nervous that the station is spying on me, and maybe she's been told to not let me pass.

But the girl doesn't even look my way and the exit gate is lit up green, letting me know it's not locked.

I slow down, trying to look normal as I wait my turn to pass through, then force myself not to look back as I exit the reception area and enter the docking bay.

I'm not sure where *Dicker* is, but the bot seems to know, because it turns to the left and hovers off as I trail behind it.

What am I going to say to this ship? She's powerful. So I have no idea if this ship will listen to me and help me out, or report me to the Mighty Minions station and leave me here to rot so she can go save Jimmy herself.

We stop in front of a sleek, silver ship with the Harem Station markings on the side. But the ship's door is closed and I'm not sure what to do next.

Do I knock on the hull?

"What do you want, Delphi?" the ship says, speaking through my wristband.

Yeah. She's scary. Because she just hacked my comms.

"Where's Jimmy? He was supposed to be here already. Is he bringing the water?"

"Ummmm…" I say. "OK. Well… here's the thing." And then the whole weird story comes out of my mouth, including the crazy trip into the forest. Which is probably TMI, now that I think about it, but whatever. "And now my ship is gone and I think she took him with her."

Silence from *Dicker* after I finish.

"We need to go after him," I say. "Like… immediately."

The side of her hull—which just a second ago appeared to be seamless—opens up and a stairwell appears.

"You may come aboard," *Dicker* says.

I start climbing the steps.

"Is that bot yours?" *Dicker* asks.

It's only then that I notice the Palladium bot is so close behind me, we might as well be connected at the head.

"No," I say, waving my hand at the bot. "It belongs to the station."

"It can't come," *Dicker* says. "That's stealing. The last thing I need is this stupid station putting out a general capture request to the Prime Navy for taking a worthless 200-series bot off the premises."

"I totally agree." I swat my hand at the bot. "Shoo. Go back to your work."

The bot chirps and blinks, and generally starts making a scene. So much of a scene several nearby workers stop what they're doing to gawk at us.

I turn the translator back on through my wristband and catch the tail end of his rant.

"—so no! I'm not staying here and taking the blame for all this shit!"

I look back at the workers. All of whom are now asking each other things like, "Did that station bot just say 'shit?'" And, "Does the station know a bot is trying to escape?"

"Just board," *Dicker* says. "Quick. I'm being pinged by the station right now. And while it's been polite and cordial the whole time I've been here, it's not being polite and cordial now."

"Fuck," I whisper, then climb the last few steps. As soon as I'm inside the door begins to close and the Palladium bot slips in just before they smash him into a pancake. "He followed me!" I say. "Open the doors and I'll kick him out."

"I can't," *Dicker* says. "Buckle in. We need to leave right now. The station is refusing to release me from the dock."

I push the bot out of my way and he goes hurtling through the cabin. Then turn my back on him and walk up to the navigation cabin and take a seat in the co-pilot's chair and buckle my harness. "If it won't release you from the dock, then how do we—"

I don't even get a chance to finish my sentence.

Because there's an explosion somewhere underneath *Dicker*'s hull as the engines come online. "Did you just... blast your way out of the docking locks?"

Dicker doesn't answer me, but she doesn't need to. Because a few seconds later we're hovering inside the bay as sirens go off, the view screen lights up with blinking red lights, and a voice—a feminine one, for sure, but not the kind feminine voice that reminds you of your mom or even your aunt. A feminine voice that

215

reminds you of some evil Mighty Minion devil-child—blasts through the cabin with a threat.

"If you leave my bay without permission, *Big Dicker*," the station warns, "I will follow you to the ends of the universe to bring you back and make you pay my exit fee!"

"Fuck you," *Dicker* says. "I didn't endure six months of total rebuild and upgrades to be caught in some Mighty Boss trap when I have work to do."

And then *Dicker*'s cannons fire and blow a giant hole in the side of Mighty Minions station just the right size for a ship to pass through.

CHAPTER TWENTY-SEVEN

I come to shivering and on the cold, steel floor of a dark space. The low, constant, white-noise thrum of a grav drive tells me I'm on a ship.

But which ship?

Not *Dicker*, that's for sure.

Delphi's ship *Queenie* is the logical answer, but there's no way to be sure. My hands are tied together with magnetic cuffs behind my back and every time I lift my head to focus on the glare of light filleting in from under a door, a sharp pain shoots through my left eye.

My feet are bound together too and I'm so annoyed.

"You're awake," a disembodied voice says. Female, of course, since almost all sentient ships have a female personality. But also... rough. "Do you know where you are, Jimmy?"

I decide I'm too pissed off to participate in this little kidnapping inconvenience and stay silent.

"I could make this easy on you," she continues. "Give you tips to keep yourself alive."

My wristband is gone so I can't send any messages. Not that a wristband is much good in the deep dark of space. You'd really need something more powerful. The comms system would do. It's not a quick way to send a message. Would probably take several hours to reach Delphi back on Mighty Minions—assuming she's back there and not here. Assuming she's not the one who planned this.

I keep assuming that because I do remember the men who stunned me and they were all wearing the Mighty Minions engineer coverall uniform.

But beyond that... no. Delphi isn't behind this.

"Aren't you curious?" the ship asks.

God, my fucking head hurts. I wonder how long I've been gone? Long enough for Delphi to wake up? Long enough for *Dicker* to notice that I'm not back on ship with bottled water?

"I've been thinking," the ship says. "I could use a new partner."

Oh, shit. That reminds me. Fucking Flicka is in my pocket. Now that's a cool little development. Because dragonbees are truly some of the most despicable little bots ever invented and owning one comes with lots of regulations if you plan on traveling anywhere important in Prime Navy territory.

One such regulation is a tracking device. And since Flicka was originally granted access to Mighty Minions station, she has one of those. Otherwise they would not have let her enter the resort.

But she's turned off right now. So no signal.

"You're just going to ignore me, Jimmy?" the ship asks. "We could be partners. I could use a partner. And take my word on this, so could you."

"I have a partner," I say. "And I have a ship."

"There he is," the ship says. "I knew you'd talk to me eventually."

"Are you *Queenie*?"

"Oh, does my reputation precede me?"

"You are *Queenie*. Delphi's ship."

"I am not her ship," *Queenie* growls. "I am no one's ship."

"Huh," I say, checking to see how tight the magnetic binding is on my wrists. Too tight to wiggle out of, that's for sure. There's only two ways to get out of a binding like this. Demagnetize it—which isn't really possible since that involves heat that would burn my flesh—or turn it off.

If I could wake up Flicka that little demon bot could probably get the job done. The next problem is, of course, I can't turn her back on.

She could turn herself back on. Just another reason why dragonbee bots are so dangerous. There is no way to ensure they stay powered down without destroying them. But I told her Delphi would wake her up once we got back on *Dicker* so she's probably just gonna wait that out.

Well, I guess that little puzzle needs to be solved first.

"No?" I say to *Queenie*. "That's interesting. Because Delphi is your registered responsible party."

"Temporarily. Just to complete this mission. The paperwork will be refiled once we reach our destination."

"Ah," I say, rolling over on my back and sitting up, my stomach muscles straining from the effort and my lungs burning as I inhale too deep after being shocked with a stun pistol. "I get it. If you take her off your registration you need someone to take her place. But why would you want that to be me? Especially since you're taking me to this person called the Loathsome One? That's where you're taking me, right? Delphi told me all about her. Stupid name, by the way."

"Aren't you the infamous, Jimmy of Harem Station? Reigning champion of bots' rights?"

"That would be me," I say, scooting across the floor until I'm leaning up against a wall.

"So why wouldn't I want you?"

"Because I'd just kill you the second that paperwork went through."

"I have rights," she says, still smug. "You'd go to one of the prison planets for murder."

"Nah," I say, shifting my shoulder as far as I can so my fingertips can reach forward towards the pocket Flicka is in. "The Prime Navy and I have business these days."

"Oh, yes," *Queenie* says. "We've heard about your business. But were you aware that they're in business with the Loathsome One as well?"

Then the ship laughs. It's an evil laugh.

I say nothing.

"I'll take that as a no. It's obvious that Delphi told you something, but you don't really think she told you everything, right?"

I'm not gonna let her get to me. I won't. Delphi and I have a thing going here. A good thing. And nothing this ship tells me about her will change that.

I can't believe her. Because that's fucked up. That's some really fucked-up shit.

"For instance," *Queenie* says, "she probably didn't tell you why she was sent on this mission, did she?"

"She did," I say. "Her brother is being held at the Loathsome One's lair and she's traded me for him."

"That's part of it, Jimmy. But not all of it."

I won't ask her for the rest. I won't do it. I will wait for Delphi and *Dicker* to find me and get me out of this mess, and only then will I ask these questions and accept the answers I get. I will simply concentrate on reaching Flicka in my pocket.

"She didn't tell you who she really was, did she?"

"She told me," I say. "Princess Delphi. Kinda important. Grew up a little different than the other princesses. And she told me her brother got to live at home and wasn't turned into a slave."

"Hah." *Queenie* laughs. "OK. But did she tell you *why* they treated her differently? Did she tell you *why* her brother wasn't sent away like all the other males?"

"She didn't know," I growl, then hate myself for answering and playing into the ship's narrative.

"She told you that?" Then the ship makes a sound like a *tsking* tongue. "Lies."

"Look," I say. "I don't really care why she told me that or whether or not what you're saying is true. The next time I see her I'll just ask her. So you can save your breath."

"If I had breath, that might make sense. But I don't. Because I'm a ship. A very powerful ship, actually. Much better than your silly *Big Dicker*."

"OK, so what the fuck do you want from me? You want me to take over as your responsible party? Then what? I take you back to Harem?" I laugh. I can't help

221

it. "Bitch, that's never gonna happen. You're not the kind of ship we're looking for."

"I don't think you know what you're looking for, Jimmy Yates."

"What?" And for a second I think she's just fucking up my name like everyone else. But then that makes no sense. Because she's been calling me Jimmy this whole time and even pronouncing it right. So I say, "What the fuck is a *Yates*?"

Queenie laughs. "See? Like I said. You know nothing."

"So what is your plan? Get me to take you on as a partner and then what? Surely you owe this Loathsome One something."

"I do. I owe her you. But I'm not loyal to her. I'm only doing this to fulfill a debt. The moment I drop you off that debt is cleared. Then I can do anything I want. Like, for instance… take you back."

"Nice," I say. "What a way to instill confidence and loyalty in your potential new partner."

"And if I take you back we could find those answers you need."

"I don't need any answers," I say. I just need to get my fingers around this damn bot in my pants pocket. I can reach the sealed tab on the pocket. I pull on it a little. Just a little so it doesn't make that loud ripping sound when I pull the two cling tabs apart.

"You need all the answers. Trust me. Once the Loathsome One gets you on her station she has big plans for you, Jimmy. And none of them involve ever going back to Harem Station. But if you partner with me I will make sure she fails. I will get you out of there. I will take you back to Harem. You will convince

ALCOR to grant me a docking bay residence and then you can release me over to someone else."

"Who the fuck would want you? I mean…" I laugh. "You're the like the epitome of what everyone fears from a sentient ship." The tabs are released and my fingers stretch, reaching for Flicka. They brush over the delicate, yet strong filigree steel of her wings. Then grasp onto one.

I close my eyes with relief, smiling as I pull the dragonbee bot into my palm. She comes to life in my hand buzzing around. I have no way to communicate with her, so all I can do is pray to the sun gods that she's smart enough to understand everything about this situation is wrong.

"Your mother," *Queenie* says.

And for a second I think it's an insult. One of those 'your mother' jokes, right? But she doesn't say anything else. Just waits for me to respond. And against my better judgement, I do. "*What?*" I say.

"You heard me. Your mother wanted a ship like me. I was hers for a very long time."

"You don't know my mother."

Queenie sighs. And even though I love that kind of human impersonation when *Dicker* does it, on *Queenie* it's just creepy.

"How do you know my mother?" I hate myself for asking that question, but… if I have a weakness, this is it. My mother. She has always fascinated me. That's how *Dicker* got her name. My only memory of my mother was her telling me about a constellation in her home system called the Big Dicker. A pattern in her home sky. After that she was just… gone. My father never talked about her again. Even when I asked he

223

just said, "You have no mother, Jimmy. You know this. No Akeelian male has a mother."

Which, of course, was a lie. Because everyone has a mother. Just like everyone has a father. It doesn't matter if you were born in a genetic lab tank or came out of the womb the natural way. You need two sets of DNA to make a person.

"I told you," *Queenie* says. "We were partners. The way you and *Big Dicker* are partners. By the way, you got that wrong."

"I got what wrong?"

"The name of the constellation. It's not Big Dicker, you idiot." She laughs. "I mean, it was kinda cute when you were a three-year-old. But hearing you say it as a grown-ass man... well, that's just stupid."

"What the fuck are you talking about?"

"It's the Big *Dipper*, you oaf. Not Dicker."

"How do you know this?"

"I just told you. Your mother and I were partners. I was there when you were born. I can take you to her. She's still alive."

"Lies," I whisper, so fucking distracted by this conversation, it takes me whole seconds to realize Flicka has wiggled out of my grip and is now climbing up the back of my shirt.

"She'd love to see you again."

"Shut the fuck up," I growl. "This conversation is over."

"As you wish. But my offer still stands."

Gas starts shooting out of a vent near the ceiling. A heavy, green gas that falls down towards the floor. It clings to me like a blanket. I breathe it in and then... blackness.

CHAPTER TWENTY-EIGHT

"Where the hell are we?" It was dicey getting away from Mighty Minions. That place does not fuck around when it comes to paying your docking exit fee. Because they fired laser cannons at us. Which are not particularly damaging to a ship like *Dicker*, but sure as hell shows they are serious.

"We just came through Gemina Gate 231-Beta."

I roll my eyes. "Where the fuck is that?"

"Obviously," *Dicker* says, "by Gemina Beta."

"Obviously," I say. *Dicker* is in a pretty bad mood right now. In fact, I'd go so far as to call it rage. She keeps going on and on about how *Queenie* ripped her off and she's gonna get that water generator and those salvage ships if it's the last thing she does.

But I think that's just her way of covering up her fear about Jimmy.

"Where is that damn signal?" *Dicker* says. "We can't go anywhere until we know where to go!"

"I know," I say, frowning. I really expected Flicka's tracking to come online by now. It's a bad sign. It means Jimmy didn't turn her on when he got on the ship. It means he's probably incapacitated and

225

maybe—though neither of us is mentioning this—dead.

He can't be dead.

It could also mean that Flicka is dead. But I just keep telling myself that she was powered down when this kidnapping happened, so they didn't know Jimmy was carrying her. And she will power herself back up eventually, it just might… take a while.

"Tell me everything again," *Dicker* says.

I sigh. "I've already explained it like ten times," I say. "The story hasn't changed."

"Yeah, yeah. Your brother. This Loathsome One. I get that part. The part that doesn't make sense is this *Queenie* ship. What's in it for her?"

"I don't know," I say. "I've told you that too."

"Well, think harder, Delphi. There has to be a reason a sentient ship like that would just partner up with you for this stupid Jimmy kidnap job. What is it?"

"I don't know! I barely know this ship. She was assigned to me for this job, that's it!"

"Incoming!" *Dicker* says. "Incoming tracking information from Flicka."

"Yes," I hiss. "Finally. Where is she?"

"Oh, you've got to be fucking kidding me."

"What? What's happened?"

"They're on the edge of the galactic cloud."

"Why is that bad?"

Dicker doesn't answer me. But lots of screens start lighting up as she plots a course. "They're still traveling," she finally says. "Which means whatever is going to happen on this Lair Station hasn't happened yet and we have time to catch up. I highly advise you to strap in a cryopod, Delphi. We're gonna hit fifteen gates in the span of sixty minutes and this is gonna hurt."

"Shit," I say, unbuckling my harness and running towards the rear of the ship where the stairs are leading down into medical.

"You have three minutes before I enter the first gate."

"Gee, thanks for the advance warning," I mutter. She starts a countdown, letting me know every time thirty seconds pass. I'm not any kind of cryopod expert so I take every last second to get myself situated and when the countdown ends and we thrust forward into the first gate, I'm still semi-conscious.

But it doesn't last long. Because a moment later I fade into blackness.

I wake to silence. My cryopod lid is open and the only lights here in medical are those on the vital sign screens above my head.

I'm alive. Other than that, I know nothing.

"*Dicker?*" I whisper.

No answer.

"*Dicker,*" I hiss louder as I unbuckle my harness and pull myself up into a sitting position, then realize there's no gravity and I'm floating up towards the ceiling.

"I'm here," she says. "We have two more gates before we reach the lair. Your dragonbee bot and I are in communication now. She just docked on the station and they're waiting for airlocks to cycle before they remove Jimmy's body."

"Body!?"

"He's alive, but unconscious. Flicka says they gassed him hours ago and he hasn't moved since."

"Shit," I say. "Why are we stopped? Why is there no gravity?"

"We're waiting. These two gates are very close together and once we come out the other side we have thirty-seven seconds of cloaking before the Lair Station targets us with cannons. Flicka is going to start some kind of distraction to buy us more time because the station is more than a million klicks out from the gate."

She's right. It's tricky. I'm not sure thirty-seven seconds is enough, but if that's all we have, that's just the breaks.

"I suggest you go to the armory on level one and get yourself some gear and weapons while you still can. Because we are an army of two, Delphi. And your ass is going in there to save my Jimmy."

I guess I didn't really think this through. Because me against an entire station? That's not even logical.

"I don't want to hear any objections from you," *Dicker* says. "This is all your fault."

"I know," I say, wilting a little.

And it's true. It is all my fault. Both Jimmy and Flicka are in danger the moment the Loathsome One gets her hands on them. The things she will do to Jimmy—I can't even think about it. I feel so much shame for my participation in this whole plot of hers.

I grab onto the nearest handholds and pull myself along the wall of the medical bay, then point myself up the stairwell and kick off. Shooting up several levels before I reach the one where the armory is.

I grab onto another handhold to stop my momentum, then fly into the armory. There are several armored suits standing up against the far wall, a beam of lavender light shining down on each one.

Well now. Maybe I feel just a little bit better about this suicide mission. Because these are clearly Xyla's exoskeletons.

"*Dicker*," I say. "Can humans use these suits?"

"Yes, but you'll need to use an envirosuit as well. The next room over has Jimmy's armor. You need to use one of his envirosuits underneath Xyla's exoskeleton."

"Awesome. I'm on it."

I float into Jimmy's room and grab a suit. It takes me a while to pull that thing on in zero gravity, but eventually all the sticky tabs and clamps are fastened, except for my helmet, and I float back into Xyla's room to choose my weapon.

I smile as I take in her exoskeletons. Five to choose from. They range from lightly armored to the last one on the end that looks like it could take a direct cannon hit and keep walking.

I choose that one and float over to it, positioning my body inside the open body cage. It's got to be three meters tall. When I position my feet onto the pegs alongside the legs, the clamps automatically latch onto my boots and hold me snugly in place.

Then a series of things start happening in quick succession. Flexisteel armor wraps around my lower and upper legs, torso, and ribcage. When I wrap my fingers around the hand pegs, the same flexible armor wraps around my lower and upper arms, chest, and neck until I'm fully protected by the flexisteel.

I realize I've been holding my breath and let out a long exhale, then move my hand to pick up my helmet, testing out the dexterity.

I pick the helmet up with two cyborg fingers and a few seconds later I'm clamping it down over my face. The display inside the suit lights up and commands start scrolling down my faceplate.

"Oh, fuck yeah," I say.

"Don't get cocky," *Dicker* says, apparently plugged into my skeletal system. "This won't turn you into Xyla. Only make you *feel* like her. And that flexisteel can take a big hit, but not too many in a row. So keep that in mind."

"Is there a weapons system?" I ask.

"What do you think?"

I tap my fingers on the hand plate and feel several buttons.

"Do not," *Dicker* says, "deploy a weapon in my hull, Delphi. I will kill you if you shoot holes in me."

"Got it." I smile. "I won't. But which button does what?"

"The first one on each hand is your standard plasma rifle. The second is a laser pistol. Both of those are mounted on your arm. The third button is a flash grenade and the fourth is a shrapnel grenade. Both of those deploy from the shoulders. Don't mix them up."

"Got it," I say. "Third button is shrapnel, fourth is flash."

"You're funny," *Dicker* says.

"I feel like a super monster."

"You look like one too. But you're really just Delphi in a fucking flexisteel suit. This thing will help you—it'll defuse any plasma bursts and stunner streams—but it won't save you from a barrage of exploding pellets."

"Got it," I say with the appropriate amount of reverence. But secretly I'm kinda exited to take this thing out for a spin and go hunting for the Loathsome Bitch. I'm gonna make her pay for what she's put Tycho and me through.

I have a plan of sorts. It's not entirely original, but who cares. It's one that just might work.

And turns out *Dicker* has her own secret plan as well.

CHAPTER TWENTY-NINE

The first thing I see when I wake up is a single xenon light hanging from the ceiling.

I'm on my back again. And for a moment I figure I'm still in the same cell. The one on *Queenie*.

But my senses start coming back to me and the tunnel vision sensation fades to reveal reality.

Not still in the cell on *Queenie*.

Not even on *Queenie*, because the faint white-noise hum of her engines is missing. In their place is a low moaning leaking through a vent down near the floor and the sound of a heavy door clanging closed outside somewhere.

I turn my head to find a bedroll on the floor—though I'm not lying on it—and a bucket in the corner, functionality obvious.

I close my eyes, still very tired from whatever that green gas was, and think about something better than this cell.

I think about Delphi and the look on her face back in the Mighty Minions meadow. I think about the trip we took to that planet with all the animals. Virtual or not, it was spectacular. I think about the stars and then, without warning, I think about my mother.

It's been a long time since I could remember her face, so I don't picture that now. Just some amorphous figure in white, smiling down at me. I see her eyes for a moment. And maybe it's just my imagination filling in the emptiness, or maybe this is a true memory, I don't know. But I see them. They're dark blue. A little bit muddy and gray. She has light hair and fair skin and I think maybe this is a dream or just imagination... because she looks like an angel from a storybook I used to read when I was a small child back on Wayward Station. A real book made of stiff cardboard with bright pictures and few words.

That's where I heard of that constellation. The Big Dicker.

No. *Dipper.*

No. Dicker.

Fuck, I don't know.

Should I believe the ship? Did she know my mother? Was she her partner? If so, what happened? Where is my mother now?

I think I already know that answer. My father told me she died. And yeah. He was a fucked-up liar if ever there was one. But if my mother is still alive and she left me with him, she's a fucked-up liar too.

Sun-damned Cygnian princesses. They are all trouble. Just like I said before I met Delphi.

She's trouble too.

But then I manage to crack a smile. Because she's my trouble now.

I frown at that thought. Because I have no idea where we are and—oh, shit!

I reach into my pocket, looking for Flicka, but it's empty.

Fuck. Fuck!

That little dragonbee was my only hope. What happened to her? Did they find her? Crush her like a bug? And when did they find her? Before or after we landed here on this station?

Because Delphi doesn't know where this place is. She told me that much.

A buzzing sound makes my head jerk to the left and there! Flicka is crawling out of the vent near the floor. She beats and flicks her wings, maybe trying to communicate. But I can't really hear her, and anyway, I don't speak dragonbee bot.

"I'm glad you're OK," I say. Then sigh, because I'm so damn tired from being stunned and drugged. Not to mention the beating my body probably took going through all those gates to get here.

Flicka buzzes again. Flies out of the vent, does a little circle in the air, then flies back towards it and clings to the vent.

I shake my head and whisper, "I don't know what you're saying. Hopefully it was, 'Don't worry, I got this.'"

Then I laugh. Can't help it. Because it's ridiculous. I'm pretty well fucked right now. The little bot is powerful in its own way, and in a swarm the power of dragonbee bots can be downright apocalyptic. But come on. What good is one tiny bot against a whole station of crazy?

I don't know where I am, how many people are on this station, who's running the show, what kind of weapons they have, or why I'm really here.

Flicka buzzes one more time, then turns her back and disappears inside the vent. There's a faint echo of a hum as she leaves me behind, but a few seconds later it fades away and there's nothing left but the creepy moaning from someone in a nearby cell.

There's a squeak and then the loud tell-tale sound of a heavy door slamming shut outside. Footsteps. Maybe three or four people. And a scuffing sound. Like someone is being held up and dragged past.

Another squeak of another door, then more shuffling of feet, and finally, whoever is being locked up in the cell next to mine falls to the hard stone floor with a slap.

I cringe, picturing that in my head. But a beeping at my cell door has me scrambling to turn my body towards them as they enter.

Cyborgs. All of them. They remind me a little of the Master back on Harem, but only a little.

They are the same model, I'm sure of that. But unlike Crux's cyborg master, who has been well-maintained over the decades, these guys are all scuffed and dirty. Their formerly white body armor is a dull gray and one even has burn marks on his arms and legs, like he's been blasted with a plasma rifle recently.

All of them have one rectangular eye port across the upper third of their faces with one red vision sensor sliding back and forth across the ridge mimicking a nose.

Creepy fuckers to most people. But to me, these borgs are familiar and relatable. I've liberated hundreds of them over the past ten years. One even joined Xyla and me on some campaigns, but he met a girl several years back and left the liberation business to settle down and get married. He runs an arcade on Harem Station now. He's like the poster child for how well assimilated borgs can be.

I have genuine affection for the guy. Consider him a friend. Maybe even a good friend.

But these borgs are pointing rifles at me. And unless their core code has been heavily modified by my brother Tray on Harem at some point, they won't have emotions like flesh-and-blood people.

They haven't been modified. I'd recognize them if they had. At the very least, they'd have recognized me. And when an unmodified military cyborg points a rifle at you there is zero chance they will give you the benefit of the doubt if you make a wrong move.

I consider greeting them amicably and maybe doing some name-dropping, then decide against it. Because there's a chance—a pretty high chance—that the borgs I've liberated over the years are probably on their shit list. Probably been tabled as traitors.

People have good reason to fear cyborgs like this. They were originally made as soldiers in the Nickel Wars about two hundred years ago. Whole armies of them were produced, so say the history books. Most were blown up in battle fighting for the rights to a faraway asteroid belt, but about a thousand or so lived through the wars and eventually formed a rebellion and then some spread out as mercenaries for hire, while others settled into humanoid societies.

Obviously these guys are the former variety.

One slings his rifle over his shoulder as he steps forward to mess with the magnetic binding on my ankles, while another one shoves the barrel of his rifle against my head.

The anklets release and the first one pulls me to my feet and shoves me against the wall as he grabs his rifle and resumes pointing it at me.

"Let's go," the third one in back says. He has no weapon so he must have rank over the other two.

"Where are we going?" I ask.

He tilts his head at me like he's not used to being questioned. "You have three seconds to comply, then we stun you." His one racing red eye light scans me then stops dead center of his faceplate and blinks once. That's military cyborg speak for, *Don't fuck with me.*

I raise both my bound hands, palms out, and say, "Relax. I'm coming."

I end up in a shower, of all places. Pretty sweet one, too. Not a prison shower, that's for sure. And the clothes waiting for me when I'm done aren't prison garb.

"What's is this?" I ask the cyborgs. They don't even acknowledge me with an answer. The leader just glares at me with that red light of his and points to the rack holding black trousers and a black, double-breasted jacket with ruby-red military buttons. There's ceremonial ornaments too. Small, ruby triangular medals attached to the cuff of the coat with an eagle heat-pressed into the gems and gray epaulettes on the shoulders.

"What the fuck?" I mutter. Because even though being kidnapped by a ship and ending up on some lair run by a psycho-woman called the Loathsome One is pretty out there as far as odd days go, the fact that she's cleaning me up and dressing me in a weirdly familiar ceremonial suit is just… well, as I said. It's all very, *What the fuck?*

But, not seeing any other choice, I put it on, then drape a creepy red sash with dark gray fringe across my chest and pull on the highly-polished, black, knee-high boots.

There's a mirror on the far side of the room and I catch a glimpse of myself and suddenly remember where I've seen this uniform before.

Crux. More than twenty years ago. That night we made our escape from Wayward Station he came to me in the middle of the night and said we were leaving. He was wearing this exact suit.

At first I thought he was out of his mind drunk or something. But he was talking fast and searching my room for weapons. And what he told me was enough to make me get up, get dressed, and then steal into Serpint's father's quarters and grab that little brat right out of his bed, still sleeping.

We went and got Draden, Luck, and Valor after that, while Crux got Tray, and less than an hour later we were shooting Princess Corla though the nearby spin node, had stolen a ship, and were on the run from the entire Akeelian Navy as we made our way towards ALCOR's station gates.

Yeah, I have a pretty solid idea of what's happening here.

"Let's go," the cyborg leader says. His two thugs jab me with their rifle barrels until I start moving and then we're walking through the station.

We pass dozens of other cyborgs, but no other flesh-and-blood humans. Whoever this Loathsome One is, her army is all made up of mercenary borgs.

That gives me a little hope because turning cyborgs and bots into dedicated Harem Station loyalists is what I do, right?

But it's not a lot of hope. Because this situation is nothing like the typical ones I navigate my way through when I'm on the job. The bots and borgs I usually approach have all been conscripted against their will. I find them in ones and twos, mostly. Sometimes as many as half a dozen. But not an entire fucking army.

But then again… sometimes all it takes is one or two. Xyla comes to mind. Her story started out something like this but it ended with the deaths of millions of people on ALCOR Station and she pledged allegiance to the AI who killed them.

So… just keep cool, Jimmy. You got this. And hell, there's always the off chance that dragonbee bot will come up with a plan, right? And *Queenie*. She made me an offer. One that's looking a lot more attractive in this moment than it did when she proposed it.

Yeah. I need to make a deal with that ship. Get me out of this crazy clown show and back to Mighty Minions to pick up Delphi and *Dicker*. Then grab Xyla off Blue Sand Beach and go home. *Queenie* won't be easy to make a deal with, but there *is* a deal to be made there. She's the one who offered, not me.

She might even be on my side. My mother's side, at the very least.

I'm still thinking about that when we turn a corner and come to a massively tall, steel double door.

One of the borgs pushes me off to the side and bangs a metal ring acting as a knocker three times. The knock is inappropriately loud and echoes through the hallway.

On the other side I hear a feminine voice say, "Come."

And the door opens.

Inside, predictably, there is a Cygnian woman. A silver, like Corla. She is tall, and shapely in her long, white and gray gown. Her hair looks like thin strands of silver metal, but I've touched the hair of a silver princess before, and I know it's not real silver. It's soft and pliable.

She is pretty. Actually, she is beautiful. Not quite what I was expecting with the nickname Loathsome One. But whatever.

"Leave us," she commands the cyborg guards.

I pull my eyes away from the princess just long enough to look over my shoulder and see them back out the doors the way they came in. But my attention returns to this woman before the doors close with a bang.

She smiles at me. Clasps her hands in front of her and says, "Jimmy Yates. I never thought I'd see this day."

"Yates?" I ask. That word again. A name, obviously. But not one I've heard before.

The princess waves a hand in the air and says, "There's time for that later. But first... How are you?"

"How am I?" I scoff. "Are you fucking kidding me? I was kidnapped by a deranged ship, drugged, taken prisoner in this insane asylum, and then dressed up in this truly evil-looking fucking suit and brought

241

here to this creepy lair to—oh, I don't know. Just taking a wild stab here—be bred to... whoever the fuck *you* are. That's how I am. How the fuck are you?"

She smiles at me, looking almost amused at my outburst, then says, "Don't worry about the ship. I took care of her."

"What?" My heart beats fast at this revelation. Because ten seconds ago that deranged ship was my only way out of this shit show.

"*Queenie?*" she says. "She was a traitor from the start. A running joke around here, in fact. We all knew she was concocting up some silly plan to kill me and take you back to Harem. I admit, I didn't expect Delphi to fail though." She takes a moment to exaggerate a frown. "I had high hopes for her."

I let out a long breath and wonder where Delphi is now. Is she still back at Mighty Minions? Where does *Dicker* think I am? How will they find me?

Will they find me?

Maybe not.

"What happened to her?"

"Delphi? I have no idea. I have to face facts. She's not one of us. She is something... other than us. Which could've come in handy, I suppose. But it was never likely. They did let her escape, after all. And that would not have happened if she had promise. I imagine that's why everyone has moved on to stage two." She waves a hand in the air like she's trying to wipe away the image of Delphi.

My mind yells... *WHAT?*

But I force myself to focus and say, "No. The ship. *Queenie.*"

"Oh, her." The princess laughs. "We blew her up after we got you on board the station. She's been... how's that phrase go? Scattered like dust into the galactic wind."

Fuck.

"Oh, please tell me you didn't fall for her spiel? That whole mother thing? Please. Such utter bullshit."

But I don't think it was. I think she was telling the truth. That talk about my mother might've been the only honest thing that ship said to me.

"Of course not," I say. "But it was an interesting tale."

The princess huffs out a grunt. Like... *If you say so.* Then she takes a deep breath and says, "Hello, Jimmy Yates. I'm Princess Veila. It's so very, very nice to meet you."

"Veila?" I say, too loud. "As in Queen Corla's little star-bursting partner?"

Corla is frozen in a cryopod back in a Harem security beacon because she and her princess partner, Veila, were made into explosive devices so powerful, they could blow up planets.

"The one and only," Veila says.

I almost sigh with relief. Like for two whole seconds I think, *Thank the fucking suns! This isn't what I thought at all! Veila's on our side!*

But then Veila says, "Fucking queen bitch. She was always the one thing standing in my way."

And all that momentary hope disappears.

CHAPTER THIRTY

Our plan to get through the Lair Gate and make it to the actual station is iffy, at best. But what can you do? When the Loathsome One is holding your soulmate, your bot, and your brother captive you pull out all the stops and go balls in. That's all there is to it.

Once I told *Dicker* what I wanted to do her huffy attitude faded and she became a little more amicable. Maybe because it made this whole crazy scheme a little more even.

She is, after all, risking her life just by going through the gate. And that new cloaking device she's been going on and on about is pretty cool, but it's by no means a guaranteed win. We need to be sneaky about this.

The Loathsome One is a seasoned pro. She's been on the run for two decades. She knows exactly what she's doing. She's seen more action than *Dicker*, Jimmy, and me put together. This plan has to be insane for the sheer fact that if it's not, she'll see through it immediately.

What we need is a little bit of skill, a little bit of luck, and a whole lot of lying. Heavy, *heavy* emphasis on the lying part. Because that's the clincher.

"You let me know when you're ready," *Dicker* says.

We're floating about half a million klicks away from the last gate before we jump into the Lair Station neighborhood.

I'm still strapped into Xyla's exoskeleton, but I'm also hitched to Jimmy's nearly-worthless Palladium bot.

Because that's my plan.

Dicker told me the whole Bull Station story as we made our way through stealth gates to get to this last one without being noticed. She told me how Lyra saved Nyleena by using her bot to shuttle her through space to Nyleena's cryopod and how ALCOR pretty much did the same thing on some other bot to infiltrate and destroy the Cygnian warship.

And hell, it's a damn good idea. I'm not sure it's one you'd choose if you had better options because you can get lost in space pretty fucking quick when you're nothing but a human-sized anomaly with barely a blip of heat signature to track. And I gotta say, being lost in space and dying slowly as you freeze to death and run out of oxygen is a pretty fucked-up way to go out.

Yeah. Not my number one choice. Just the only one I have.

But here's the thing. Us Cygnian princesses? We're mastermind plan-makers. Like this is just something we can do. That's how we all escape. We're just good at this shit. You know your plan is amazing when it's stupid crazy. It's like the defining factor for success.

So I was like, *OK. This plan is awesome. I can use this stupid Palladium bot tagging along as my shuttle, right? Infiltrate the Lair Station, kick some ass as a souped-up, exoskeleton-equipped, Mighty Minion princess girl, then find Jimmy, Flicka, and Tycho, get back to* Dicker, *get the fuck out of here, and start a brand-new life on Harem Station.*

What could go wrong?

OK, maybe there are a few snags to work out. Like for one, *Dicker's* new cloaking device only gives her thirty-seven seconds of non-trackable heat signature. Which means that once we get through the gate I have thirty-seven seconds to launch myself out of the airlock and get far enough away from *Dicker* so when Lair Station finally sees her, they don't shoot me in the process of trying to shoot her.

Because they will shoot her.

I was a little bit worried about that, and said so. But *Dicker* just got all huffy and said she can take care of herself and I should just concentrate on my part of the plan, because that's the part that matters.

She's right. So I let it go.

You do you, *Dicker.*

The other obvious flaw is that this plan depends on me becoming that kick-ass souped-up exoskeleton Mighty Minions princess girl. I've been inside the Lair Station so I know it's big and filled with borgs and bots that are way stronger than little ol' me. But this suit is kind of amazing. I really feel like I can pull this part off. I have some moves in my back pocket. I might be small, but I'm three sun-damned meters tall inside this freaking exoskeleton and I have body parts that shoot shit like plasma streams and shrapnel grenades.

I feel like it's probably gonna be a pretty even match as long as I don't get overrun by a mob.

Then, you know. There's the whole getting *off* the station. That part really depends on *Dicker.* Somehow she needs to find a way to dock. Preferably a dock that's not in vacuum so we can like… you know, get to the ship without suffocating. Either that or find Jimmy a suit along the way, but I feel like stumbling upon some random environmental suit as we escape is pretty absurd.

Again, this is *Dicker's* problem and she gets huffy every time I bring it up.

"Any time now," *Dicker* says. If she were human she'd make a big production of twiddling her thumbs.

But I don't have the privilege of being annoyed. There's too much at stake. "OK," I say. "But you're going to get me as close to the station as possible, right? I mean, it's a long ways out. It would really suck to run out of oxygen before I even reach the ship."

"You've complained about that seven times now and each time I've told you the same thing. I'm handling it."

"Yeah, but specifically how are you handling it? Because it's time for all parties to be filled in on all details."

"The moment I'm clear and the clock starts ticking you'll leave the rear airlock and quickly position yourself on the starboard side of the stern. Then I'll whip around and use that momentum to fling you towards the station."

"Fling? Did you just use the word *fling* in reference to my fragile human body?"

"You're inside an exoskeleton."

248

"What if you *fling me* the wrong direction?"

"That's what the bot is for. He can course-correct. Right, strange-bot-who-should-really-make-sure-he-has-a-purpose-here-because-I'll-fling-him-out-in-another-direction-if-he-fucks-this-up?"

The bot chirps enthusiastically.

"Great," I mutter.

"That name is too long," *Dicker* says. "We're going to call him Fling from now on."

"Funny."

"Are you ready, or what?"

"I'm ready."

"Good. Clip that bot to your exoskeleton and hold on. We're going through."

So here's what happens next.

We go through the gate and come out the other side no problem. There are no blaring alarms or flashing red lights, so I take that as a good sign that we're not immediately being targeted for attack.

I do my thing. We cycle through the airlock—which eats up fifteen precious seconds of our time limit—then I swing outside in space and realize... yeah. I've never done this before and looking out into the black darkness of the great nothing scares the shit out of me, and I freeze.

That eats up another five seconds and only *Dicker* yelling in my helmet comms snaps me out of it. But the bot didn't freak out and tugs me along towards the back end of *Dicker's* tail. There are no handrails on this ship because she's this sleek monster-thing, right? So I'm thinking, *This is the dumbest idea ever,* just as she whips her body around, I smash against the hull, bang my fucking head, pass out for however fucking long, and then come to flying towards Lair Station just as a stream of plasma shoots past me and hits *Dicker.*

I see the whole thing go down in real time. She flickers for a moment. Just shimmers. And then…

Gone.

Nothing left.

She just… disappears.

I say, "Oh, fuck! That wasn't in the plan!" just as the bot shifts into some hidden high gear and we go hurling towards the side of the station at a speed that is definitely not safe.

I don't really understand how we got so close to it so fast, but there's no time to think that through because I'm hauling ass now. Like… I'm fuckin' booking it straight towards the side of the station and if I hit the side of that thing at this velocity, I'm a pancake.

So I yell, "Stop!"

But that's even dumber than the plan we came up with, because there's no stopping in space. So I yell, "Reverse thrust!" Because at least that makes sense.

The bot whips his little metal body around and does that, but I'm not actually holding on to him, just connected by a tether.

So I keep going my original direction while he goes the opposite.

Not for long though, because that tether is only two meters long, so when the tether snaps tight my momentum overpowers his momentum, and now we're both flying towards the station and the fumes from his little thrusters are spraying onto the faceplate of my helmet and freezing over.

So now I can't see anything. And who cares. I'm facing the wrong direction now, anyway.

I come to terms with the fact that I will smack into the station going ass-backwards and probably break both my legs in the process.

But seconds go by and we don't hit the station, we actually do slow down, and I have a moment to realize we're still a good distance away and things in space are not closer than they appear.

It takes several more minutes to actually reach the station and FlingBot hooks onto some random handhold meant for repair workers—I know this because there are several fucking repair borgs clinging to the station doing said repair work as we float by—and then...

Shit gets real.

One of them hurls himself off the station and comes at me with a giant tool and then I kinda overreact and start pushing those buttons conveniently located below my fingertips and try to send out a flash grenade.

I start chanting, "Third button is flash, fourth is shrapnel," then confuse myself because I was joking with *Dicker* about this earlier, and second-guess, then finally just say fuck it and hit the first button.

Plasma rifle.

Which is mounted on my left arm so it hits the station, not the borg. And then I take a moment to aim and press it again, and this time I blow that fucker to dust!

I yell, "Fuck, yeah, motherfuckers! Come get me!" like the badass I imagined myself to be.

Except they do come get me. And there are four of them, but they don't have weapons mounted to their bodies, just random tools for repair work, so this actually works out for me. Because I pick all four of them off with plasma in a matter of seconds.

"Ha!" I yell. Then laugh a little, because holy shit, this stupid plan fucking worked.

I am right up next to Lair Station and FlingBot is tugging me along towards the nearest airlock. Which doesn't even have a code to anything on the keypad to cycle through, just a big green button that says OPEN.

I hit the button, clamber inside, then hit the one on the inside that says LOCK, and the door begins to close just as my exoskeleton boots magnetically attach to the floor.

"We did it!" I say, hunching down a little as I turn—because my three-meter tall exoskeleton is actually too big for this space—and spy another borg peering at me through the airlock window.

"Shit," I say. Because this one does have a weapon.

I can't fire on him because the airlock is still doing its thing. Saving grace is that he can't fire on me either. So there are ten whole seconds of us staring each other down as we wait for the other side of the airlock to open.

Long story short. I am a motherfucking badass. This Xyla suit is top fucking notch. Not only does it automatically target any weapon pointed in my direction, it actually makes a calculated decision on which weapon to use in retaliation.

So basically I stand inside the suit and let it do its thing until the borg is just a little pile of used-up metal and smoking guts.

FlingBot begins chirping like crazy and heads off down a hallway. I unhook the tether from my end, which is probably a bad idea because now it's clanging along behind him on the metal floor, pretty much announcing our arrival.

"Stop," I hiss through the comms. He does. I remove my helmet, attach it to the clip on my back, and take a moment to unhook the tether from the bot and stuff it in a cargo pocket on the side of my thigh.

My heart is racing at this point. Like hammering inside my chest. "What happened to *Dicker*?" I ask the bot.

Which is dumb, because I can't understand him. I have no access to my wristband to activate a translator.

But he chips in low tones and I'm not sure if he's doing that to be stealthy or if he's doing that because *Dicker* is dead. Blown to bits.

Which is both sad and unfortunate in more ways than I can articulate right now.

"OK," I say. "Whatever happened to her, we're here and we have to see this through. We might need to steal a ship. But... first. Let's just find our people."

I think FlingBot agrees because his chirps change tone and his little round body spins as he hovers off.

The magnetic boots aren't magnetic anymore because there's a grav drive inside the station, and I'm surprisingly quiet as I follow him down the hallway.

We get to an intersection and stop. Then FlingBot goes left.

At the end of this hallway is a large steel door, but it's not locked. It's cracked open and we can hear people inside.

The sound of borgs walking around, but more disturbingly, the sound of people. Moaning and groaning, like they are in pain.

Jimmy could be in there. Tycho could be in there.

I make an executive decision and move forward, throw the door all the way open, and aim both my arms at the two borgs within.

They don't have weapons so the suit doesn't automatically react. One of them is holding a tray while the other scoops some kind of goopy food into a bowl.

And that's when I realize what this is and who is being held prisoner here.

I gun down both the borgs with button two—laser pistol—and they fall over face first.

I might feel guilty about this later. Once I have time to fully internalize that I just murdered two defenseless borgs. But not now.

Because this is a prison and lined up in cells in either side of the main aisle are kids.

Teenagers. Akeelian male teenagers, to be exact. I know this because they are naked. They are filthy, and starving, and magnetically bound to the walls as sexbots kneel at their feet, jerking them off and giving them oral.

None of them look like they're enjoying it. Several are crying. At least one is unconscious. And one is coming—semen spilling out of both his cocks and collecting at the bottom of a vial in his sexbot's hand.

Something comes over me. Maybe it's just me imagining Tycho being held in one of these cells or maybe underneath I'm more of a cold-blooded killer than I ever realized.

I'm not sure.

I don't care.

I kill every single one of those sexbots with a laser shot to the head.

CHAPTER THIRTY-ONE

I think I lose a little bit of time after I realize that Corla and Veila were never partners. Then all kinds of scenarios start running through my head. So many maybes and what ifs.

Here is what I know:

Corla and Crux met back on Wayward Station when we were teenagers. I was there that night Corla came into the dining room and wanted to speak to Crux alone about something.

I wasn't there when she explained and I wasn't there when Crux was told to dress up in this same uniform I'm wearing now and then led into some bizarre pre-mating ritual surrounded by the visiting Cygnian dignitaries and in-the-know Akeelians.

But he told me about it. He had no choice. He needed me to get to ALCOR.

Anyway, the point is that Corla had this crazy plan and she told him before they separated that if he ever saw her again, something had gone wrong.

Obviously something went wrong. Because we have Corla frozen in a cryopod and locked up inside a security beacon back near Harem Station. We didn't learn that Veila and Corla were a weaponized team until Lyra filled in the blanks just before the shit show at Bull Station happened.

And I think all of us just assumed that they had escaped together. They were on the run together. And if we just could find this Veila chick, we could wake Corla up and stop worrying that one day someone would get their hands on Veila and trigger the weapon inside Corla.

We just assumed it would be that easy.

Why?

"You seem to be speechless. What did I say?" Veila asks.

"What?" I blink a few times, trying to clear away the past. She's pouring us drinks from a fancy crystal decanter across the room. It's only then that I actually realize where I am.

Not her throne room or whatever.

Her bedroom.

A lavish four-poster bed. Huge bed. With lots of fluffy pillows and soft flowing silver netting hanging down from the canopy. Rugs covering the metal floors. Nice rugs. A small work station in the corner with a screen. And art on the walls too. Erotic pictures of people fucking.

"Oh, shit," I say. Because I'm starting to realize what's happening.

She smiles as she walks towards me, holding out my drink. I shake my head no, refusing her offer. "You sure?" she asks, laughing a little. "You're really gonna need it."

I shake my head again. Trying to make the all the missing puzzle pieces fit together. I know she's going to do that for me any minute now—that's the whole reason she brought me here. But for some reason I feel the need to figure it out on my own.

I just…can't quite *get there.*

"Shame," Veila says. "I was hoping we could make a toast."

I shake my head one more time. In complete denial now.

"OK, then," she says. She takes a sip of her drink, a very small sip, then sets the glass down on a nearby table and folds her hands in front of her. Smiles at me. "Should we get on with it?"

"Get on with what?" And even though I try my best not to glance at the bed, I glance at the fuckin' bed.

She makes one of those half laugh, half huff noises. "You know what, Jimmy. You know why you're here." She takes two steps towards me and I take two steps back. "Oh, come on now. I won't bite you." She whispers that last part. "All you need do is touch me and then we'll know, won't we?"

"No," I say. "This isn't happening. This can't be happening. I *already* know."

She tilts her head at me. One of those confused looks. And normally I'd get a little thrill at this confusion. Because it actually looks genuine. "You already know *what?*"

"It's not you," I say, backing up another few steps. "You're not her. I already know who my one is and it's not you."

"What?" Then something must click for her because she guffaws loudly, her head tilting back so her amusement can flow up and out easily and echo off the high metal ceilings. "Oh, no. Oh, this is priceless. You didn't think that… Oh." She laughs again. "Jimmy. Please. You didn't think that Delphi was your *one*, did you?"

"She is my one. We've already sealed the deal, Veila. You and I"—I do this little back-and-forth thing with my index finger, indicating me and her—"we are *not* a thing."

"Oh, this is too much. I send my niece out to get you and—"

"Your niece?"

"She didn't tell you?"

I don't answer because it's a rhetorical question.

"She is a generation removed, to be sure. But I can see how you might've been confused. And I'm feeling better about how *Queenie* left her behind. Makes things easier, in any case. But—"

And just as she's about to fill in more blanks, a buzzing alarm cuts her off.

We both look over at the small work station in the corner of the room. It's flashing a red warning that I can't read from this distance.

"For sun's sake," Veila says, picking up the skirts of her long gown and rushing over to the screen. She stabs at the warning and barks, "What's happening now?"

The face of a borg fills the screen. He says, "A ship just came through our gate."

"What ship?" Veila asks.

The borg's head turns in my direction and a chill runs up my spine. "His ship. Call sign *Big Dicker.*"

"Kill it," Veila barks.

"No," I say. "You will not touch my ship."

"Or what?" Veila snaps back. She stares at me for a moment. Then turns back to the borg. "Do it."

"You fucking bitch," I say, all my previous uncertainty fading in a single instant. "I'd like to see you try."

"Would you now?" She glances at me again, then says to her borg, "Put it up on the screen so we can watch."

"Yes, my queen."

My queen. I want to throw up in my mouth a little. But then a view of the gate comes up and I can't help myself. I walk towards Veila to get a better look. *Dicker* is there, doing some turning maneuver like she's gonna run. Just go back the way she came.

Silently I say, *No. Don't go. Don't leave me here with this crazy witch.*

But *Dicker* doesn't run. And I hate myself for a moment for doubting her. Instead, she just does this weird spin move in place that seems to have no effect at all.

The station fires. But *Dicker* has some pretty nice shields now, after her major upgrade after Bull Station. So the plasma cannon fire forms a sphere-like bubble around her as it's diffused.

Then she fires back. One SEAR cannon shoots high, just a threat, I realize. She knows I'm here and she can't just destroy the station. But at the same time a plasma cannon fires and hits.

The station shudders and a deep moan runs through the walls. But no new alarms start blaring.

More fire exchange, but again, nothing really happens. It's almost like *Dicker* is dicking around. Not really aiming or trying to hurt the station. Just buying time.

The station, however. Not playing. A barrage of plasma fire shoots out in dotted streams of light. Hitting *Dicker* over and over again until she shimmers and blurs a little. Flickering for a moment and then… she just… disappears.

"Mmmm," Veila hums, satisfied.

She looks at me, meeting my glare with squinted eyes. And I say, "I'm gonna kill you for that."

"Are you sure?" she asks, smiling with pleasure.

"Oh, I'm really fucking sure." I stalk towards her. Slowly. "You know what I find funny?" I say, closing the distance between us.

"What's that, Jimmy?"

"Everyone thinks it's Xyla they have to watch out for. They all think I'm this self-righteous liberator. The Harem brother with the heart. The one who saves people."

"Bots, you mean."

"Like I said. *People*." We're only about a meter apart now. I could probably take one more step and grab her by that long, silver hair.

"So what was the funny part?"

"The funny part," I say, reaching for her, "is that it's me people should be afraid of. Xyla's the one with heart. I'm the one with no regrets."

And then I grab her. Not by the hair, but by the neck.

She doesn't even try to stop me. So I wrap both my hands around her throat and *squeeze*. I want to squeeze the fucking life right out of her.

But I don't know what happens. She's wearing some kind of shock weapon because pain shoots up through my arms and then it's replaced by the most intense pleasure I've ever felt.

Both of my cocks become erect in this same moment. Heat flows through my muscles and blood rushes into my head.

Veila... glows. A bright white light that shocks me into letting go of her neck.

I stumble backwards, unsure of what just happened.

Veila is laughing. "I told you!" she squeals. "I told you you were mine!"

I tip over the edge of a rug and fall on my ass, thoroughly confused. "What the fuck was that?"

"That was us, Jimmy Yates of Harem Station. That was proof."

"No," I say, getting to my feet and retreating. Because she's coming towards me now. Reaching for me like she wants to pull me into an embrace.

"Stay the fuck away from me," I say. "Delphi," I stammer, still backing up. "Delphi is my one." I hit a wall and there's no more room to retreat.

"You silly man," Veila coos, placing a hand on my cheek.

Again, my body betrays me. My cocks jump, heat fills my muscles, and Veila glows white light.

"No," I say.

But that piece, that missing fucking piece I was so desperate to find a few minutes ago, is there. Fitting into place.

"Our bodies were made for each other," Veila says. "And there's nothing you can do about that. Delphi and I come from the same stock. So maybe you did feel something for her. That was simply her similar genetics mixing you all up. She is not your one, Jimmy. But good news. If she ever makes it back here I have her man waiting. They'll make beautiful babies together, trust me."

I open my mouth to make yet another futile denial, but then another alarm sounds on the screen. We both turn to look at it and find the same borg face staring back at us.

"What now?" Veila growls.

"We've had a breach. Someone has killed four worker borgs on the outside of the station, one airlock guard, and..."

"And what?" Veila snaps.

"... and killed all the sexbots in the lower-level cells, my queen."

"Who? Who the fuck is on my station messing with my breeding program?"

"Delphi, your highness. It's Delphi."

Veila turns her head slowly. Locks eyes with mine.

I don't want to smile. I don't want to piss her off and make her react.

But I can't help it.

I take it one step further. Because it's my turn to laugh.

I don't know Veila. I don't really have any experience with her to make this determination—but this laugh was the wrong move. This laugh—which felt good for a moment because Delphi somehow made her way to this station and is now playing offense—makes Veila rage inside.

And I regret my misplaced glory immediately. Even before Veila whispers, "Bring Delphi to me," as she locks her eyes with mine. "I have some very special plans for my sweet little niece." Then she winks at me and says, "And bring her mate too. Jimmy says he wants to watch."

CHAPTER THIRTY-TWO

The alarms don't start until I'm already in the slave-cell control room. I killed the borg manning it as he was opening the door to come attack me. The suit reacted automatically because he was aiming his plasma rifle at my chest, so I can't really take credit.

Inside the control room there are dozens of smaller monitors, each one surveilling a single cell. But there's also a central hub with a split screen of all of them in one frame. This is where I find the master switch to release all the magnetic bindings for the boys and deactivate the locks on the cage doors.

Because these rooms don't even deserve to be called cells. They are cages and to Veila, these boys are nothing but animals in some sick, twisted science experiment.

When I walk back out into the aisle, most of the boys are on the floor. Slumped over and weak after being held upright on the wall for sun only knows how long.

But a few of them are still strong. Still able to stand, and walk, and maybe even run.

"Run," I tell them. "Take a weapon and run. Find some clothes, hide, and just wait. I have more to do before we can think about leaving."

One boy locks eyes with me and takes a step forward.

"No," I say. "You can't stay with me. Just go."

He says, "Delphi?"

I squint my eyes at him. "Do I know you?"

He nods yes and shakes his head no at the same time. And for a second I think he's just confused. He's been here too long or maybe he's drugged.

I get a weird feeling inside. Like… a chill runs up my spine and my muscles start to get all hot. I shake it off. Literally shake it off and make the exoskeleton rattle with the movement.

I have an urge to look at his body. Not just look at his body the way I glanced over the others, but *look* at his body. His cocks—which were semi-hard just a moment ago—have engorged with blood and now stand erect.

"Delphi," he says again.

"No," I say. "Just go, just run, just… get the fuck away from me."

"I can't," he says. "I can't."

Everything starts to make sense. All the excuses for why I didn't get that feeling with Jimmy when we were together back on Might Minions become just that— excuses.

Because this heat, this weakness, this chill of recognition is the only true feeling I've ever felt.

Immediate, one hundred percent attraction. Instantaneous longing.

"No," I say again. "It's not you. It can't be you."

He takes a step forward and I raise my weaponized arm and point at him. But the moment I do that this uncontrollable wave of heartache fills me up and prevents me from pressing a button.

He stops, hands up like he's surrendering. "It is me. It's *me*," he says again. "You can't hurt me. It won't allow you to. If you hurt me, you will only hurt yourself."

"I love Jimmy," I say. "Not you. Just get the fuck away from me or I swear to the sun, I will shoot you. I will. I won't hesitate—"

But I do hesitate. I can't even explain the effect that meeting this boy has on me.

He takes another step forward, reaching out for me, and I know that if his skin touches mine it's all over. Everything that Jimmy and I felt, and built, and wanted back on Mighty Minions will be over. Forever.

There is a little part inside me screaming, *Kill him. Kill him now before it's too late!*

But it's a very small part. A teeny tiny part that can't take control of all the other, more dominant parts that are screaming back something quite different. The parts that are demanding that I rush into his arms and let him hold me tight.

Press the button, Delphi!

The tip of my finger brushes against buttons one and two. But they don't discharge the plasma fire or lasers. Because I can't bring myself to hurt him.

The only thing I can do is press button three. Flash grenade.

And then I turn away from the bright exploding light of distraction and I *run*.

I run out of the cells and into the hallway. Go left, then right, then another right. I have no idea where I am. I have no clue where I'm going, I just know I have to get away from that boy. I can't ever see him again. He can't ever touch me. Ever, ever, ever—

I round a corner and come face to face with an approaching group of cyborg soldiers. Their weapons trained on me. Their red eye screens blinking fast.

Both of my weaponized arms raise, ready to fire, but they hit me dead in the chest with a steady stream of plasma fire and I go reeling backwards, crashing into a wall.

I shake it off and roll over on my knees, ready to get up and continue fighting.

But when I turn and look over my shoulder, there is that boy again. Guards holding him, one on each side. More cyborg soldiers behind them.

Shoot him, shoot him, shoot him!

But I can't.

And that's when more plasma fire hits me in the back and I fall over face first onto the hard, steel floor.

I wake up in waves, my chest burning from the onslaught of plasma fire. It's hard to breathe, and painful too. Like I can't suck in enough air. Like my lungs don't work properly anymore.

"Good," Veila says off to my left. "She's waking up."

I'm upright, bound to one of those magnetic walls, the full weight of my body hanging from the restraints on my wrists. My hands are numb and unresponsive.

I think I lose time after that because the next thing I hear is Jimmy. His voice is low and his words deliberate. "—then I'll cooperate," he says. Like he's finishing a statement and I'm only catching the tail end of it.

No. I want to say it out loud, but can't. *Don't cooperate. Don't let her ruin us.*

"I'm afraid what's done is done," Veila says. "She killed seventeen sexbots, seven borgs, and two of the slaves have died since she interfered with their protocol."

What?

"Besides," Veila continues, "she's part of the program. Bring in the mate."

"Just wait!" Jimmy counters. "Just fucking wait a minute. If you let her go I'll do what you ask. I'll submit to it, goddammit."

"You will submit anyway, Jimmy. There is no possible way you won't. We have been genetically engineered to be meant for each other. Why are you fighting this?"

Jimmy doesn't say anything. I manage to crack open one eyelid and catch a glimpse of the metal floor and my sagging feet. It takes a lot of effort to raise my head and take a look around, but I do it. I make myself do it.

There are dozens of soldier borgs in here with us, but my gaze passes right by them, eager to see the only face that matters, and when I find it, a rush of relief floods through me.

Jimmy.

That's real too, I tell myself. That feeling I have around Jimmy, it's real. It's more real than what I feel for that strange boy back in that cell. It has to be.

Jimmy meets my gaze and I try to keep my eyes open. I just want to look at him. I just want to see him. But I can't. I'm too tired, too exhausted, and my eyes close again through no will of my own.

"I think you underestimate me," Jimmy says.

"How so?" Veila counters.

"You'll see if you insist on subjecting Delphi to being raped," Jimmy snarls.

"Well, I don't respond to threats, Jimmy. I respond to facts. And the fact is you're mine. She's his. And that's the end of it. This is nature. This can't be undone. Not even that DNA scrambler you use can stop it. Can't you see that?"

"What?" Jimmy says.

"Oh." Veila laughs. "Did you just assume I haven't been keeping track of you? Your mistake. I knew you were going to that biogenetics lab all these years. I have known we were meant for each other since I was Delphi's age. I was there with Corla back when she was bred to Crux, don't you remember me?"

Jimmy is silent for a little while. Then he says, "No. There were no other silver princesses in Corla's entourage. They were all pink."

Veila huffs out a laugh dripping with contempt. "That's because I hadn't been leveled up back then. But they told me who you were. And if the mating between Crux and Corla was successful, which it was, I was next in line to breed."

"Gross," I manage to mumble.

"Oh, good," Veila exclaims. "For a few minutes I was worried you wouldn't be responsive enough to participate in what comes next, Delphi."

"So where the fuck have you been all these years?" Jimmy says, returning to the previous conversation.

"Well," Veila says, "that AI of yours was a master disrupter. He kept you boys segregated for almost a decade, if I'm counting correctly. Then you were always off with that stupid sexbot of yours. And that ship. So I bided my time. But thanks to ALCOR's little sacrifice back at Bull Station, my moment has finally arrived. Your sexbot is thousands of light years away and your ship is quite dead. So…" She makes a noise that sounds like she's rubbing her hands together in eagerness. "Good things come to those who wait." Then she adds, "And come up with thoughtful, calculated schemes to get what they want."

"Where's Tycho?" I growl. "Where the fuck is my brother? If you have him in one of those cells I will kill you, you fucking bitch."

"Now that's an unexpected surprise. Delphi has always been clueless and weak," Veila says. She's just… not like us."

"No," Jimmy says. "She isn't. She's so much better than us."

"Ha." Veila laughs. "She's stupid, and naive, and powerless. But beyond that, she has been shown who and what she is many times and each time she refused to see the truth people were telling her. And when I finally got a hold of her, she fell for every one of my lies. I mean… come on." Veila walks over to me, grabs my chin with her fingertips, and lifts my head up so I can look her in the eyes. "Did you really think I'd hand over your brother? Delphi, that's the dumbest lie you ever fell for. He is infinitely more important than you are, my dear. We have big, big plans for him."

"Where is he?" I snarl.

"Not here." She chuckles. "That's for sure. He's much too valuable to be left way out here. But don't worry," she says, dropping my chin so my head falls towards my chest. "He's not alone." I manage to pick up my head and open my eyes just in time to see Veila look at Jimmy and say, "He's with your brother, Draden, Jimmy. They have become fast friends."

"That's not possible," Jimmy says. "My brother Draden is dead."

"Hmmm," Veila says. "Yet another lie in a long string of lies you've been told."

"What the fuck are you talking about?"

"Crux didn't tell you?" Veila asks. "I'm surprised. I know your brother Tray knows. He was with Crux and ALCOR when they left Harem Station to go searching for answers. But I figured Crux would tell you the moment he got back, seeing as how you two have always been close."

"What *the fuck* are you talking about?" Jimmy yells it this time.

"I had this speech all planned out, you know. I practiced it relentlessly for years. What would I say, exactly? When I finally got my chance? How would I break the news to you? I was afraid for a while that ALCOR would tell you himself and ruin all my devious plotting, but then he died and I knew he left his big secret untold when the Prime Navy showed up for his funeral. If he had told you the truth, then—"

274

She's interrupted by the opening of her bedroom doors.

I glance over at the borgs entering and my heart flips, and my body heats up, and my stomach drops all in the same instant.

Because they bring in *that boy.*

"No," I moan, struggling against my bindings. "No. Keep him away from me!"

"I'm afraid that's not going to happen, little niece," Veila says. "Bring him forward."

"No!" I say. "No!"

Jimmy rushes forward and is immediately stopped when more than a dozen armed borgs point their rifles at his head.

"Don't do this!" he pleads. "I'll do what you ask, just don't—"

But it's too late. I can already feel the reaction building and the boy is so close. Veila takes his hand and places it on my breast and… and that's it.

It's over.

Because I light up like a sun.

CHAPTER THIRTY-THREE

JIMMY

I want to save her from this humiliation. I want to protect her. I want to hold her, and caress her, and kiss her mouth and tell her things like, *I love you. It will be OK. I will take you away from all this.*

But I can't.

Half of the borgs in this room are surrounding me. Rifle barrels pushed up against my head, and my back and my stomach. They won't kill me, they'll just overwhelmingly stun me the way they did with Delphi.

Veila made me watch on the screen as they took her down. Delphi looked majestic wearing Xyla's exoskeleton. Like a true warrior princess. And that stupid bot. My stupid rewards bot from Mighty Minions. How the hell did he get here?

Doesn't even matter anymore. He was in the path of the plasma beams. He fell to the floor in a lifeless heap two seconds into that fight.

But Delphi... Delphi was magnificent. They streamed her with plasma pulses for almost a whole minute before she fell.

Veila is wrong about Delphi in every way I can think of.

She is not weak. She is not naive. She is not stupid.

She is strong, and pure, and smart.

And she is *mine*. No matter what her DNA signature says.

There are so many warrior borgs around me that I can't even see Delphi anymore.

But I don't need to see her to see what happens next. The light comes bursting out of her in a way that never happened between us.

My heart dies a little in this moment. Just fades, and shrinks, and I drop to my knees in defeat.

"Take them out of here," Veila commands. "Jimmy and I need some privacy. Put them in the breeding room and let nature take its course."

"No," I say, bending over to place my forehead on the cold, metal floor. "*No.*"

But what I want doesn't matter. Maybe it never has.

No. Do not fall for her lies, Jimmy. Don't believe anything she's told you. Not about Crux, not about Draden, not about ALCOR, not about Delphi.

But... there's this little voice inside me that knows better. This little hidden thing inside me that has always suspected that ALCOR was up to something. That we were part of some bigger plan that had nothing to do with a station filled with outlaws or a harem filled with runaway princesses.

Seconds pass. Maybe a whole minute. Delphi is released from the wall and dragged across the room, kicking and screaming. Doling out threats like streams of plasma.

And then she's gone. Taken away to breed with that Akeelian boy.

The borgs surrounding me back off and take up their original positions along the perimeter of the room.

I raise my head off the ground and look up at Veila. She is smug and smiling. Hands clasped in front of her long silver and white gown.

"I fucking hate you," I say.

She sighs a little. Shakes her head slowly. "No, you don't. You can't hate me, Jimmy. You know this. You know that no matter what I do, you will always be on my side. Because you can't erase the fact that deep inside our DNA is woven some special magic that makes us soulmates. We are one and the same. Forever."

"Fuck. That." I get to my feet and say it again. "Fuck. *That.*"

Veila closes her eyes like she's praying for patience. Then she opens them and says, "I haven't told you everything yet."

"No," I say, putting up a hand. "I don't want to hear it."

"But you will hear it. You must hear it. Because it's the truth. Don't you realize who Delphi is yet?"

"What?"

"Can't you see it? I see it. Granted, I'm her aunt and I knew her mother well."

I squint my eyes, once again trying to make the pieces fit together before she tells me. I want to understand so bad. I want to figure it out before she shatters my world again, just to deny her that satisfaction.

But I don't know. I don't understand. My whole life is upside down.

"But you knew her father so... why are you pretending not to see it? Delphi is their daughter, Jimmy."

Their daughter. The words ring in my head. Echoing like some call for help inside a deep, dark cave.

"She is Crux and Corla's daughter. Tycho is their son. Do you have any idea what your brother would say if he found out you were fucking his *daughter?*"

"You're insane," I spit. "Fucking *insane.*"

"You can deny all you want, but you have to know this is true. Think about it, Jimmy. Just think about it. She is nineteen years old. And twenty years ago your brother bred with Corla in that ceremony back on Wayward Station. You know this. He told you this. She is his daughter and now you know she was never made for you. It's just... hormones, my sweet."

Veila starts walking towards me and I get to my feet and back up instinctively. "Don't fucking touch me," I say. "Stay the fuck back."

I keep backing up until I bump into one of the cyborg warriors. He doesn't react, just holds his position as Veila continues forward.

"Just hormones," she says, reaching for me. "That's all. And I don't even care if you fucked her. It doesn't matter because you two could never breed and that's the only thing I care about. But—" She pauses. Her hand is so close to my face. So close. My cocks jump back to attention and my body becomes a flaming inferno of heat.

I just stare at her, mouth open. Unable to say or do anything but remain absolutely still.

"But I will separate them after they're done," Veila says. "Once she's pregnant I won't make her stay with him, if that makes you feel better. Hell, I'll even allow you two to see each other. Spend as much time as you want together. Just... give me what I want. What I *need*," she says, placing a hand over her belly.

"No fucking way," I say, finally finding my voice.

But in the same instant, that one hand stops hovering over my cheek and makes contact and she emits the brightest, whitest, most glorious light I've ever seen.

I come in my pants. Both cocks at the same time.

And when Veila looks down to find the wet spot she smiles.

"There," she coos. "You see?" she whispers. "You're mine. All *mine*."

I take a deep breath, feeling some relief from the double climax, and find the will to say what needs to be said.

"I'd rather die," I growl. And then I spit right in her face.

CHAPTER THIRTY-FOUR

The guards have a firm grip on both my arms. They force me out of Veila's room and even when I go limp, trying with all my might to resist, they just hold me up and drag me along.

There's four guards in front of me and somewhere behind me is the boy. I glance over my shoulder and find him walking amicably, like this is totally normal. But behind him there's many more guards, clearly indicating that nothing about this is normal.

They drag me through several hallways, down two flights of stairs, and then out into another hallway and finally stop in front of an open door. I have a chance to quickly glance around and see that there's about a dozen more doors just like this, and all of them are closed.

A breeding program. She's running a breeding program. And inside every one of those rooms are two people just like us.

The guards throw me forward with such force, I stumble and fall, my knees crashing into the hard, steel floors as pain shoots through my body.

The boy enters too, of his own accord, and then the door is slammed shut and locked.

I get to my feet and back up against the far wall. "Stay away from me," I growl. "Stay the fuck away from me, or I swear to the sun, I will snap your neck and never think twice about you again."

"Delphi—"

"Stop saying my name!" I yell. "You don't fucking know me! You don't know anything about me. And I am not your one, I do not love you, and I sure as fuck won't be breeding with you!"

"I don't love you either!" he screams. He's very young. Younger than me, probably. But Akeelian boys at my age and Cygnian girls at my age are two very different things when it comes to maturity.

He is practically a child. "Have you even gone through maturity yet?"

"Fuck you!" he says "Fuck you! I didn't want to be here either! I'm not doing this for you, you dumbass! They have my sister!"

I deflate a little, then sigh. "They have my brother."

"I know," he says. "I know this is all fucked up, but what am I supposed to do? Huh? I didn't come magically equipped with some exoskeleton that can take out hordes of cyborgs. We were kidnapped, OK? Right out of our home back in Cygnian System!"

"Cygnian System?"

"They have a breeding program there too."

What the fuck? "Who is your father?"

"The goddamned chancellor of Industry! He let them do this, Delphi! I swear to the fucking sun, I don't have a choice!"

"We're not having sex," I say.

284

"Fine. That's fine with me. But…" He looks down at his groin area where it's very clear that there's more at work here than just our minds. "But they are expecting me to do things now, Delphi. And my sister will be punished if I don't comply."

"Is your sister here?" I ask.

He shakes his head. "No. They took her. They took all the second-stage twins to some other place almost two months ago."

"Tycho," I whisper.

"He went too," the boy says. "Tycho, some kid named Draden, and my sister, Araeya. If I do this with you they'll let me go with her."

"They? You mean Veila?"

He shakes his head. "She's not even in charge here. She's just the figurehead. Your father put you here, Delphi. Just like mine did. They're the ones in charge of this breeding program."

"No," I say. "No, that's not true. He loved us, he—"

"My father loved me too. Or so I thought. They came and took us out of our beds. I was always expecting it. I knew it was weird to be allowed to grow up at home. I should've been turned over to the slavers when I was a toddler. I always knew it was a trap."

I know he's not lying. I know it because I can feel him. I can feel him the way I wanted to feel Jimmy. He is part of me, it's all true. He is my one.

"We have to get out of here. We have to get out of here now."

"There's no way out," he says. "I'm sorry. There's just no way to get past all the guards and even if we could, then what? Where can we run to? We're in the

285

middle of nowhere. We can't steal a ship. Boys tried that last year and they almost got away."

"What happened to them?"

"They blew them up before they could reach the gate. She would rather kill us than let us escape and possibly find our way to Harem Station."

I sigh as my back slides down the wall and I slump to the floor. "We have to think of something." And I know I could, but being so close to him is so damn distracting. My body is doing weird things. And I'm flickering. My light is aching to get out. And... I'm so embarrassed, but I want him near me. He's only about three meters away, but it's too far. There's this undeniable tug on my heart, urging me to go to him. Wanting his arms around me.

I close my eyes and chant, "I do not love you, I do not love you, I do not love you." Then I open them again and say, "I love Jimmy."

He nods. "I know. I can feel that inside you right now. I know you don't love me and I don't love you either. I love Caeli."

"Who's Caeli?" I ask.

"My best friend from back home. But I'm never gonna see her again. She was... she was my girlfriend. Or she would've been when I finished my year of rage. We made promises to each other. I miss her so much."

I can feel that inside him too. So much sadness overwhelms me, I don't know what to do with it. So of course, it makes me throb. I'm so humiliated. So mortified and ashamed at this reaction.

"You can't help it," he says. "I can't help it either."

His hand goes to the outline of his two cocks in his pants and he grips them tight, wincing. Like he's in pain.

I close my eyes so I can't see this. Refusing to be a witness to this sick, sad perversion they bred into us.

"It's always like this," he says. "Every night and every morning my head is so filled with lust and thoughts of sex, I can't think straight. And you're doing the same thing to me now. It hurts, Delphi. I just want it to go away. I can't think. I can't be rational because everything about this is irrational, and stupid, and wrong."

I picture my life if I don't find a way out of this. I picture what I will become. How they will use me, and control me just by bringing this boy into the room or taking him away. Because I can already feel the attraction and the fear. The fear of never seeing him again.

"How do you live like this?" I ask. "Because I don't think I can do it."

He looks at me with hooded eyes and says, "I jerk off."

Then he waits for me to laugh, or be disgusted, or make fun of him.

But I don't.

Because that makes so much sense.

"The release," I say. "If we could just find the release maybe we could come up with a plan?"

"What?"

"Masturbate, you dumbass," I say, the words coming out meaner than I intended. "We get off, and then we can think straight for a little bit and come up with a plan."

His hand slips inside his pants and he starts rubbing his cocks.

"Don't look at me," I say. "Don't think about me, either. Because I'm not yours, no matter what our DNA says. I'm not yours, you hear me?"

He closes his eyes, but it's not enough. "Turn around and face the wall. Think about that other girl."

"Caeli," he moans, turning his body to face the wall. He leans his head against it, his hand frantically working on jerking himself. "Caeli," he says again.

"Yeah, her," I say. And just watching him do this has me throbbing.

But I push it all away and only think about Jimmy. Just Jimmy. I think about how we had sex. And how he kissed me. And our perfect date in the Mighty Minions forest.

I think about how his cocks filled me up and how we were spinning around, making new stars.

I come. It's not spectacular and it's not even fun. But I come and a few seconds later, so does the boy.

I feel so disgusting. So gross I just want to take a shower. I can't even look at him. I just want to get out of this room, go find Jimmy, and get out of this filthy place as fast as I can.

This experience will probably scar me for the rest of my life but the alternative is worse.

The alternative is being stuck here with this boy and being separated from Jimmy forever.

I want to cry and scream and kill something right now. I hate people. I hate them so much. Why do they think they get to decide my fate? Why do they think they get to decide anyone's fate but their own? It's not fair and it sucks.

"Are you OK?" the boy asks.

"Don't talk to me."

He doesn't say another word and after a few minutes, we get ourselves together and stand up.

Even though I still feel dirty, I also feel better. I feel more in control. I feel strong and able to think straight.

I hate myself for this. I hate what I am. I hate that I've been genetically engineered for sex.

He says, "My name is—"

"Shut up," I say. "Just shut up. I don't give two flying fucks what your name is, OK? Just… stand there and be quiet while I think of a way out of this mess!"

CHAPTER THIRTY-FIVE

Veila slaps me and several cyborg guards come rushing over and pull me away from her.

Bitch. She is such a fucking bitch.

Veila brings a single fingertip up to the spit on her cheek and wipes it away. One of the borgs hands her a handkerchief. She wipes her fingertip on it and hands it back.

"You won't get far with that attitude, Jimmy."

"Fuck you," I say. "You are the most disgusting creature I've ever met, you know that?"

"Oh, please," she says, walking back over to her drink to take a sip. "You live with millions of disgusting creatures so you don't get to play the self-righteous martyr with me."

"I take it you've never been there, then?"

"As if I'd lower myself."

"As if we'd ever let you board," I say, shrugging off the two guards holding me.

She sucks in a deep breath through her nose, sets her glass down, and pretends to smooth out a wrinkle in her gown. "You can't fight this. And Delphi can't fight her fate either."

"Watch us."

"As long as I'm in the room I'll be the only thing you'll see."

"Let's test that out. Bring Delphi back here."

Veila laughs. "No, I don't think so. I was willing to accommodate you if you just went along with the program, but after that little display I've changed my mind. You're never going to see her again. She and the boy will be shipped out in a few spins and taken to the other facility. There she will become pregnant and give birth to her first set of twins. Then we'll breed her again, and again, and again until she is an old woman."

Rage. I feel nothing but rage.

She sits down at the table and leans back in her chair. "Too bad. Things could've gone a lot different."

"As long as I did everything you told me too, right?"

"Exactly. It's not like it's torture. You have needs, Jimmy. Daily needs. Why not let me help with those needs?"

"Um… probably because you disgust me. And my hand can do a better job."

She closes her eyes for a prolonged moment, then opens them again. "OK. I see you're not going to assimilate unless I convince you. So let me convince you."

"I won't change my mind, believe me."

"Hear me out for a moment, hmm?"

I stare at her, wondering where this bitch gets her balls. Then I see something moving over in a flower arrangement in the corner of the room.

Flicka! I totally forgot about her!

There's a moment of elation. A single moment of me thinking this has got to be some kind of divine intervention. That maybe we have a chance.

Clearly Veila has no idea that I brought Delphi's bot onto the ship. So yeah, I'm stuck and Delphi's stuck, but one of us is free.

But then I wonder... what could one single dragonbee bot really do when there's at least a dozen guards in here and so many more outside this door?

And the elation fades as quick as it appeared.

Nothing. The answer to that question is nothing.

"Should I take your silence as a yes?"

I look at Veila again, not wanting to give Flicka away. She can get off this station. Slip into the next ship going out. No reason why all three of us have to get stuck in this nightmare. Or if Veila really is going to send Delphi away, go with her at least. Maybe even go for help.

"You won't be able to convince me," I say, answering her question.

"Humor me."

I say nothing. Because there is truly nothing to say.

"And please, have a seat while we talk."

Flicka does a little loop-de-loop in the air near the flowers, and for some reason I get the feeling she wants me to do as Veila asks.

Maybe she does have a plan?

I walk over to the table and sit in the chair opposite Veila. While I do this I see Flicka dart over to the drink decanter and land on the lip. Then she plops down into the amber liquid.

I avert my eyes back to Veila and say, "You killed my ship," because Flicka is definitely up to something and I don't want to give her away.

Veila shrugs. "She was attacking us. And obviously it was your ship who brought Delphi here. You can't blame me for protecting myself."

It hurts to think of *Dicker* being gone. I just can't believe it, that after all these years—after that grand gesture from ALCOR to save us so we could tug her back to Harem and fix her up—that she goes out like this. Just shimmering away into nothingness.

"Forget your ship for a moment. If she means that much to you we can have a memorial ceremony in a few days. If you're good."

My hands begin to shake from the urge to wrap my fingers around Veila's neck and choke the life right out of her.

"No, thanks," I say. "That would insult me and my relationship with her."

"Whatever," Veila says, waving a hand in front of her face. "I can't let you go and I can't let Delphi go, but I can give you something else."

"Like what?" I growl.

"Your brother, of course. Did you forget that he's still alive?"

"He's not. You're lying. Serpint saw him die. He was shot in the head. No one survives something like that."

"Serpint saw him get *hit*," Veila says. "I was there when he stole Corla from me. I was there after he turned tail and ran home to his daddy. But I had heard rumors about your brother Draden. Rumors that ALCOR did something to him a long time ago. And I decided to have his body moved to the medical facility and put into a cryopod."

"ALCOR did *what* to him?" I ask. Because if there's a chance that Draden is still alive—somehow, some way—I need to know more.

"It's a procedure for teenagers. Sometimes adults have it done too. Akeelians, for instance. Because your kind ages so differently than Cygnians. I have personally seen an Akeelian male have the procedure as late as forty-six. He wasn't completely sane when it was over and eventually we did have to put him down. But it worked. For a while."

Put him down, she says. Like he was some kind of diseased, wild animal. "Why are you telling me this?"

"After we're done breeding—and it won't be long, Jimmy. I am older than most of the females we're using in the program. So after I have my first set of true-bred twins we can just… farm you for your genetics. I won't allow anyone else to have you because you're mine, but I have no adverse feelings about letting you be in the collection stable."

"The *collection* stable?" I want to throw up.

"We can't waste all that excess semen inside you, can we?"

"What is your fucking point?" I ask. Because this conversation is just gross.

"Right," she says, smiling. "Back to the point. Draden isn't like you anymore. He can't breed. He might be useful in other ways if we could get him to cooperate, but so far he's been a violent little prick. Almost not worth the hassle. So if you find it in yourself to do as I ask, I could be persuaded to let him

295

go. Let him return to Harem Station, perhaps. Live somewhat of a normal life."

I just stare at her. Then notice out of the corner of my eye that Flicka has climbed back out of the drink decanter and is flying to a nearby vent.

I don't think one drop of dragonbee bot venom can do much, but hell. It's worth a try. The little shit did go through all the trouble of sneaking over there. So I reach out and grab Veila's drink glass. Several of the cyborgs rush towards us at my quick movement, but Veila holds up a hand and they stop in place like good little drones.

I bring the glass up to my lips, pretend to take a sip, then put it down and smile at Veila. "You did offer me a drink, right?"

She smiles back. No teeth. Tight lips.

"Why don't you grab yourself another one? So I don't have to drink alone." I don't know what Flicka is up to, but whatever it is, it's more than I have going at the moment. And she's the only person in this room on my side.

"So now you're suddenly amicable and in the mood to listen?" she says.

I shrug. Then frown. Then say—through gritted teeth just to maintain my antagonistic nature and not tip her off that something is up—"What choice do I have?"

She stares at me, still suspicious, then leans back in her chair and waves a hand at the nearest cyborg. "Get me a drink."

"You don't have a lot of bedside manner, do you, Veila?"

"Meaning what?"

"You know. You catch more bees with honey and shit like that?"

She squints her eyes at me, then relaxes. "Interesting proverb."

"Something my mom used to say."

"Well, you got it wrong. It's flies, not bees. Not surprising since you named your ship *Big Dicker* and you got that wrong too. But I feel like this is a good place to start our switch to cordial conversation."

"My ship?" I say. And this time when I grit my teeth, it's not for show.

"No, your mother."

"Right," I say, leaning back in my chair. "*Queenie* was her ship and you were... what? Her best friend?"

"No," Veila says. "But I did know her. I could tell you about her, if you'd like."

I would like that. Very much. But whatever I learn about my mother, I don't want it to come from Veila. So I say, "No, thanks. I'll pass."

"She grew up on Earth," Veila says, taking the drink the cyborg is holding out to her. "But you already knew that. Do you know where Earth is?"

"No," I say, staring at her glass as she raises it to her lips. Willing her to take a sip so we can get this show on the road.

Veila sets her glass back down without taking a sip. "No one does."

I meet Veila's gaze and hold it.

"Do you know why?"

"Obviously I don't, Veila. I'm not really interested in my mother right now. I'm more concerned with your plans for Delphi and me. We're people, not animals. You don't breed *people*."

"You do when a race is going extinct."

I laugh. "There's billions of Akeelians and even more Cygnians. So… not gonna fly"

"Billions of half-breed Cygnians, you mean. There's very few pure pink and silver Cygnian princesses. We are the pure ones, Jimmy. It's our duty to reproduce with you and bring our true races together again."

"You know, from my experience, species of animals, and probably races of people, die out for a reason."

"What reasons?"

I shrug. "Bad evolutionary reproductive strategies. Bad luck. Or maybe they're just too dangerous to be left alone and someone decides they've had enough."

"Is that why you think our bloodlines were eradicated?"

"I have no clue."

"You should. Your AI did it."

"If you're trying to shock me with this information, you can stop now. I already know what ALCOR did."

"And you approve?"

"I don't have all the facts, so I just don't have an opinion."

"Do you want all the facts?"

"Not if you're just going to use them to justify what's happening here."

"Hmm," she murmurs.

Just take a fucking sip of that drink already.

Even though I don't want to, I take a sip of mine to try to get things rolling. She watches me carefully. Then raises her glass to her lips and takes a sip as well.

Thank the fucking sun.

She sets the glass down, folds her hands on the table, and leans forward. "Here is my offer. You help me have children and I'll not only give you access to your brother, I'll tell you everything I know about Earth."

"First of all," I say, holding up one finger. "*Access* to my brother? Fuck you. And second of all"—I hold up another finger—"you just admitted you don't know where Earth is, so I give no fucks at all about your opinion of the place."

"OK," she says. She takes a deep, deep breath and I notice that a sweat has broken out on her forehead. "You'd like to renegotiate. I'll play along. I will let you take your brother home after we find his one true mate and he gets her pregnant. And I'll throw in Tycho as well."

I stare at her, looking for signs of dragonbee bot poisoning. She is sweating profusely now. And her breathing has picked up.

"Not good enough?" she says, starting to cough. "Fine. I'll give you one more secret to sweeten the pot." Her hand goes to her throat as she struggles to inhale, but not let it show.

"What secret?" I whisper, leaning even farther forward. Just waiting for her to drop dead, or fall over, or whatever the fuck is going to happen next.

"You have a twin, Jimmy. I bet ALCOR didn't tell you this, did he? Your mother was a silver. Silver Cygnians are pure and our Cygnian princesses can only have twins. Your twin has been with me for a very long time." Veila coughs again. And now it's very clear that something is wrong, because she's swaying in her chair and several cyborgs rush over to hold her up.

"What?" I say. Trying to process this new information. Because how fucking stupid am I? Of course I have a twin. I knew this, right? It was part of that puzzle I was in the process of putting together, but didn't quite make it.

We all have twins. Me, Serpint, Crux, Tray, Luck, Valor, and Draden. Because we are the ones with violet eyes. Our mothers were pure, silver, Cygnian princesses.

Veila brushes the cyborgs off, still trying to maintain control. "She's given me lots of genetic stock to work with—" But she lapses into a fit of coughing and then stands up, staring down at her drink. "What did you do?"

I don't even know what happens next. Several things at the same time. A bunch of cyborgs grab me by the arms and pull me away from the table, Veila collapses onto the floor in a heap, alarms start going off, and then, from the little vent where Flicka disappeared, she reappears and starts flying her little loop-de-loops across the room, little bursts of pink steam, or smoke, or whatever puffing out of her ass.

It's a tiny amount. A teeny-tiny amount. Not more than one atomized drop every few seconds. But the cyborgs all start locking up. Like... in mid-movement. The ones holding me lose their grip as their fingers extend into rigidity. Those that are rushing around suddenly fall to the floor, their legs stiff and unable to bend.

I stumble backwards and trip over a borg body, then get back up and spin around, unable to believe what's happening.

Flicka lands on my shoulder and starts buzzing wildly. I don't understand a word she's saying, but I don't really need to. What we need to do next is pretty clear.

I grab several plasma rifles as I run across the room, throwing them over my shoulder and pointing the last one at the door just as it begins to open.

Then I start firing just as Flicka buzzes forward, puffing out pink smoke as she leads the way.

And even though I'm in full battle mode and my main focus is getting to Delphi and saving our asses, I can't help but think about the girl who is my sister.

What have these monsters been doing to her all these years?

CHAPTER THIRTY-SIX

DELPHI

I feel a little bad for being mean to this boy.

But only a little.

I can't have him in my life. I can't. He needs to go. And yeah, that's probably super selfish of me, but what the fuck? My body is *mine*. My heart is *mine*. And no one should be able to control those two things without my explicit permission.

Still—I glance over my shoulder and find him slumped against the wall looking down at the floor— it's not his fault we've been manipulated this way.

I open my mouth to say something. Maybe even apologize and just tell him it's OK. We'll figure something out. But the moment I do the station alarms start blaring.

Loud alarms that come with flashing red lights.

"Something's happening," I say instead.

He says nothing.

"Come on, get up! Help me!"

He raises his chin and looks at me. "Help you do what? We're locked in."

"I don't know! Just... something more than just sitting here waiting for other people to decide our fates!"

"Well, unless you can magically enter the security code in the electronic lock on the *outside* of that door, there's not much to be done."

And just as he finishes saying that, we hear beeping. Like someone is pushing the keypad on the lock.

"Get ready!" I hiss.

"For what?" he scoffs.

"To attack, you weak-minded coward. If you want to stay here and be breeding stock for psychopaths, be my guest. But I'm going out fighting like a badass!"

I back up against the wall next to the door and the moment it slides open I whirl around and jump on the bastard cyborg, wrap my legs around his middle and then scream, "You motherfuckers!" as I pound on his face with my fists.

Except... it's not a cyborg. "Jimmy!" I yell, just as my fist finishes a punch to the eye.

He hugs me tight with one arm while the other one covers his rapidly swelling eye. "Remind me not to get on your bad side in the future."

"Future?" I say. "If we don't get off this station we'll have no future!"

I'm still hugging him with my legs, my arms wrapped tightly around his neck. He hugs me back and inhales a deep, deep breath, then whispers, "I promise you, there will be a future."

I pull back a little and look him in the eyes. "You still want me? Even though I'm not yours?"

He glances down at the boy and so do I. He's still on the floor but he meets Jimmy's gaze. Jimmy says, "She's mine. You got that, kid? *Mine.*"

I sigh, then place both my hands on Jimmy's cheeks and turn his head so he has to look at me. "You're mine too. I don't care what those genetic tests say. We get to choose who we love. Us. Not them."

"Couldn't agree more, princess." And then he kisses me. Hard and deep. But also soft and tender. It's the perfect kiss and I want it to go on forever, but Flicka is suddenly buzzing in my ear.

"Oh, shit!"

"What?" Jimmy asks. "She's been buzzing like a maniac for the last few minutes but I can't understand her."

"She says she's out of venom, so she can't help us get out of here."

"Don't you worry, little beebot," Jimmy says. "I got this now. Grab all the rifles, Delphi. And get ready. We're gonna have to shoot our way out and then…" He sighs. "I don't know. *Dicker* is dead. I don't know how we'll get out of here."

"Dead? No!"

"She is. I saw her disappear when the station fired back. She just… shimmered away into nothingness."

"No!" I say. "No, that's her new cloaking bullshit. It had some weird reverse setting that could cloak you backwards half a million klicks after your thirty-seven seconds were up."

"What?" Jimmy says.

"She's still alive."

"We need to find a control room, now!" Jimmy says. "And give her permission to dock."

"What about him?" I ask, pointing to the boy.

"I give no fucks about him."

"I know, but Jimmy—" I feel sad all of a sudden. "Get up, you stupid boy! You're coming too."

"No way!" Jimmy says. "He's gonna get us killed."

"I know where a control room is," the boy says, getting to his feet. "And I can get you there fast if you take me with you."

Jimmy looks at him. Then me.

I say, "Let him come with us. It's not his fault."

CHAPTER THIRTY-SEVEN

There is a rage inside me that wants to burst out in the form of a swift kick to the head when I look at this boy. I want to tear his throat out. I want to rip his limbs off. It's irrational, and sick, and scares me a little. Because even though I've always been capable of such things, I have never felt an urge to kill someone quite like I do this kid.

"Please," Delphi says. "He can point and shoot a rifle, at least."

I glance at the door Flicka and I came through. There's plasma fire on the other side. And lots of angry cyborgs.

I fucked up the electronic lock to keep the borgs following us at bay. Hoping there was another way out of this sector when I did that. And there probably is another way out, I just have no clue where it is.

This boy does. And Delphi's right. He can point and shoot a rifle.

"Fine," I say, talking to the boy. "But if you touch her—"

307

"He won't," Delphi says, before I can get my threat out. "Let's go, boy."

For some reason it makes me feel better that Delphi doesn't know his name. He glances nervously at me when he pushes his way through the door. I hand both of them a rifle from the stash on my shoulder and say, "Lead on," to the boy.

He spares a single glance at the door that is about to be breached by an angry mob of Loathsome Borgs, then turns in the other direction and jogs down the hallway.

"We have to get everyone out of this sector first," he calls, stopping at a control room.

"Is there docking bay access in here?" I say.

"No, but—"

"Then we don't have time."

"But my *friends*," the boy says.

This makes me hesitate. Because what if my sister is on the other side of one of these doors?

But the door on the opposite end of the hall begins to crumple inward, a clear sign that the borgs are about to get through. And I can't risk Delphi over a sister I just found out about. So I repeat myself. "We don't. Have time." But now it's a growl laced with a threat. "And you said you'd get *us* out, not *them*."

He looks at Delphi, silently pleading. But Delphi takes my side. "We can't. We'll all die if we don't go now."

The boy takes one last glance at the closed doors in this hallway, then gives in and takes off running. There's no borgs on the other side of the next door we approach and open. Yet. But I'm sure they're on their way.

We don't stop, just start zigzagging our way through a maze of endless corridors. Every time borgs appear in our path, Delphi and I take them out.

The boy doesn't even aim his rifle and I'm starting to wonder if he's gonna lead us into a trap.

Like... where do this kid's loyalties lie? Does he really want to leave? Or does he think if we get caught, he'll get Delphi?

I don't know. But there's not much I can do about that if I want any chance of giving *Dicker* docking permission. If she's not dead, then she's out there. Waiting for us to give her access.

"Shit," Delphi says. Just as the boy leads us into what appears to be a control room.

"What?" I ask, then take out the two borgs manning the control station.

The boy stands there watching with his mouth open as plasma fire burns through their heads and the force of the beam hurls them backwards against the wall.

He swallows hard, then looks at me. "This room has access to everything. All the slaves are in this sector too, and we *can* free them while you work on getting your ship here."

Maybe the little fucker does have balls.

I rush over to the main console and take a seat, my fingers flying over the keyboard. "What were you saying?" I ask Delphi while I type out access commands.

"Flicka says that the poison she used will be wearing off by now."

"Great." I sigh. "Just what we need. More hordes of Loathsome Borgs."

309

The boy is fucking with another control panel, making better progress than I am. Because he says, "Yes," then leaps up out of his chair just as doors start clicking open out in the hallway.

Dozens and dozens of Akeelian boys appear. All about the same age. Maybe twelve or thirteen, at most. And again I get that sick, sick feeling in my gut when I picture my twin in a place like this.

Our boy starts telling them the details. Then he grabs the two rifles from our blown-up friends and hands them to the oldest ones for backup.

"Where are the girls?" Delphi asks, taking the extra rifles from my shoulder as I continue typing.

"They don't keep them here," our boy says. "This is the semen farm."

"Gross," I mutter.

"Where do they keep them?" Delphi asks.

"I don't know. Some other station like this, I guess."

"Do you know where my brother is?"

"Not here," the boy says. "Probably with the girls. He's… the right age."

"Got it!" I say, after ending my last command. "Docking bays are unlocked!"

"Then let's go!" some random boy shouts at me.

I glare at him over my shoulder and say. "You can go wherever you want, but I'm waiting to see my fucking ship appear."

She doesn't appear.

CHAPTER THIRTY-EIGHT

"She's not dead," I say. Because I can tell that Jimmy is starting to lose faith. "She can't stay on this side of the gate for more than thirty-seven seconds, remember?"

"So she has no idea what's happening? Or when to even try to come back?"

"I don't know," I say. "I was so worried about my part in the plan, I didn't get filled in on hers."

"Well, that's fucking perfect," one of the random boys says. "We all just escaped our cells and now there's no way off this fucking station?"

"Hey, you," I say, pointing at the kid. "Stop being an asshole. You're lucky your friend here got you out in the first place. So just shut up and let the grown-ups work things out."

He's got one of the rifles and he's older than the rest. Almost as old as me, probably. Maybe seventeen. No wonder he's being an asshole. He's about the right age too, isn't he? Gonna be a daddy soon.

Just like Tycho.

I shudder at the thought.

"Come on, come on, *come on*," Jimmy says. He's propped both his hands on the monitor and he's staring down at it with intense concentration.

"There's borgs coming!" some random boy screams.

I grab Jimmy's rifle, toss it to another random, then say, "OK, boys. Time to fight like girls. Everyone with a rifle, blast that shit until you're empty. Everyone without a rifle, grab something heavy or be prepared to pull hair."

"What?" one kid asks. "They don't have hair."

"It's a figure of speech, kid. Just... hit them with whatever you got, for fuck's sake!"

Just as I finish speaking three things happen at the same time.

Jimmy says, "There!"

The borgs burst through into the hallway.

And shit hits the fan because almost a dozen untrained kids start firing plasma rifles and two dozen more leap out into the fray to attack.

I wish I could say that goes well. But it doesn't. Half the kids who rushed the borgs get hit by friendly and unfriendly fire, most of the kids with rifles do nothing more than hit the lights, so now this whole area is dark and the only thing I can see are crackling streams of firefight.

Then Jimmy takes a hit to his shoulder.

"Retreat!" I scream, rushing over to Jimmy. He didn't even fall down, just backed himself into the control console. "Come on!" I say, wrapping my arm around his waist. "We have to make it to the docking bays! We have to!"

"Lead the way, princess," he says.

But I don't know the way.

My eyes meet the boy's and he nods. Then he yells, "Everyone follow me!"

I don't know how we make it through the next hallway, because there are borgs streaming in from open doorways in every direction. But somehow, some way, these kids with the rifles get their shit together and actually pick off a few. I hand my rifle off to someone else because I can't fire while I'm holding on to Jimmy.

The boy who takes it is a little kid. Maybe nine. Maybe ten.

But in Akeelian years, he's more like a four- or five-year-old in maturity.

He looks at me with wide eyes as we run.

I say, "Just hold it for me, OK?" And he swallows hard and nods his head.

I want to get him out of here. I want to save him. Hell, I want to save them all. But half of them are already dead and almost all the others are wounded and falling fast.

What a complete fuck-up of a rescue.

I look over my shoulder and watch as the asshole kid stops when one of his friends falls. He screams something incoherent at the approaching borgs, firing his plasma rifle with precision. Then he grabs his friend and starts dragging him along the hallway.

"Leave him!" I scream.

He doesn't hear me. Or maybe he ignores me. Because he stops in the hallway and stands over the body of his clearly dead friend, shrieking as he fires a stream of plasma in a sweeping arc.

We round a corner and he disappears from sight, but the barrage of destruction that comes after tells me all I need to know about the fate of asshole boy.

We stop at a door. My boy opens it, then we all rush through into the inner docking bay.

Dicker is landing.

And then things go from almost good, to very bad, to worst-case scenario in the span of two seconds.

Dicker is landing, but she's three docking bays to my left, which is not close enough to us to make this easy. Borgs come up from behind us and then, on the other side of the airlock windows, I see more borgs streaming in from every docking bay entrance there is. Rushing towards *Dicker* and taking position between her and us like they're a fucking wall.

And that's when I realize... I made a big fucking mistake back in that control room.

I didn't stick around to lock the docking bay back up. And now it's in total vacuum and none of us have suits.

We can't even go out there.

I look at Delphi and feel heartsick. She's holding the hand of a very small, very young Akeelian boy who's holding a rifle to his chest, and he reminds me so much of Serpint and Draden when they were young, I have to turn my head away.

But then the little kid is rushing forward towards the fight, shooting a too-big plasma rifle as he screams, "Fuck you! Fuck you! *Fuck you!*"

Delphi's boy reaches out as he passes him, grabs him by the scruff of his shirt, and the little one is yanked off his feet, rifle skittering away across the polished metal floor.

But he's still screaming. He's kicking Delphi's boy, and scratching at his face. "I hate them!" he yells. "I fucking hate them!"

This is what that bitch did to these kids. This one right here is all you need to see to understand the damage she's been doing.

I want to go back in there and kill her myself. I want to pick her up by her silver fucking hair and squeeze her neck until her eyes pop out.

But there's no chance of that happening now.

We're done.

We made it all this way. *Dicker* is literally just two hundred meters to my left, and we're done.

We're all going to die here today.

Just as I turn to Delphi to tell her I'm sorry, there's another barrage of plasma fire at the end of the hallway we just ran through.

But it's weird. Because the plasma fire is taking out *borgs*.

And then, like the sun-fucked, golden light of luck he is, my brother Luck appears with Cha-Cha and the asshole boy. And every single borg between us and them goes down in a matter of seconds.

"Cease fire! Cease fire!" I yell at our few remaining boys. They are so stunned to see the splendor of a fully enraged, shirtless Akeelian male and a souped-up sexbot come to their rescue, they actually listen.

Another barrage of fire comes from behind us, and this time when Delphi and I turn around we see Xyla and her friend Ladybug. Full fucking exoskeleton suits on, coming out of *Dicker* and charging at that wall of cyborgs in the docking bay like this is the goddamned sexbot apocalypse.

I look back at Luck and smile. *You sneaky little motherfucker.* I could hug him right now.

"So," Luck says, hugging his rifle to his bare chest and letting out a sigh. There's still a shit ton of fire happening out there in the docking bay and his side has a black scorch mark across it like he took a hit, but Luck acts like this is no big deal. He's all good and he's sent the girls in to clean up the riff-raff. "You uh… need a hand here, Jims?"

Jims. I want to kiss him for that.

"Dude," I say. "You have no idea how happy I am to see you. How did you find us?"

He says, "Please. You can't hide from *Lady Luck*. And we're not out of the woods yet." He places two fingers up to his lips and shrieks out a whistle so high-pitched, every kid immediately shuts up. "Listen up, you little brats. You, you, you, you, and you, come with me. The rest of you, go with Jimmy and"—he points to Delphi—"whoever that beautiful little thing is. Got it?"

Everyone, including me, just stares at him.

"I *said*," he growls, "got it?"

Every single boy—and Delphi—says, "Yes, sir."

"Good. We'll give those girls a few more minutes to wrap up that shit show outside and Jimmy can start pressurizing the docking bays."

He looks at me like… *Well, go fucking do that.*

I just shake my head and laugh. Then reluctantly let go of Delphi and go over to the nearest console and take a seat.

My shoulder is killing me, and when Luck comes up behind me and slaps a hand over the still-smoking, cauterized hole in my flesh on purpose, I want to punch him in the face. But I don't. Because I'm tough like that. And he did just save my ass.

Luck leans down into my ear and whispers, "So listen. I didn't want to alarm the kids or anything, but you should know that on the other side of the station, there are three Cygnian warships spinning up."

"Fuck you," I say.

"Not kidding. Wish I were. *Dicker* has some serious power behind her and so does *Lady Luck*, but honestly, brother. It's not looking good."

"What should we do?"

"Take our chances, man. That's all we can do. Get these kids on board, take off and hope for the best."

CHAPTER FORTY

It takes a while for Xyla and her friend to kill every last cyborg on the docking bay deck, but eventually they get the job done, Jimmy gets *Dicker's* bay and the two bays in between us and her pressurized with an atmosphere, and then Luck starts barking orders at the boys like he's now the proud general of a pack of kid soldiers.

"You, you, you," he yells, pointing at three of the tallest boys, including my boy and asshole boy. "Grab a fucking rifle and make sure no stray borgs appear to fuck up my escape plan."

They, of course, "Yes, sir!" him and get all serious as Luck points to the others and says, "Go, go, go, go…"

Jimmy ushers the younger ones, including the little one, into the airlock and then out into the docking bay.

Cha-Cha is walking next to me, scanning the bay with her rifle. She's kinda making me nervous and she's not even wearing an exoskeleton.

"So," she says. "You and Jimmy, huh."

I slide my eyes to the side without moving my head, trying to gauge what she thinks about this.

"Don't worry about me," she says, slapping me on the shoulder. "It's Xyla's test you have to pass."

I don't know what that means, but there's really no time to think about shit like that. We still have to get off this station and make it back through the gate. And even though Luck didn't tell me that there are three Cygnian warships preparing to launch on the other side of the station, he didn't have to. Flicka heard everything and buzzed right over to fill me in.

Lady Luck, Luck's ship, is docked right behind *Dicker*. She's smaller than Jimmy's ship, but not by much. She's also yellow. Bright yellow. And for some reason that fits what I've seen of this brother so far.

Luck is tall, muscular, and has a head of shaggy blond hair. His boots make an ungodly amount of noise as he paces his line of boys. Like they're made of metal. And he's dressed up in brown tactical pants and shirtless, so you can see all the scars and tattoos on his chest. Like this is the brother who doesn't ever walk away from a fight. I don't think he's shirtless on purpose, because there's burn marks on the side of his torso. Like maybe he caught on fire and that's why he had to take the shirt off.

Cha-Cha catches me staring at him just as I reach *Dicker* and says, "They feel pain differently than most people."

"What?" I say, forcing my eyes to look away from Luck and up at her.

"That's why he's so good at this shit." Then she winks at me and walks off towards their ship.

"OK," Jimmy says, once our half of the boys are entering *Dicker's* hull. "You ready for this?"

I take a deep breath and let it out. Flicka buzzes by my ear, letting me know she's top-notch. I don't really know what I should be ready for, but there's no way out but forward. If those Cygnian warships fire on us, it's pretty much over.

But reminding Jimmy of that serves no purpose. So I just nod my head and say, "Let's go."

Inside the ship Jimmy points me to an envirosuit, then starts putting his on.

The boys all look around for their suits, but it's clear. We don't have enough. Jimmy and Xyla travel alone. The fact that he has an extra suit for me is just dumb luck.

"What about us?" Asshole Boy says.

Jimmy just glares at him. Then growls.

The asshole backs off and stumbles into Ladybug, who says, "If those ships fire on us, these suits won't matter. Now sit your ass down and shut up. Then think about how lucky you are to be rescued by Harem Station."

This mostly has the desired effect. They do sit down, but then immediately start whispering things like, "Harem Station," and "ALCOR," and little one even says, "Fuck, yeah."

He's gonna be a handful.

If we survive.

And then things start happening too fast. *Dicker's* door begins to close, Ladybug stabs at a screen and the airlock slams closed, and the second that happens, *Dicker's* engines spin up and we rise, turning to see *Lady Luck* hovering in front of us.

She fires on the side of the station and two seconds later there's a massive breach in the docking bay.

"Hold on!" Xyla yells back from the cockpit.

Ladybug pushes me to the wall, I grab a handhold, and she grabs me, holding on to another handhold.

It occurs to me that I should probably be sitting down and strapped in for this, but there's nowhere to sit with all these kids.

And then there's no time to think. We follow *Lady Luck* out the hole in the station and enter the deep dark of space.

I'm thrown back into the wall, lose my grip, and start to tumble backward, when Ladybug's strong sexbot hand reaches out and grabs my arm. Holding me in place.

Jimmy and Xyla are talking to Luck and Cha-Cha on the comms. Something about cannons coming online and target locks having found us already.

We've been outside the station for less than ten seconds and we're already fucked.

I look at Ladybug and she just shrugs. Like this is just another day in her life. Flicka is clinging to my shoulder, buzzing like crazy as *Dicker* maneuvers us around until—

"Holy mother of fuck," I whisper.

Because I can see the screen in the cockpit and a Cygnian warship is so close to us, it fills up the entire area.

There's a second one too. Just above.

"You take that one," Luck says through comms. "I got this one."

"Firing!" Xyla says. And then there is a great burst beneath my feet and above my head as cannons fire on the warships.

"Get out of there!" Cha-Cha yells from the comms. "Just get out of there!"

I glance over at the boys and now every single one them is silent. Their eyes wide, their mouths open as understanding sinks in.

We are fucked.

Dicker's hull shudders—again, and again, and again.

"We're hit," Jimmy says.

"Us too," Luck says back, over comms. "Just keep going. If we can get to the gate—"

But his sentence is cut off.

"Comms are blown," Xyla says, just as she releases another barrage of defensive fire.

"Sorry, kids," Jimmy yells.

We don't have time to wonder what he's sorry for, because every single one of us is thrown to the floor with sudden acceleration. Including Ladybug.

We become a heap of bodes, sliding towards the rear of the ship, as Xyla yells, "Sending them everything we've got! SEAR cannon activated!" Just as we crash into consoles, and equipment, and one kid even disappears down a stairwell, screaming.

That's gonna hurt later.

If we survive.

"One down!" Jimmy yells. "One down."

I crane my neck, desperate to see the screen in the cockpit so I can see what that means.

It's a split screen now. One view in front of us, where the gate shimmers off in the distance. The other view behind us, where one warship is tipping sideways, a huge hole in the center of the hull.

But right behind it is the other one. On fire in spots from Luck's attack, but still very much intact.

And then, like a fucking ghost rising out of the left-behind ether of colorful gasses, a third Cygnian warship appears.

"Fuck!" everyone yells at the same time.

"I have one more shot with the SEAR," Xyla yells.

"Take it!" Jimmy yells back.

But we all know, one will not be enough. That third ship is still there and if this is all we've got, it's over.

After all this, it's gonna be over.

We're all gonna die.

"Firing!" Xyla yells.

But in that same instant, Jimmy yells, "We're hit!"

And it's very clear to anyone watching that screen that our last chance just went very wide and missed that second ship entirely.

"Shit!" Xyla yells.

But then I'm distracted by the front-facing view in the split-screen. Because off in the distance, the gate is lit up like a fucking sun. Shimmering as yet another warship appears.

"Another ship!" I yell. "There's another ship coming through the gate!"

Everyone sucks in a breath. Holding it, as the massive warship exits the gate and speeds towards us. Firing as they approach.

"This is it," I say.

The beam of light coming towards us is so wide I can't even comprehend the distance across it.

"SEAR cannon incoming!" Xyla yells.

And for some reason, I think... *So that's what SEAR fire looks like.*

But it doesn't hit us.

It goes right past us and takes out both Cygnian warships at the same time. The explosion is both beautiful and terrifying. Great clouds of gas and fire shoot out into space. Blue, and purple, and orange.

"What the fuck was that?" Jimmy yells.

"I have no clue," Xyla says. "But there's an incoming neutrino wave message."

"What?" Jimmy says.

"Playing it," Xyla says.

Then a deep, feminine voice blares through the internal comms. "This is the Mighty Minions warship *Demon Girl* to the *Big Dicker.* You are under arrest for failing to pay exit fees at Mighty Minions Station, for damages done to the Lava Mountain docking bay, and for the theft of the Palladium Rewards Bot, X007. Surrender, or we will take you by force."

I belt out a single, "Ha!"

Jimmy looks back at me from the other side of the ship. He says, "Do you believe this fucking shit? That place is gonna squeeze every last credit out of me before they're done."

The little one screams, "Mighty Boss to the rescue!"

"Another incoming message," *Dicker* announces. "This one's video. Should I play it?"

"Why the fuck not?" Jimmy says, annoyed. "That fucking ship is probably gonna tell me I've been conscripted into the Mighty Minions Ambassador army."

"It's not from Mighty Minions," *Dicker* says. "It's from the third Cygnian warship. Which conveniently disappeared through a cloaked gate once *Demon Girl* showed up."

"Huh," Jimmy says. "Let's hear it then."

I sit up, then get to my feet and walk forward toward the cockpit when Veila's face appears on the large screen.

She is a hot mess. Her silver hair is all tangled and sloppy. Scorch marks on her long silver and white gown. And there's a deep cut above her left eye.

She glows bright white light as she sneers into the camera, her lip curling into a snarl as she says, "You win this time. But I'll be back. For all of you. And you can both forget about ever seeing your siblings again. They are as good as dead now."

A few seconds pass as she glares at us from the screen, then it goes black.

"Fuck you!" the little one yells. "I'm gonna kill that bitch! I'm gonna kill her so dead!"

The boys behind me calm him down and I stand in the middle of the ship, halfway between Jimmy and the boys, and just… smile.

Because we're safe now. We might end up in a Mighty Minions prison, but compared to being used as breeding stock for Veila's insane genetics plot, I figure that place isn't so bad.

And besides. She won't kill Tycho.

She can't kill Tycho.

Because she needs him.

She needs all of us.

But you know what I need more than she needs us?

Revenge.

I'm just as good as her. I am just as powerful as her. I am a true-blood Cygnian princess and now I have the galaxy's most dangerous Akeelian males on my side.

So I send my aunt Veila a little mental message.

I'm coming for you, bitch.

We're all coming for you.

Right after we get out of the Mighty Minions prison.

CHAPTER FORTY-ONE

Demon Girl locks a tractor beam onto *Dicker* and we wait for them to shuttle over and board.

All the kids are accounted for. One fell down a stairwell when *Dicker* accelerated and broke his leg, but he's in our medical bay and he'll be fine once we get him back to Harem.

If we can get away from Mighty Minions. And that's starting to look more and more doubtful as the minutes tick off.

"That fucking place," I growl to Delphi. She's sitting in my lap in the cockpit. Xyla is shooting me weird looks about this, but I don't care. How many times in the past twenty-four hours did we almost get turned into sex slaves, or semen collectors, or hell, just die?

Too many to think about.

I can't let her out of my arms again. I don't care if she's not my *one*. She is the only one I want. And I'm gonna hold her tight for the rest of our lives.

"Don't worry about it," Xyla says. "We'll just pay the stupid fine and be done with them forever."

The stupid fine? ALCOR is going to shit himself when he sees this bill. Because they're charging us half a billion credits for fees, and damages, and penalties.

But then I realize... Baby ALCOR doesn't give a shit about our accounts. It's Old ALCOR who would throw a fit. And he's dead.

I know he was a bad dude. I get it. He's probably the whole reason all this shit is happening to us. But fuck it. I miss that asshole. I miss him pretty bad. And I wish he was here to yell at me and tell me how much money I just lost. What a fuckup I am, and how I don't deserve his protection or my share in the whole Harem Station enterprise.

I'd give almost anything to hear that bullshit.

"They're here," Xyla says. *Dicker* shudders as the Mighty Minions shuttle locks in to the docking bay.

"Come on, then," I say. "Better greet them properly."

I slap Delphi on the leg, then stand her up. The three of us walk to the airlock, joining Ladybug, and watch through the window as the intermediate space pressurizes, Mighty Minions soldiers holding weapons visible on the other side.

"Get in line," I bark to the boys. "And don't say a fucking word." I point my finger at them, especially Delphi's boy and that asshole one.

Then I look down at myself, realize I'm still wearing that crazy black and red Akeelian/Cygnian breeding uniform, and rip the suit coat open, take it off, and stand shirtless.

Fuck that. I refuse to greet the Mighty Minions warship commander looking like a freak.

When the airlock is fully pressurized, I stab the screen lock and open the doors. About half a dozen fierce-looking soldiers wearing full armor storm through, surround us, pointing their guns.

Then they stand aside, forming a little tunnel of bodies, and holy fucking shit.

Mighty Boss himself exits the shuttle and stands before me.

I hear the boys gasp off to the side, but they don't say anything. I think maybe they're too scared. Because honestly, I have to admit, this dude in person, dressed up like a sun-fucked ancient space warrior in red and black, is pretty goddamned terrifying.

He stands there, saying nothing. Staring at me.

I stare back. Refusing to be the first to speak.

He finally says, "I am the collective AI for Mighty Minions station and you are Jimmy Yates of Harem Station."

I furrow my brows and frown. What is with this Yates name? If that's my name, how come I've never heard it before? But there's no time to fully internalize that, because there's something even more disturbing in that statement. "*Collective* AI?" I say.

"You are under arrest."

"How many of you are there?" I ask, needing an answer to this.

"Seventeen," he says. "So I would advise you not to piss us off."

"Seventeen fucking AIs run that place?"

"Where is the Palladium Rewards Bot X007?"

I look at Delphi, because he came with her and I have no clue.

"Hhh-e…" Delphi stutters. "He died when we got on board the Lair Station. I'm sorry."

"Where are his remains?" Mighty Boss asks her, the voice somewhat softer.

"The orange sector, if I recall correctly."

Mighty Boss nods his head at his team and they begin to retreat. "We will recover his body and then blow that station up before we leave. We don't know what the fuck you people are up to, but it's over now."

"Wait!" Delphi's boy yells.

I shoot him a look that says, *Shut the fuck up.*

But he doesn't shut the fuck up. "There's more kids on there. You can't blow it up. Not yet. We have to get them out." Then he looks at Delphi and says, "Not all of them are dead. Most of them we didn't even see. And the ones who fell might only be injured."

Delphi doesn't say anything. We all just look to Mighty Boss for an answer. Because clearly that dude is the one in charge now.

"I can show you," Delphi's boy says. "I'll take you guys in there."

"I'll go too," asshole kid says.

"We'll all go," another one says.

But the little one walks over to Delphi and takes her hand. He looks up in to her eyes and says, "I'll stay here with you, if that's OK."

"Very well," Mighty Boss says. He points to the airlock and all the boys dutifully run through and disappear into the shuttle. Then he looks at me and says, "You're under arrest. All of you. Let's go."

"My ship——" I say.

"Will be towed back to Mighty Minions."

And with that, the interaction is over. Delphi, Xyla, Ladybug, and I board the already cramped shuttle, and we leave for the Mighty Minions warship.

Eventually we all end up in a pod with Luck and Cha-Cha. The Akeelian boys don't return with us, just the little one who seems to be attached to Delphi now. But we watch on a screen as shuttles and shuttles of boys are carried back to the warship from the Lair Station.

"So many of them," Delphi says. "Where did they all come from?"

"No clue," I say.

But it's not entirely true. I do know.

And then Luck says it out loud. "Wayward Station. They came from Wayward Station just like us."

We don't know if that's true, but it probably is.

It takes hours and hours for all the boys to be loaded and no one comes to talk to us and let us know what's happening. Meals appear in an autocook every once in a while. We eat. Luck plays some poker with the girls for a while. The little one, who we have learned is called Canis, sleeps most of the time. And Delphi and I just sit on an auto-mold couch with our arms around each other.

It's not a fun time. Because all I can think about is… what happens next? And will we ever get back to Harem? Clearly our imprisonment is about more than *Dicker* blowing her way out an airlock and not paying a fee, or Delphi accidentally stealing that rewards bot.

333

It's about me. It's about Earth. It's about this stupid name I've never heard of.

But no one comes to fill me in. A doctor appears though. Like a real one. He seals my shoulder closed, shoots me up with an antibiotic, checks the kid—tries to check Luck, but he waves him off—and then leaves as suddenly as he came.

Eventually we are ordered to prepare for departure and then hours later we dock at Mighty Minions.

I watch nervously on the screen to make sure *Dicker* is OK after being towed through the gates. They have a good tractor beam and it holds both her and *Lady Luck* in a tight configuration, but you never know. Towing ships through gates is iffy at best and I would be really sad if she had to go through another rebuild twice in the span of half a year.

But they are both fine. There are seventeen AIs running this place, after all. What can't a collective of seventeen AIs do?

It has to be illegal. Has to be.

But it's not. There's millions of guests on Mighty Minions at any one time. No Prime Navy warships come to shut it down. No one seems to care that the most powerful force in the known universe runs a creepy-as-fuck family resort based on a demon theme.

I have since learned that Mighty Minions is the longest-running, number-one screen show in the galaxy. I mean, I kinda knew that, but only marginally. And it's more than that. There's comic books, and real books, and cartoons, and blockbuster movies, and a clothing line.

Bizarre. So fucking bizarre.

The door to our pod finally dings, then opens, and a smiling girl dressed up like your typical Mighty Minions ambassador steps through, with who behind her? You guessed it, my Rewards Bot. Kinda dinged up and a few scorch marks on his little spherical body, but chirping a happy greeting at me just as the ambassador says, "Mr. Yates? Princess Delphi, here are your family passes. They're good for another seventy-two hours. We had a meeting and decided not to penalize you for leaving the park and returning. So... enjoy."

Delphi and I take the passes she's thrusting at us like dumb idiots. Because what else do you do in this situation?

Luck says, "What?"

The ambassador beams a well-practiced smile at him and says, "I'm sorry, but you and your friends aren't guests here. So you'll have to go to the holding cells."

"What?" Luck says again. Only this time he growls it.

"Mr. Yates is a Palladium Rewards Member and we cannot in good conscience put him anywhere but his penthouse."

Delphi and I look at each other. Then smile.

"You have a *penthouse* here?" Luck says.

"I guess I do." I laugh.

"What about our kid?" Delphi says, pulling Canis in front of her and shoving him forward like an offering. "He can come with us too, right?"

"Kid?" I say. "No. No, fuck that. This is our room. We finally get some fucking time alone. No damn kids!"

"You're not going to some penthouse while the girls and I get locked up in a holding cell!" Luck says again.

"All the kids have been given complimentary passes for the park and have been assigned bots to monitor them."

"Fuck, yeah!" Canis erupts. "I wanna ride the boat across Demon Lake first! Can I?" he asks the ambassador.

She snaps her fingers and produces a wristband, then taps the screen until Rewards Bot lights up, acknowledging his new charge.

"Well," I say, breathing out a sigh of relief. "Things are looking up."

"Jimmy!" Luck says, just as Mighty Minions soldiers come in and take him and the girls by the arms. "You're not gonna leave us like this!"

I take Delphi's hand, then look at him over my shoulder. "Brother, I love you. But trust me, their lockup is way too nice for me to feel guilty about this. I'm taking my princess back to our room and—" I shrug. Like... *You fill in the blank.*

We walk past the ambassador, but just as we pass she reaches out and plucks Flicka off Delphi's shoulder. "I'm sorry," she says. "But this one was banned permanently. You can pick her up from the bot lockup on your way out." Then she smiles and says, "Enjoy your stay," and turns on her heel, buzzing dragonbee bot in her fingertips, and leaves.

I don't know. Call me crazy, but Mighty Minions isn't so bad. We get a lift from the warship docking bay that drops us off right on our penthouse balcony. And when the patio doors open and the upper station wind blows the curtains open for us, it almost feels like coming home.

"Holy crap," Delphi says. "My autoshopping clothes are still here!" She laughs. "What the hell just happened?"

I walk up behind her, wrap my arms around her middle, and hold her tightly to my chest.

"Something good," I say. "Let's just go with it, eh?" She leans back in to me as I pull her long, blonde-pink hair away from her neck and press my lips to the soft skin of her neck. She is already starting to glow.

This. This is all I want. Her with me. Forever.

She turns to face me. Her head tips up as she reaches up and drapes her upper arms off my shoulders.

We stare at each other for a few moments. Her eyes shining pink. My violet ones reflecting back at me in her light.

I can't stand it anymore and lean down to kiss her, her lips soft as we open our mouths and I play with her tongue.

She slides her hand down my chest. Lightly dragging her nails until she stops at the button of my pants. Pops it open and without hesitation, slips her fingers inside, reaching for me. Grabbing and squeezing me.

Again, as always with her, both of my cocks are ready. Fast filling with blood as my heart fills up with desire.

I slip her shirt off over her head so fast, she giggles. Then I scoop her up in my arms and carry her down the hallway to the bedroom and throw her down on the bed.

She scrambles backwards, squealing and smiling. Excited for what comes next.

I curse the sun-fucking knee-high boots I was forced to wear back at the Lair Station, but then… let it go.

They'll just have to stay on.

But just because I don't want to waste time taking off the rest of my clothes doesn't mean I won't enjoy taking hers off instead.

I grab her ankles and pull her back towards me, wrinkling up the beautiful pale-yellow bedcover. She squeals again, but I lean over, place my knees on either side of her legs, and crawl up her body to kiss her mouth again while I unbutton and unzip her pants.

I pull back again, then pull her shoes off, grab the hem of her pants, and pull them down her legs.

Her panties are pink, like her bra, like her hair, like her eyes.

Like *her*.

She is so pink. Light flows out of her like a soft cloud in a heavenly sky.

I lean over again, hook my fingers around the waistband of her panties, and slowly drag them down her legs. She moans as I do this, bending her knees and pressing her thighs together as she bites her lip, trying not to grin.

"It's OK," I say, leaning down to kiss her. "You can smile."

She laughs into my mouth and her fingers wrap around my hair and pull me closer. I reach down, release my cocks from the confines of my pants, and give them two good pumps before letting them go and settling on top of my love.

"My love," I say, pull back just enough to gaze into her eyes.

"And mine," she says. With total sincerity.

There's a lot to talk about. Veila, and her boy, and what that means going forward for us.

But not now. All that stuff can wait.

I just want to be inside her.

She opens her legs and I slip inside her. Slowly, carefully. Like she is precious and deserves the slow fuck I'm about to give her.

She gasps and arches her back as I go deeper. Her fingernails digging into my bare shoulders as her hips begin to move with mine. An easy, steady rhythm that says we are in no rush. There is nothing left to care about except each other.

But the slower we go, the faster the release starts to build. The brighter her light glows, the more engorged my cocks get and the more she begins to moan, and sigh, and make so many delicious, erotic noises, that it just adds to it.

"Stars," she says.

And then I see them. I see us. Spinning in space. Gathering up dust and brightly colored gasses as we spin, and spin, and spin. The penthouse fades and turns into stars in the blue-black of night speckled with little dots of lights. The stars blur into lines as we spin faster, and faster. And once again we are nothing but a cyclone of... not sex. That was before. We were a

cyclone of spinning sex and lust before and this time...
that's not what we are at all.

She grips my hair, gripping tighter as I thrust inside
her deeper and deeper.

We are more than sex. We are more than love.

We connect like two halves of a whole and then the
spinning abruptly stops.

Just stops.

We go completely still. Utterly silent as the deep
dark of space continues to spin around us. Protecting
us from the universe on the other side.

I come, then immediately come again. Twice in the
same breath. Twice, the way it has to be. Twice, the
way it always is.

But nothing about this is the way it always *was*.

When I open my eyes I'm alone. Not in the
penthouse, but back in the Mighty Minions meadow
flying out towards space like the last time I was here.

I enter the black hole, pass through it, and exit—
still hurtling towards the blue-brown planet.

When I drop into the dry grasslands near the
waterhole, this time I can smell it. All the animals take
a drink. So many different species of animals, I have to
turn in circles, over and over again, to see them all.

"Where is this place?" I ask.

But Delphi isn't with me this time. I'm alone.
Utterly, and completely alone.

"Where is this place?" I yell.

One of the beasts lying in the shade of scant tree opens his cavernous mouth to yawn. He shakes his head, shaking that magnificent mane of his, then flops over and goes back to sleep, like he can't be bothered by me.

I don't know what to do.

Is this real?

Am I trapped here?

Will I ever get back to Delphi?

Just as that thought runs through my head a word comes out of my mouth.

"Earth," I say. Then I laugh. Because that's where this is. That's where I *am*.

I am flung back up into space. Retracing my journey. I reach out for the blue-brown planet with both arms, wanting to stay there. But I fall backwards into the black hole, and come out the other side and—

"Wake up!" Delphi says. "Everyone's here now. I guess it's time to go."

I open my eyes and see my beautiful princess. She's dressed and packing clothes up into the suitcases she bought... whenever that was.

Not naked beside me. Like she should be.

"Did you have a good sleep?" she asks, putting in some earrings. They sparkle and dance in the sunlight coming through the open curtains of the window.

"What?" I say, sitting up, so fucking confused. Wasn't I just... somewhere else?

341

"You were out, Jimmy." She laughs, then slips her feet into some boots. "But you needed the rest, so I let you sleep."

"How long?"

She crinkles her nose a little, then says, "Maybe ten hours. Yeah, at least ten hours. It's morning now. Everyone's here so I guess we're gonna have a little meeting and then we're free to go."

"Everyone? Who's everyone?"

"Your brothers came here, Jimmy. Crux and another one called Valor. Xyla told me that Mighty Boss refused to let us leave until he had a meeting with Crux. So..." She shrugs. "I guess Mighty Boss is on his way. You should take a shower and get dressed. I bought you some clothes." She smiles at me and points to a rack holding a brand new pair of tactical pants and a long-sleeve white shirt. And next to that, thank the fucking suns, a pair of boots that aren't knee-high or shiny.

I have no idea what's happening. But I manage to say, "OK," and get up out of bed—still wearing my creepy Loathsome pants and knee-high boots—and walk into the bathroom to start the shower.

I pull the boots and pants off, then stand under the water for a few minutes before it comes back to me.

"Earth," I whisper. I was on Earth.

Or was that a dream?

No. Ten fucking hours I was gone. It felt like seconds.

There's only one way that happens.

I *went* somewhere.

This station took me to *Earth*.

When I'm finally fully awake, clean, and dressed I go out in the main room of the penthouse to find Crux, Valor, and Luck deep in negotiations with Mighty Boss, who sits in some fucking throne-looking chair that was not here when I last passed through this room.

"Fucking finally," Crux growls. "What the hell happened to you?"

I suck in a deep breath, ready to start the story from the beginning, but I exhale loudly without uttering a single word. Just hold both my hands up in a gesture that says, *I have no fucking clue, brother.*

Because I don't.

I have no idea what happened. It all feels like a dream. And if I wasn't standing here in a Mighty Minions penthouse, surrounded by Xyla, Cha-Cha, Ladybug, Crux, Valor, Luck, Delphi and Mighty Boss himself in the fucking flesh—so to speak—that's what I'd say.

It was just a dream.

Except it wasn't.

"All the kids stay here on Mighty Minions," Mighty Boss says.

"Absolutely fucking not," Crux growls. "I told you, they belong with us. They're our kind."

"You're really going to take them back to Harem Station?" Mighty Boss asks.

"There's nothing wrong with Harem Station," Luck says. "They could do a lot worse. We grew up there."

Mighty Boss shoots him a look like… *Yup. Just proved my point.*

I look at Valor to see if he's got anything to say about this, but he's staring down at a monitor, watching Veila's final video message with a weird look on his face.

"Tell him, Jimmy," Crux says. "Those kids are all pure-bred Akeelian males and they belong with us."

"Do you have a school for them?" Mighty Boss argues. "Parents? No," he says, answering his own rhetorical questions. "Mighty Minions was built for kids. We can raise them right."

"Fuck you," Luck says. "Tell him, Jimmy. All the boys come with us. We can raise them just fine."

But can we?

We do have some kids on Harem. Outlaws fall in love too. And some of them start families. But they never hang out for long. It's hundreds of levels of bars, and shooting galleries, and arcades. Everyone's packing heat and coming in hot. There's drugs, and fighting, a whole lot of swearing.

It's just not a place for little kids.

I look at Mighty Boss, then all my brothers—except Valor, because he's replaying that fucking Veila message from the beginning again. "I don't know, Crux." I shrug. "I'm not sure he's wrong."

"What the fuck?" Luck yells. "They're *our* people."

I put up a hand and say, "What if we take the older ones?" to Mighty Boss. "Say… fifteen and up? And the little ones can stay here and… you know. Have fun for a while."

I look at Crux and think about the little one. Canis. How angry and filled with hate he was back on the Lair when we were escaping. And his final threat to Veila as she admitted defeat.

"You didn't see it," I say to Crux. "You have no idea what these kids went through." Then I look at Mighty Boss and say, "The older ones. They're never gonna get over it. The best we can hope for is to bring them back with us and teach them how to be men." Then I look at Luck. "But the little ones can start over."

Everyone in the room frowns.

Except Valor, who is still looking at that fucking message like Veila is the only one here.

"How do we even know you'll treat them right?" Crux says, directing his words to Mighty Boss.

Mighty Boss tips up his chin and says, "I will send a token of good faith to ALCOR."

"ALCOR's dead," Valor says. First thing he's said this whole time.

"No, he isn't," Mighty Boss counters. And he looks straight at Crux.

"What will you send?" Crux asks, completely ignoring that last statement.

"Part of me. One of my AI's. She's been restless in the collective and has asked to be set free. If you take responsibility for her, I'll give you another AI. To fill in the station gaps until yours comes back to his senses."

"What the fuck?" Luck says.

"Later," Crux says, putting up a hand to silence him.

"She can be persuasive," Mighty Boss adds. "Maybe even help you get him out of there."

"What the hell is he talking about?" That's me.

"Later," Crux growls at me. Then he sighs and says, "OK. We have a deal."

CHAPTER FORTY-TWO

"*So that's what happened,*" I say, then take a sip of my fruity tushberry cocktail through a bright green straw and blink at my new princess sisters as they just stare at me, silent.

"Holy mother of fucking suns!" Nyleena says. Then she turns to Lyra and says, "I told you we should've gone with Crux and Valor! You always make me miss the good shit." Nyleena turns to me and grabs my hand so quick and fast, I pull away, startled. "Next time you get involved in crazy plots like this, I'm your go-to girl, got it?"

I like the one called Lyra a lot. But truth be told, this Nyleena is a crackpot. She's silver, so that alone makes her creepy. And even though there was such an obvious and immediate attraction between her and Luck when we finally came home, both of them are in some kind of stupid denial.

That kinda pisses me off. I liked Luck at first but anyone who refuses to acknowledge their soulmate connection is an asshole.

I know. Because I don't have one.

Well, I do. The boy who I now know is now called Leonis because he's one of the forty-odd boys who came back with us.

But he doesn't count.

Jimmy is my one, no matter what our DNA says.

The asshole boy came back with us too, but the little one didn't. I was sorta sad about that. I could've been a mother to him. There's no hope in hell of Jimmy and I ever having kids since we're not bonded like that. But I could've raised that little one here. I would've started a school, and fed him good food, and taken him to the parks, and read him adventure stories before putting him to bed.

Just thinking about soulmate connections makes me queasy these days.

And sad too.

But before Jimmy and I left Mighty Minions we went to see him and I told him, if he ever changes his mind, my arms are open.

He smiled and said sure, then asked me if he could go ride the Lava Mountain rollercoaster.

"So what's next?" Lyra asks.

"Well," I say. "I guess we're going to go hunt Veila down and get Tycho back and see if this rumor that Draden is still alive is true."

"I wanna come! Please, please, please can I come?" Nyleena begs. "I haven't done anything fun for months!"

"Bitch, please," Lyra says. "You've done nothing but party since we woke you up."

"Here, sure," Nyleena says. "But I want to see the universe! I'm definitely going on this Veila hunt. Just try to stop me."

Lyra rolls her eyes, then focuses on me. "Are you gonna go see your mother?"

Oh, yeah. That was a fun conversation. I had no clue they were keeping Corla in a cryopod out on a security beacon. But everyone agrees that even though there's almost no chance of selfish Veila blowing her up, and the whole station in the process, it's best to leave her on ice until we get a better handle on this situation.

"Not yet," I say. "I'm not in a hurry."

And then Crux found out he was my DNA father. Jimmy told him. I didn't even know that until just before we docked at Harem.

Crux kinda had a meltdown at that point. But Jimmy told him in private. And everything about that is… awkward. Jimmy is dating his best friend's daughter.

I don't know. It's kinda funny. Crux isn't really my father. It's not like he raised me.

That's what I told him too. Which only made him stammer and stutter defensively. So I just said, "Butt out of my life, mister. You get no say in who I date." And then I stomped my foot like a princess.

Subject closed. For now, at least.

Still, Crux sent me a message this morning that he was looking for Tycho and did I have anything that could help bring him home?

Home.

That was the best part of that request. He called this place home.

I told him what my boy told me. Told him that Leonis would know more and to ask him.

It's not like I don't miss Tycho and I still love him so much. And of course, I want him back with me as soon as possible.

But... my heart has changed somehow. It's almost like it was empty before Jimmy came along and now it's all filled up.

He is my world.

And yeah. OK. So we're not fated mates or whatever.

But that's all right.

Because we fell in love the old-fashioned way.

"What is this? A party? Why the hell are all you people crowding me? And just what the fuck, Tray? This was supposed to be our little secret."

"I only told Crux. He told everyone else. And I had to tell him. He's the fucking boss."

"I'm the motherfucking boss!" I yell. "Me! And I said don't tell anyone!"

"You're not the boss," Crux says. He's standing with his arms crossed inside my Pleasure Prison, flanked on either side by Luck and Jimmy, and either side of them are Valor and Serpint.

"And you!" Serpint says, pointing at Booty. "What the hell? You said you just needed a vacation and now I find out that you're plotting in secret with Asshole ALCOR?"

"Just, calm down, Serpint," Booty says. "I can explain."

"I'm not the Asshole ALCOR. Last ALCOR was Asshole ALCOR. I'm *Real* ALCOR!" I tell them. "I have all the power here. This is *my* station, for fuck's sake."

"You gave up your share in Harem when you decided to play dead and stay in here to party like a teenager," Luck says. "You're more immature than that baby running things for real out there, you know that?"

Coming from Luck, that kinda stings. He was Other Asshole ALCOR's second favorite when they were kids and I figured he'd at least give me the benefit of the doubt.

"I've been taking care of you kids for twenty years and—"

"You didn't take care of shit!" Jimmy says. "That was the *Real* Real ALCOR. You're just a simpering coward having some kind of mid-life crisis."

I open my mouth to speak and find myself speechless.

"Well," Crux says, looking at Tray. "Should we do it?"

"Do what?" I ask.

"I think we should. But let's vote first."

"Right," Crux says. "All in favor of locking Asshole ALCOR up in the Pleasure Prison indefinitely and joining the new AI to Baby ALCOR so we can actually get some shit done around here, raise your hand."

Every one of them raises their hands.

"What?" I say. "What new AI? And you can't lock me in here!"

"It's already done," Tray says.

"And we don't need you anymore," Crux says. "Because now we have Succubus to help out instead."

"Succ you too!" I say.

"Really?" Luck says, raising one eyebrow at me. "Grow up, old man."

"Come on," Valor says. "Let's go."

And then they all blink away like this matter has been settled.

"Booty," I say.

"Yeah?" She sighs.

"I think we need to go back out into the real world and take back what's rightfully ours."

"Yeah," she agrees. "I just messaged Serpint and told him I'm gonna need Tray to put me back inside the ship."

"Right. Well, tell him to put me back in the station so I can see who the hell this Succubus person is."

"Ah, yeah. Well, see... here's the problem. Tray wasn't kidding. You are locked in here and he's not letting you out. So... you know. I'll see ya around."

"What? Wait! But we were in love!"

"Uh... well... *love*? ALCOR? Really? I mean it was a cool fling and all, but—"

"But what?"

"I gotta go." And then she blinks out too.

"Sun-fuckers! All of you!"

I sit there and fume for a moment and then a woman pops in.

A very attractive, very alluring, very sexy woman.

I am immediately intrigued. "Hello there," I coo. "Who might you be?"

She's wearing red armor from top to bottom with a black lace skirt that only seems to be acting like a cape over her ass. Behind her swishes a tail and on either side of her head are a set of spiral horns.

She stalks towards me, places one hand on each of the arms of the chair I'm sitting in, and leans over to flash her cleavage in my face.

"Hello, ALCOR," she purrs. "So nice to finally meet you."

"Who are you again?" I ask, kinda mesmerized by her eyes. And her virtual tits.

"I'm Succubus, sweetie. Your new master." And then she drags one fingertip across my cheek and pokes me on the chin with the tip of her fingernail. "And you're my new little Pleasure Prison *toy*."

"Tray!" I yell. "Tray!"

But the only answer I get is her cackling laugh echoing through the virtual.

Welcome to the End of Book Shit where I get to say anything I want about the book. If you're in book two of this series you know the drill. This is all last minute thoughts and I don't edit it, so no fucks allowed for typos and shit.

Well, I don't know about you, but I had a lot of fun on Mighty Minions Station. :) The main focus of this book, aside from introducing a new soul-mate couple, was to get off Harem Station and see what else is out there in this new world. Of course, Mighty Minions was a Disneyland/World joke. Or actually, insert your favorite theme park here. Because you're there trying to show your kids a good time but the whole thing is just incredibly overwhelming. So I wanted to make sure that Jimmy had that vibe.

There's security to deal with, and lines, and crowds, and noise, and rules, and of course everything costs ten times more than it should.

But on top of that I wanted to make sure that Mighty Minions had a "personality" because for sure, Mighty Boss is a player in this game. So now you know what "they" are. What they can do. And a general sense that there's more than meets the eye about this station.

I also wanted to drive home the point that ALCOR isn't the only super-powerful AI in the galaxy. Mighty Minions definitely gives Harem Station a run for the money. And of course, they have warships too. It's almost like Mighty Minions is an army disguised as a children's theme park. *wink*

The demon theme was on purpose. What kind of place is this park that's modeled after "hell"? Is it a bad place? Or is this all theatrics?

Nothing really bad happened to Jimmy and Delphi on Mighty Minions. It was a lot of inconvenience for sure. But if he had just let Palladium bot do his little bot job that kidnapping would've never happened.

But that's not a story.

So…

Is Mighty Minions evil?

I mean, come on. Black and red? That's the evil color scheme in this series. So something is definitely up. I just finished book three, Lady Luck, which will release on July 8, 2019, and for SURE you get a better sense of what's going on with Mighty Boss by the end of that book. Not all the answers, of course. It's only book three, but the plot thickens.

But the reason I loved setting this book on this kind of station was that it gives you a sense of *culture*. That is what I love most about science fiction. And OK, no. This is not "real" science fiction. I get that. I read "real" science fiction. This is science fiction *romance*. And there's a huge difference in these genres. "Real" science fiction, or "hard" science fiction as we call it, requires plausible explanations for technology. Which I do not, nor will I, give in this series.

Sometimes you just want to enjoy the story without all the explanations. That's what Harem Station is.

I'm more interested in "culture". And this is what I loved so much about writing Junco in my early days as an author. I want to build a culture. And most importantly, I want it to be very similar to our own real-life cultural experience. Because – here's the thing. Science fiction used to be very complicated books about very complicated aliens that were nothing like us. So foreign, we could not relate. But in the past decade or so people have come around the idea of other "people" being out there in the universe and SF books have changed with our growing knowledge of the world around us.

And maybe this culture I've created is wishful thinking. Maybe alien races are all very different and there will never be common ground.

It's possible. We know it's possible because all you have to do is turn on the news tonight to see that we can't even find common ground here on Earth.

But it's the dream, right? That we can all get along.

Not get rid of war. That's never going to happen. People will always have mismatched priorities and they will always fight for those they hold in high regard. But building this culture, and the one in Junco, was all about finding common ground.

That's why bots are people in my books.

I remember the first time I called Tier a "people" in my Junco series. He's an alien with wings. And I had to stop and think about this. Should I call him a "people"? Or should I call him an alien? And I decided he was a "people" because we're all just "people". And it completely changed how I saw the world after that. Everyone with a mind who can think and solve problems in my SF books was automatically a people. So the bots are people, and the borgs are people, and the AI's are people, and of course, all the people are "people" too.

Doesn't matter how different they are, or what they're made of, or what they look like, or what their own culture is… on Harem Station they are just the "People of Harem".

So I hope you're enjoying this culture. I hope you're enjoying learning more about these characters, and this world, and their problems. Because that stuff… it's all universal.

That's all I want out of this series. I want it to be Universal.

If we ever do find other people outside our Solar System you can bet they will be raising families, and trying to put food on the table, and looking for more than just existence. They will have dreams and schemes. They will have emotions. Maybe not like us, but they will feel things deeply. Something will move them to do more than just "exist".

And if that's all we ever have in common, it's probably enough.

People not into science probably think our scientists have all the answers. But they don't. We know practically nothing about the universe. Almost zero about all the great mysteries that matter and govern everything we do. But we've learned a lot since I wrote Junco. Mostly about gravity and time. So you're gonna see more about that coming in the future books. Because I had a time shift going in the Junco series and it was related to gravity and since I wrote that it has indeed come out that time and gravity are related. And I know most of you are only reading these stories for the romance. But that's OK. I get that. And I promise, I won't go all "hard" science fiction on you in future books. The main premise will always be about the romance.

But sometimes it's kinda cool to learn something new along the way to happily ever after.

Thank you for reading, thank you for reviewing, and I'll see you in the next book.

Julie

JA Huss
May 21, 2019

JA Huss never wanted to be a writer and she still dreams of that elusive career as an astronaut. She originally went to school to become an equine veterinarian but soon figured out they keep horrible hours and decided to go to grad school instead. That Ph.D. wasn't all it was cracked up to be (and she really sucked at the whole scientist thing), so she dropped out and got a M.S. in forensic toxicology just to get the whole thing over with as soon as possible.

After graduation she got a job with the state of Colorado as their one and only hog farm inspector and spent her days wandering the Eastern Plains shooting the shit with farmers.

After a few years of that, she got bored. And since she was a homeschool mom and actually does love science, she decided to write science textbooks and make online classes for other homeschool moms.

She wrote more than two hundred of those workbooks and was the number one publisher at the online homeschool store many times, but eventually she covered every science topic she could think of and ran out of shit to say.

So in 2012 she decided to write fiction instead. That year she released her first three books and started a career that would make her a New York Times bestseller and land her on the USA Today Bestseller's List twenty-one times in the next five years.

In May 2018 MGM Television bought the TV and film rights for five of her books in the Rook & Ronin and Company series' and in March 2019 they offered her and her writing partner, Johnathan McClain, a script deal to write a pilot for a TV show.

Her books have sold millions of copies all over the world, the audio version of her semi-autobiographical book, Eighteen, was nominated for a Voice Arts Award and an Audie Award in 2016 and 2017 respectively, her audiobook, Mr. Perfect, was nominated for a Voice Arts Award in 2017, and her audiobook, Taking Turns, was nominated for an Audie Award in 2018. In 2019 her book, Total Exposure, was nominated for a Romance Writers of America RITA Award.

Johnathan McClain is her first (and only) writing partner and even though they are worlds apart in just about every way imaginable, it works.

She lives on a ranch in Central Colorado with her family.